HARD PLACE

HARD TO LOVE: BOOK ONE

EMILY GOODWIN

Hard Place: Book One in the Hard to Love series

UNCORRECTED ARC

Copyright 2019
Emily Goodwin
Cover photography by Lindee Robinson
Editing by Contagious Edits

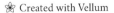 Created with Vellum

To anyone who is struggling...don't give up. There's always tomorrow.

CHAPTER 1

HARPER

B eing a mother is a complicated thing.

I remember the day I went from only having to take care of myself to having to care for something completely helpless as if it were yesterday. I'd read all the baby books, downloaded all the apps, and lurked through a few message boards, but nothing prepared me for how completely terrifying it would be. Some days I still can't believe I was allowed to take those precious baby girls home with me, that medical professionals entrusted me to raise them, care for them, and keep them safe.

I bring the glass of dark red wine to my lips, shuddering at the taste. I don't like red wine, but this shit has the highest alcohol content compared to others from the same brand, and at three dollars a bottle, it's not like I expected to feel like the beginning of an orgasm was coming on when the wine spilled past my lips.

All I wanted was a slight reprieve from the slow suffocation my dear friend Mr. Anxiety causes. I take one more sip of wine, looking up from the small kitchen table. The finish is wearing off the surface, and no matter what I use to clean it with, I cannot get the pink paint that's splattered across half the table off.

I lay my hand on the table, splaying my fingers and letting my eyes fall shut for a moment. Mom's voice rings loud in my head, telling me everything's going to be all right. She truly believed things would work out for those who worked hard and had a kind heart.

She believed it up until the day cancer stole her life.

Inhaling, I open my eyes and look around the small apartment. The girls just fell asleep for the night, and I came into the kitchen with the intention of doing the dishes that are overflowing in the sink. Toys are strewn about the living room, and I'm not entirely sure I have clean underwear to put on for work in the morning.

I need to clean but can't find the energy, though I'd rather clean than open my computer, log into my bank account and see how much money I *don't* have. Grabbing the wine, I suck down another mouthful and hope it doesn't come back up.

"Ugh, that's disgusting," I grumble to myself and put the glass back down. Taking a steadying breath, I swallow the lump in my throat and open my computer. Money's always been tight, but things are tighter than normal right now and looking at my bank account is only going to make it worse. Why remind myself that I don't have enough to cover the rent that's due soon? I know my credit card bill is higher this month than last, and thinking about all the interest I'm paying makes me sick to my stomach.

I desperately need a break from work, and would love to have a day or two to just stay home and finally have time to play with the girls. The guilt from telling them no every time they ask me to play with them weighs on me, but if I want to pay off my debts and have a chance at putting anything into savings, I'm going to have to pick up another shift or two this weekend.

My legs hurt from treading water, and I'm barely keeping myself above the surface. Yet it's not just me who will drown if I stop, if I give in and let myself rest for even half a second. Because as I'm madly kicking my legs to stay afloat, I'm holding my children up, one in each arm.

If I go down, they'll go with me, and I will not let my children slip below the surface. Everything I do, I do for them.

Closing my computer, I get up and tiptoe into the girls' room, grabbing the dirty clothes from their floor. Sneaking out so quietly a ninja would be impressed, I silently click their door shut and take the laundry to the closet at the end of the hall. I should have taken a load downstairs before bedtime and stuck it in the washing machine.

Dropping in the girls' clothes from today, I stare at the overflowing basket, thinking. It would only take me five minutes or less to grab it, run down two flights of stairs, and start the washing machine. I'd be in the same building, and the girls wouldn't even know I left.

But what if I got locked out?

Mugged?

Kidnapped?

What if I fell down the stairs, broke my neck, and no one found me until the morning?

Shaking my head at myself, I use my foot to push a pair of jeans out of the way and close the closet door. I'll do laundry tomorrow. It's not like I don't have enough to clean tonight anyway.

I'm halfway through the dishes when my phone rings. Drying my hands, I rush into the living room to get it, stepping and tripping over Barbies on my way.

I grab my phone and my heart skips a beat. It's Tessa, my best friend, and she's a text-and-not-call kind of person. Something terrible must have happened.

"Hello?" I ask, voice already shaky.

"Hey, girl," she replies. Music plays in the background and she doesn't sound panicked or on the verge of tears. Still, I need to be sure.

"What's wrong?"

"Nothing."

3

"You called me," I say.

"I know. Hell is freezing over. But I got great news and wanted to tell you in person."

"You do realize we're still not in person, right?"

She laughs. "This is more in person than a text. Are you sitting down? You need to sit down for this."

I go back to the kitchen table and sit down, reaching for my glass of wine. "I am now," I tell her and take another drink. I don't drink often, and I didn't eat much for dinner. I had exactly enough bread and cheese left to make three grilled cheese sandwiches. Violet dropped hers on the ground after she only took two bites, and when she picked it up, there were crumbs and lint stuck to it, thanks to my lack of cleaning the floors.

So I gave her mine, and then ate the leftovers the girls didn't. It's enough to tide me over until the morning, but this wine is going to hit me fast.

"Okay," Tessa starts and pauses for dramatic effect. "I got the girls in!"

"In? Into Briar Prep?"

"Yes!" she squeals with excitement, and for a moment, I feel excited too. Briar Prep is a fancy private elementary school and it's necessary to go there before being accepted into Briar Academy, which is an even fancier private middle and high school. I had to move into a not-so-great school district because rent is cheaper here, and sending the girls to Briar Prep was a high—very high—hope.

But then I remember that I can barely afford to pay the reduced rate at the current daycare the girls go to during the day while I'm at work. There's no way in hell I could afford what Briar charges.

"New student orientation is tomorrow. I know it's short notice, and we start earlier than the public schools, but when a family withdrew from the school at the last minute, it opened two kindergarten spots," Tessa goes on. "And I'll have the girls in my class!"

We moved here years ago only a few days after the girls' first birthday. I promised them it would only be temporary, and I'd find a way to get us back into a better area before they started school.

"I...I can't afford tuition there." I pinch the bridge of my nose and let out a defeated sigh. "Thank you, though." I swallow the lump in my throat, trying hard not to be mad at my best friend. She knows I can't afford a place like Briar Prep and getting me in only hurts. It's like giving a starving man food only to take it away.

"I know, hun," she says gently. "I got the girls in on a scholarship."

"A what?" I ask even though I heard her loud and clear.

"A scholarship," she repeats. "All expenses for the whole year have been paid, and that includes three uniforms each, fifteen hundred in their lunch accounts, and all field trips covered."

"But how?"

"Briar is trying to be more diverse to draw in more of the rich, hipster parents. I was able to expedite your application for review since you'd be a perfect demographic to add to our current year's roster."

"Is that a nice way of saying I got picked because I'm a poor, half-Latino, single mother of twins?"

"Exactly."

I take another drink of wine. "I feel like I should find that offensive yet I don't care." A smile pulls up my lips as I let the news sink in. My babies are going to arguably the best school in Chicago. "Thank you, Tess. So, so much."

"You can thank me by activating that account I set up for you."

"No way," I tell her, and drink the rest of my wine. "I don't have time to date anyone."

"Don't date. Just fuck."

5

I shift my eyes from the wine glass to the girls' bedroom door. "We both know how well that worked out for me in the past. I'm still upholding my vow of chastity."

"Harper," Tess says firmly, and I know she's going to drop some truth. She's never been afraid to tell it like it is, and even though there've been times when I wanted her to hold my hand, lie to me, and tell me it's all going to be okay, I'm so grateful to have a friend like her. "You have got to stop blaming yourself. It's been five fucking years."

"I know," I sigh and get up, putting the call on speaker and turning down the volume. This apartment is small, and it doesn't take much to wake up Penny. "And I wouldn't change it for anything. I love my girls."

"We both do, and they're a big part of why I think you should get out there again. I'm not talking about anything serious," she adds quickly. "But the longer you wait, the harder it will be, and don't even think about telling me you're happy being single the rest of your life. You love love more than anyone I know. And that includes me."

"You love sex, not love," I correct.

"That is true," she agrees with a laugh.

"Lucky for you, your lovers can't get you pregnant."

"You're free to come bat for the other team," she reminds me. "Women know women's bodies. You'll never want a man again."

"If I could swing that way, I would," I confess. "But I like the dick. I'd miss being penetrated."

"You can still be penetrated, you know," she laughs. "And if being penetrated is what you want then online dating might be perfect."

"I meant by a dick, not a knife."

"Stay away from Craigslist wanted ads and you won't go on a date with a murderer."

"You say that now," I laugh and grab a towel to start drying the few dishes I already washed. Someday, I'll have a dishwasher.

Until then, my poor hands continue to suffer because I always end up tearing holes in rubber gloves and just gave up on wearing them when I do dishes.

"Going out does sound nice," I admit. I used to love getting dressed up and going out. "Just something casual," I quickly add. "Because any guy I get serious with is going to have to check off a lot of boxes."

"Oh for sure. I only want the best for you and my godchildren."

"Thank you for that," I say and sit back down at the table. I'm too damn tired to finish cleaning, but if I put it off tonight then I'll have to do it tomorrow, and I'll want to do it even less then. "Really, Tess, thank you."

"Of course, hun. I'll email all the parent info over. There are a million forms to fill out, but if you can't get to it tomorrow let me know and I'll fill in what I can. I know you and those girls." Her doorbell rings and her dogs start barking. "My food is here."

"Thank you, Tess," I say for the hundredth time, not sure if she can hear me over the dogs barking. "See you tomorrow."

With a sigh I end the call. I force myself to wash the rest of the dishes, but I'm leaving them to air dry. I drink another glass of wine as I pick up the living room, and by pick up, I mean scoot around on my butt, dragging a Rubbermaid bin behind me. All the toys, a few loose socks, and several books all get piled into the bin.

The girls have a lot of toys, thanks to Mrs. Dembroski across the hall. She has a granddaughter who just turned nine and gives us all the toys and clothes she's outgrown. I never thought I'd still be dressing my kids in hand-me-down clothes, but buying new is a luxury we can't afford.

I saved up a hundred extra bucks over the spring and summer with the intention of using it all for Christmas. The girls are at the perfect age for believing in Santa, and I was so looking forward to getting them a good little haul.

7

But then the girls got sick and I had to take a few days off work to stay home and watch them, which put me short on rent, and I had to use the little bit I'd saved. It's so tiring to feel like I'm always sinking, to take one step forward only to be pulled yards back.

I want out of this mess. I just want to be able to breathe. To not wake up with a clenched stomach and my throat tight from anxiety. I want to be able to buy more fresh fruit and veggies for the girls.

Go see a movie on a Friday night.

Dress them in matching outfits with obnoxiously big pink bows.

Big tears roll down my cheeks, and I hate that I'm already worrying about my girls being picked on at school. The only reason we got in is to make the school look less pretentious than it already is. We're the odd ones out, but it'll be worth it in the end.

I hope.

CHAPTER 2

HARPER

"Thanks again, Dad." I usher the girls inside and close the door behind me before Skittles the cat sneaks out. Yes, the girls named the little tabby last year when Dad found her, wet and cold and shivering with fear along a curb on a busy street downtown. "I know it's early," I add apologetically.

"It's never too early to see my girls." Dad sets his coffee mug on the coffee table and crouches down, knees cracking and popping, and opens his arms for a hug. The twins groggily walk in, making him laugh.

"Put on cartoons and they'll probably go back to sleep," I say, already looking at the couch. Dad has it set up with extra pillows and blankets already. "Be good for Papa," I tell the girls, shrugging their duffle bag off my shoulder. "And please be ready and dressed when I call and say I'm on my way. We get to see your new school tonight!"

The girls respond with groans and blank stares. As much as I want them to be excited, I can't blame them. They're only five and it's fucking early. But in order to make it to the new student open house tonight, I have to leave work an hour and a half early and I can't afford to miss even thirty minutes of pay.

I hate this.

"I'm making my famous pot-pie tonight. Will you be able to join?" Dad gives each girl a kiss and stands up.

"I wish," I sigh and get hit with a ping of guilt over the lack of time I have for my family. "And you don't have to cook for us."

Dad waves his hand in the air. "I never get to cook for anyone, and these little stinkers love a home cooked meal."

I cock an eyebrow and Dad laughs.

"That wasn't a dig at you, sweetheart. I know how busy you are."

"Yeah." I yawn and plow my hand through my hair, fingers tangling in my brunette locks. I'm on the last day I can get away with not washing it and make a mental note to throw it up in bun before I get to work.

"I'll have a plate wrapped up to go for you when you get here."

"Thanks." I step in to give Dad a hug goodbye and see a stack of bills on the table with the words "overdue" in bold red letters. My stomach drops. Dad said he'd taken care of this, and I don't know why he would keep this from me, though I'm as useless as insurance, apparently.

"Be good," I tell the girls once more before kissing them good-bye. I dig my sunglasses out of my purse as I go down the steps of Dad's one-bedroom apartment and into the parking lot.

It's a hot August day and I'm sweating by the time I get to my car. My air conditioning is on the fritz and doesn't stay cool for very long. If I'm moving with the windows down, it's not much of an issue. But when we get stuck in traffic…my poor babies.

Leaving earlier than usual today helps me avoid traffic, and I get to the downtown office right on time. I'm nothing more than a glorified telemarketer, collecting research data for the city's largest PR firm. I was only a semester away from graduating with my own degree in public relations when Mom's health took a turn for the worst. I took time off to spend it with her, and then I got knocked up with the twins before I could make it back.

I still plan to go back to school...someday.

Grabbing my ID badge out of my purse, I hold it up to security and pull into the parking garage. My spot is as far from the elevator as you can get, but who am I to complain? I get a covered spot every day of the year.

"Morning, Miss Harper," Nicolas, one of the security guards says when I make it to the lobby. It's eerily quiet in here this morning. "You're here early."

"Too early," I laugh. "I am not a morning person."

"One good thing about getting here early is the coffee is fresh."

"Oh, good point. I didn't think of that. I'll definitely be needing a cup or two this morning." I yawn again as I get into the elevator, going up twelve stories. The office is quiet as well. If I weren't so tired, I might appreciate this moment, and the breathtaking view of the early light shining down on Lake Michigan.

I set my purse down at my desk inside my little cubicle and head into the break room to get coffee. I'm going to need a lot to get me through the day. Even though I was exhausted last night, I couldn't sleep. After tossing and turning for hours, I got up and went back into the kitchen to drink the rest of the wine to help me sleep.

But then I remembered I was getting up earlier than normal and there would be a good chance of still being drunk when I finally stumbled out of bed. I'll go to bed early tonight and make up for the lost sleep...I say now.

I suck down another gulp of coffee and fire up my computer, pulling up today's assignments. I have to go through handwritten responses to a survey and input the data into a computer program for an analyst to go over. Today's survey is about people's responses to a particular ad set the firm put together for a fast food chain.

Sounds fun, doesn't it?

Two hours later I get up to pee, get more coffee, and to walk around and try to wake myself up. It's very easy to fall asleep while doing this riveting work even when you've gotten a full twelve hours of sleep.

"Hey," I say to Angela, who's refilling the coffee. Coffee does go fast around here. "How's your morning going?"

She looks up and wrinkles her nose. "I'm on phone duty today."

"Ugh, fun." I give her a sympathetic smile. "There's nothing like getting yelled at by strangers bright and early in the morning. Though truthfully, I'd be annoyed with me too if I called myself at nine AM in the morning."

Angela laughs and turns on the coffee pot. We both stare at it, waiting for that first drop to come down, giving us hope we'll make it through the rest of the workday without passing out at our desks.

"Hannah, Melody, and I are grabbing drinks after work," Angela starts. "Want to join?"

"I wish I could," I say honestly. Because I do wish I could go out for drinks with my work friends. A majority of the employees working the "research floor" at the PR firm are my age or a little younger. This is an entry-level job that doesn't really require much skill other than computing data into a program. "My kids are starting at a new school and orientation is tonight."

"School starts already? I feel like it used to start later when we were kids, didn't it?"

"I think most public schools around here start a little later. This one's a private school."

"Oh." Angela's eyebrows go up, and I know she's wondering how the hell I can afford to send my kids to private school. We're not close, but she's enough of a friend to know I struggle financially. Hell, most the people working this menial job struggle considering the shit wage we get paid. "Well, that's exciting. I think?"

"Yeah, it's a great school with intense lessons but will prepare them for the next years. Remember when kindergarten was just finger painting and playing house?"

"It's not anymore?"

"Not even close. I was looking over the kindergarten standards last night and it's just crazy what they expect these kids to do by the end of the year."

Angela nods and looks from the coffee pot to the clock on the wall and back. Ever since I had the twins, I've dedicated my entire life to them, like any halfway decent mother would do. But since I'm on my own, it's even harder to find time to go out and do anything remotely adult. I talk about them too much, but I feel like I've forgotten how to talk about anything else.

"Well, maybe next week then." She sets her coffee cup on the counter next to the pot, still watching it fill. "We've been trying to get out at least once a week. August starts the unofficial end of summer and it'll be too cold to go out sooner than we know it."

"Ugh, you're right. I'm still trying to recover from that last Polar Vortex. I am not ready for winter."

"I question why I live here every winter," she laughs. "But I love this damn city too much. You've been here your whole life too, right?"

"Yeah. Born and raised." Chicago has it's good and bad qualities, but it's home. The neighborhood I'm currently in is less than ideal, but I'll get us out of there and into somewhere nicer. A big-ass house on North Orchard Street in Lincoln Park is goals, but I'll gladly settle for a third-story apartment along the lake.

Angela and I both get more coffee and go back to our desks. I squeeze my eyes closed, hoping if I give myself a ten-second break I'll be able to open my eyes back up and focus like a boss.

On this boring-as-hell project.

I'm close to dozing off again when my desk phone rings. I can tell by the lit-up number flashing at me that the call is coming from my manager, Veronica Marshall's office.

EMILY GOODWIN

"Hello?" I answer, cradling the phone to my ear with my shoulder.

"Good morning, Harper. Can you come into my office when you have a spare moment, please?"

Always fearing the worst, my heart skips a beat with fear. "Uh, sure. I'll be right in." I hang up, pulse increasing, and think back to the last few weeks. Did I do anything to piss anyone off? I don't think so, but you never know.

I'm a hard worker but have a bad habit of getting a little chatty when I'm standing in the break room, or even when I pass by someone's desk. I like to talk, and I don't get out much.

Running my hands over my messy hair, I get up and feel like all eyes are on me as I walk through the row of cubicles and toward Veronica's office. My mind is racing the whole time, going over every and anything I could have done to get myself into trouble.

The office door is closed, and I knock before reaching for the doorknob.

"Come in," Veronica calls, and I take in one more shaky breath and twist the handle. Veronica is on her computer, furiously typing away at what I'm going to pretend is a passion-filled email to her lover.

It's a weird thing I do. I make up little stories to distract myself with, though sometimes I get so into my own stories I go home and write them down and give them alternate endings in a top-secret notebook that not even my girls know about.

"Close the door behind you and have a seat," she tells me, not taking her eyes off her computer. My heart rate speeds up even more, and I can feel sweat starting to collect in beads between my breasts. I picked a great fucking day to wear this pale yellow, silk top that's less than friendly to sweat stains.

My throat gets that closed-up feeling, and it's all I can do not to shake as I sink down into a dated, yet comfortable, plaid armchair. A full minute passes before Veronica looks up from her

14

computer. She has a faint smile on her face, furthering my suspicion of her emailing a lover.

"I just got started on performance reviews," she begins, sending another wave of anxiety through me. I wasn't always this gloom-and-doom, but the thought of getting reprimanded at work is, well, awful in its own way, but puts the fear of God into me that I could easily lose my job.

And then I wouldn't know what I'd do.

"Your file surprised me."

"In a good way, I hope."

She laughs. "Yes, in a good way. You're smart, dedicated, and driven, too much so to be working a tedious job like you are now."

"I, um, always intended on going back to school and finish my degree, but it's hard with my kids being so young," I ramble and reach up to my neck, taking a little lemon-shaped charm between my fingers. It was a gift from my mother when I graduated high school. *Life gives out its fair share of lemons,* she'd tell me. *Just remember to turn them into lemonade.*

Veronica holds up her hand, silencing me. "I get it. I have three boys, all grown now, but I remember just how it was. The boys' father and I divorced when my youngest was only four, and for the next ten years, it was just me and my boys."

Leaning back in her chair, she eyes me up and down again. "Most people who take this job spend a year or two getting experience under their belts and then move on or up." She looks up at the ceiling, literally meaning people here move up one more floor to be an intern or assistant with the hopes of being hired on full-time as a publicist. "You remind me of myself," she starts again. "Which is why I'm willing to break my rule of *don't play favorites* and help you out. Well, if you'll take my help, that is."

"You've captured my interest," I tell her and let out a breath. I give the little lemon a squeeze and put my hands back in my lap, feeling a little better. I'm not getting fired or yelled at or even scolded. "But I'm not quite following."

"Mr. Harding is in need of a new assistant, starting tomorrow. The last three assistants who have worked for him have gone on to be hired full-time by the firm."

Mr. Harding built this company from the ground up. Rumor has it he will be retiring within the next year, and getting to pick his brain while bringing him coffee or organizing his schedule would be more educational than sitting through an entire semester of marketing and advertising classes.

"It would be more hours than you're currently working, but you would get a significance pay raise, be paid salary and not hourly, get two weeks paid vacation your first year, and you'd get benefits plus a handful of other incentives, like a company car to ensure you're able to run errands for Mr. Harding."

I blink rapidly, too stunned to let the information sink in. "And I'd start tomorrow?"

"Yes, Mr. Harding's assistant was in an accident last night."

"Oh my God, is she okay?"

"He, and I was told he'll make a complete recovery but had some sort of awakening and doesn't want to work for corporate America anymore." She rolls her eyes.

I nod and look past Veronica, squinting from the bright light coming through the large window. I used to dream of having an office like this, with a big desk, stark and modern decor, and huge windows that look down on the busy city below. She's the head analyst here and is in charge of all of us "researchers" on the twelfth floor.

It was the thing I wanted most in life. Get the job and be successful in my career. I thought that's all I needed to be happy. I'd be making good money, traveling the world, well, maybe not the world, but I'd escape the cold Chicago winters to Vegas or Miami. And of course, I'd have a super-hot, equally successful fiancé by now and we'd be happily planning our over-the-top wedding.

But things didn't quite go according to plan, obviously. Though now I know without a doubt there is more to life than working. There are more important things than having my name on a silver nameplate tacked to the door of my office.

Yeah, it's important to make money since you can't really live without any, but at the end of the day, it's who you go home to that counts. I used to think that my career would define me, and it wasn't until having my own children that I realized a *thing* can't define you at all. You can quit your job and get another. You can switch fields and take your career in a totally different direction.

It's not definite or defining.

"Need time to think about it?" Veronica asks.

"Yes, I mean no." More money means paying off debts. And paying off debts means being able to put money into savings and not having to live paycheck to paycheck. And being able to take two whole freaking weeks off and still get paid…sign me up! "No, I don't need more time," I clarify. "I'll take the job."

CHAPTER 3

ALEX

M*aybe I'm getting old.*
Another late night with a woman I didn't know turned into an early morning at the office. My bed was occupied last night, but my house still felt empty.

I felt empty.

Truth is, I'm over the whole one-night-stand thing. It was fun in the past, but now I find myself craving something different... something *more*. Which is ridiculous, I know. I don't have time for a relationship, and even if I did, finding one person I'd want to spend forever with—who'd want to spend forever with me—seems overwhelmingly daunting.

I suppose it's cliché to say coming from a broken home has left me doubting any sort of romantic relationship will last in the end. On the outside, it looked like we were living the dream. Rich, all smiles in family photos, and living in a big-ass house in one of the most expensive neighborhoods in Chicago.

But behind closed doors, it was a different story. Dad got violent when he drank, and I felt it was my job as the only other male in the house to protect my mom and sister. Mom, more concerned with impressing everyone at the country club, turned a blind eye to everything and didn't give a shit what happened to me or Nicole.

Mom and Dad both had affairs, and their marriage was nothing more than a hollow sham. It wasn't sacred. It didn't matter.

True love isn't real, which is what led me down the path of meaningless sex and one-night stands.

And I as laid there in my bed last night, listening to the woman—Monica, maybe? Or was it Mandi?—get into the shower, I found myself anxious to get my ass up in just a few hours and drag it to the office. I enjoy my work, and while it doesn't fill the void inside me, it distracts me from it. It's pathetic if I think about it, so in turn, I don't.

I bring my hand to my forehead and let my eyes full shut. Is the sun always this fucking bright? And who's genius idea was it to *not* put blinds or curtains up on these floor-to-ceiling windows?

Blindly reaching out, I feel for the phone on my desk. As soon as my fingers touch the cool plastic, I remember that Jason isn't here today.

Fuck me.

I'd call for an intern to come in here, but I don't know the extension to reach them. Jason always did it for me. I in no way considered Jason, my former assistant, a friend, but after working together for the last three years, we developed a good rhythm. I've been at the office a whole three minutes and already need him, but I'll never fucking admit that.

What I will admit is that I need coffee. I can sit here and grumble about it, or I can get my ass up and get it myself. Before I get up, my office door opens and I look up, narrowing my eyes.

Everyone in the office knows not to come in here without knocking. But who walks in isn't just *everyone*.

"Hello, Father." I plow my hand through my hair and lean back in my leather chair. "And to what do I owe this pleasure?"

We've had a rough relationship over the years, and working together has made it either better or worse, depending on the day.

"Where is the proposal for the Huntington project? I was supposed to look over it this morning."

Ah, fuck. Jason always brought projects and proposals to my father's desk.

"It's...it's...." I sit up and open the top drawer of my desk. I spent a week on this proposal and it's fucking gold. The clients are going to eat it up. "Fuck. Jason always took it." I open the middle drawer and find the folder in a neatly organized stack. I pull it out and flop it down on the desk.

"You need to get your shit together," Dad grumbles. "I'm supposed to be retiring within a year but maybe I should push it back. Again."

"I can handle the company."

"Can you? Because you look hungover and sloppy."

I look down at my designer suit. It's perfectly fitted, and I'm in impeccable shape, thanks to a rather strict gym routine and diet, which I completely strayed from when I was sucking Jello shots off that hot blonde's stomach last night.

"We have a reputation to uphold here," he reminds me, as if I forgot it from the other million times he's mentioned it. It pisses me off...mostly because he's right. "Put some drops in your eyes, get a coffee, and be on time for the client meeting this morning." Dad grabs the file off my desk. "And find yourself a new assistant."

∽

I slide the bill over to me and stick my credit card inside the little leather folder without even looking at the cost of lunch. We had two bottles of three-hundred-dollar Champagne, and three appetizers, and I lost count of all the dessert ordered.

But I just landed us another multi-million-dollar account.

"I'm excited to work with the best PR firm in the city," Mr. Johnson says, shaking my hand.

"We're going to do great things for your company," I assure him. "I look forward to what the future holds." We exchange more bullshit pleasantries on our way out of the restaurant, stepping out onto the busy sidewalk of downtown Chicago. The sun is low in the sky, but the air is holding onto the heat with a vengeance. I'm already looking forward to cool, crisp days of fall.

I head back to the office, riding on the high I always get from scoring a new client. Our rival PR firm had been trying to get this particular account as well, and the game of winning over clients is part of what I love about my job. It's a challenge, and the harder it is, the more satisfied I feel when I win. And I always win.

Back at my desk, I sort through my email. It's something Jason usually did for me, deleting anything that wasn't worth my time or answering the clients himself. There's an email from my father I open right away.

Subject: "Assistant: Watson, Har"

Starts tomorrow. File is in system if you want to review. If you find issues, let me know ASAP. I've already hired.

I hit reply, finding it almost funny that dear old dad is so on top of anything business-related but only remembers my birthday when his own assistant reminds him. I don't see the point in reviewing Har's file. And what kind of name is "Har"? Is it short for Harry?

Typing a quick reply, I thank Dad for getting me a new assistant on such short notice and then go back to work, getting a head start on the account I just secured.

About half an hour later, someone knocks on the door. I look up, forgetting yet again that Jason isn't out there to handle it.

"Come in," I call, and the door opens.

Marcus, one of the secretaries, inches in. He's new and is

scared of me. A lot of the new employees are. Someone else might feel bad about it, but I see it as a sign I'm a good boss. We're not here to be friends. We're here to make money.

"Yes?" I ask after he stares at me for a few seconds.

"Your sister is on the line. Should I send her through?"

I cock an eyebrow. Why the hell is Nicole calling me? Is something wrong? "Yes, go ahead."

The door clicks shut and a few seconds later the phone on my desk rings.

"Why are you calling me at work?" I say as soon as I answer the phone. I don't mean it to sound as harsh as it does, but I'm worried.

"Oh, I'm sorry, I meant to call my big brother, not my father," she spits, and the jab actually hurts.

"Fine, sorry. But what do you want? I'm in the middle of putting together a client proposal."

"And I'm about to go into surgery."

"You called to tell me that? That's nothing new for you."

"I know, but I was supposed to be leaving right now so I'll be home in time to take Henry to his kindergarten orientation, but there was a bad car accident with multiple victims. It's all hands on deck at the hospital and I'm waiting for the chopper to bring my patient for emergency surgery to save his life."

My sister is a surgeon and I'm so damn proud of her. "I still don't get what this has to do with me."

"Calvin is in Dallas for business and Mom is at a day-spa and *can't leave in the middle of my treatments,*" she says in a voice imitating our mother. I can't help but laugh. "Trust me, I feel bad asking, but is there any way you could take Henry to student orientation?"

"What about your nanny?"

"I am not going to be one of those moms who sends her kid to orientation with the nanny. The school really advises against it anyway. You're family and are one of his emergency contacts.

Plus, Henry would love to see Uncle Alex. It's been a while, and he asks about you all the time."

I wish I could help, but I have so much to do at the office. "I'm at work, Nicole."

"So am I. Please, Alex. Don't make me pull the doctor card."

"What is the doctor card?"

"The card where I remind you that I'm literally saving some-one's life and you're putting together marketing plans that if you put on hold for an hour or so won't kill anyone. Please, Alex. I feel like a bad mom for not being there," she adds, voice thinning out. "I don't want to be like Mom."

"You're nothing like Mom," I tell her. Nicole and I were raised by our nanny. Dad was at the office more often than not, and Mom...I still don't know what the hell she did or where she was. She wasn't home and wasn't involved in our lives at all. "You're a good mom and Henry is lucky to have you. You're not able to be at orientation but you *want* to be there. Mom never wanted to have anything to do with us."

"Thanks, Al."

"Of course. And I'll go. Text me the details."

CHAPTER 4

"Girls!" I turn into the parking lot, nerves freaking shot. We barely made it here on time and the girls have been fighting over a stupid toy the whole time. Dad gave them each five dollars and took them to the store. The toy they wanted was ten dollars, so they combined their money and conned their poor, sweet grandfather into believing that buying one would be fine since they could share.

"If you don't stop, I'm going to take that doll and throw it out the window!" I snap and then feel bad. The girls were excited to see me and show me their LOL Doll, but I was in such a rush I brushed them off and practically dragged them into the car.

"Mommy, no!" Penny screams. "It's my doll!"

"No, it's mine!" Violet counters and the two start crying.

"Stop it!" I scream at the top of my lungs and then instantly feel bad—again—for screaming. This is not my finest parenting moment. "Please, girls," I say. I don't try to hide the desperation in my voice. "Please, just behave. We need to be on your best behavior so the teachers will be excited to have you," I add, not wanting to tell them I'm afraid that if I come into the school with

24

a screaming kid under each arm, the school will reject us and give the scholarship to someone else.

We're a minute away, and orientation officially starts in five minutes. Assuming I can find a parking spot and get the girls out of the car in time, we might walk in with thirty seconds to spare.

The school has a tiny parking lot, with a sign saying that the spots are reserved tonight for orientation parents. I spent the afternoon filling out paperwork for my new job, and was given keys to my very own Lexus to use at my disposal.

I might look the part when I pull into a parking space, but seeing expensive car after expensive car reminds me how much we don't fit in here. I turn down the last row and see a spot at the end. I flick on my turn signal, driving slow since I'm more than a little terrified of getting a scratch on this new car.

Penny screams at her sister and kicks the back of my seat. Again. I've asked her not to at least three times on the way over. It's annoying, distracting, and could cause me to get into an accident. And the last thing I need is damage to the leather seats from children's feet. I'm not entirely sure I'm supposed to put in car seats, and I didn't ask.

I step on the brake and turn around, eyes wide.

"Stop kicking my seat!"

"I'm not," she protests, and the fact that she straight-up lied isn't helping my anger. "It's Vi."

"Vi can't reach my seat with her feet. Stop lying, Penny. And listen. Please, just please, listen." Blowing out a breath, I turn around and start forward, only to slam on my brakes when a BMW zips into the spot I was going to take.

Seriously? What an asshole. My signal was on. There was no mistaking that I was going to turn into that spot. Gritting my teeth, I drive forward, circling around the lot and taking a spot at the end. I get the girls out, hide that stupid toy in my purse, and heft them up, one on each hip, and walk as fast as I can toward the school.

I stop halfway, arms hurting. The girls are getting so heavy, and it's like they gained ten pounds overnight.

"We're going to have to walk fast," I tell the girls and hike my purse back up my shoulder. Reaching down, I take their hands and start forward again, walking as fast as their little legs can move.

And then I see him, the asshole in the BMW who took my spot. He's still sitting in his car, with his phone pressed to his ear. We slow and I narrow my eyes.

"Mommy, my shoe's untied," Penny tells me.

"I'll get it." I let go of their hands and crouch down, tying her shoe. I don't know why I thought getting the girls shoes with laces was a good idea already. Oh wait, yes I do. They were three dollars cheaper than ones with velcro.

I quickly tie Penny's shoe and then stand back up right as BMW Asshole gets out of his car.

"Hey," I call, and he stops short, looking around the lot. His eyes settle on me, giving me a blank stare.

"Yes?"

"You took my spot."

"Your spot?" He cocks an eyebrow and looks at his car. "I didn't see your name on it."

"Yeah, well, I didn't see yours either."

"Then what's the problem?" He moves a few feet toward me, but this man doesn't just walk. He saunters, and it's not like he's even trying. I'd be blind not to notice how handsome he is.

Tall. Dark hair, dark eyes, and a strong stubble-covered jawline. He's muscular, apparent under his suit, which has to be designer, I'm sure of it. He's the kind of man who can command a room just by stepping in it. I find him intimidating, and he knows it.

"The problem is I had my signal on and was clearly going to turn into it."

"I didn't see you." He comes closer again and my lips part as I suck in air. I can smell his expensive cologne and my stomach does a weird fluttering thing, almost like that feeling I got way back in the sixth grade when Tommy Stevens told me he thought my butt was cute.

But this guy...he wouldn't say the word *cute*. No, he's a dirty talker, I can tell. I just know that he'd—get it together, Harper.

Has it really been that long since I've been laid?

I look down at my girls. Yes, yes it has been that long. Cue dramatic sigh, right?

"You didn't see me?" I echo, needing to remind myself that this guy is an ass.

"Yeah, and I got into the spot faster."

"There's no way you didn't see me."

"What a shame you had to park all the way over there, and you had to walk," he says sarcastically.

My jaw actually drops. Is he implying I should be walking to get into shape? I lost the baby weight, probably due to stress and skipping meals, but besides my C-section scar, my body bounced right back to normal, and the only stretch marks I got were on my boobs from breast feeding. I wasn't able to do it long, but my boobs went from humble to *whoa*.

I take the girls' hands again. We need to get into the school before we're late. BMW Asshole opens the passenger door and a cute little boy starts to get out. "Learn to obey simple traffic laws. A signal means someone is taking a spot. Well, to the majority of the population who aren't selfish jerks," I add, wanting to get the last word in like a mature adult.

I turn and gently tug on the girls' hands to get them to walk with me. "Don't ever act like that," I tell them, making sure I'm speaking loud enough for BMW Asshole to hear me. "I've raised you better than to be rude and disrespectful."

Tessa is waiting for us right inside the doors, holding the

paperwork that she started for me, filling in everything she could. I quickly fill out the rest, writing so hastily I have no idea if any of this will be legible. Then again, I'm sure a handful of doctors' kids go here. They're probably used to the messy handwriting.

The presentation is starting when we finally get into the auditorium, which is huge, by the way. Never in a million years would I think I'd be describing an elementary school as *swanky*, but here I am, looking at the dark velvet carpet and the sparkling chandelier hanging above me.

"Isn't this pretty?" I whisper to the girls and look around for three open seats. We're the last ones here and everything is full. I scan the room one more time and find two open together, which will be fine. One girl can sit on my lap if they can't both cram into the same chair together.

We quickly walk down the middle aisle and stop at the third row from the back.

"Excuse me," I say to the man sitting at the end of the row. His face is turned down to his phone, and a cute little boy sits next to him. The man turns his head up and my stomach clenches. It's BMW Asshole.

"Seriously," he mumbles under his breath. I raise my eyebrows at him but press my lips together. There's no point saying anything to him now, especially not in front of everyone. And I have the sinking feeling I'm going to come up against more entitled parents throughout our year here anyway.

"Can we sneak in, please?" I ask and he sighs, like it's so much trouble to move his legs to the side so we can walk past. Staring back down at his phone, he angles his legs in so we can shuffle past. Penny sits in the seat next to the little boy, who introduces himself as Henry. I pull Violet into my lap only to have Penny whine that she wants me to hold her.

"I'll switch who I'm holding in ten minutes," I whisper-talk to them. "Okay?"

"I want my own seat," Violet says.

"Perfect. Then you sit there, and I'll hold Penny."

Penny slides back into the seat. "I want my own seat," she whines.

Gritting my teeth, I take a breath and look at the stage. Tessa is up there, along with a few other staff members. She gives me a big smile, helping to ease my nerves.

I zero my attention in on the stage, and just a few seconds later, the principal starts talking, welcoming us to the school. Penny moves into my lap, and Violet sits next to Henry, whispering something to him that makes him giggle. I smile, happy to see that she's making friends already.

"Shhh," I remind the kids and give Henry a wink. He smiles broadly and pushes himself back in his seat, turning his attention back to the stage. The staff is introduced, and we go over policies and procedures.

It's warm in here, and having Penny on my lap doesn't help. BMW Asshole must be feeling it too, because he leans forward and pulls his arms from his suit jacket sleeves. He neatly folds the jacket and rests it on his lap. And then he undoes the wrist button on his shirt and starts to roll up the sleeves.

Good God, he shouldn't be allowed to do that in here. I turn my head as slightly as I can, flicking my eyes from him to the stage and back again. A few other moms are looking as well, and two in the row across from us are obviously staring and talking about him.

He has muscular forearms, and seeing that little bit of tan skin shouldn't make heat flash through me. I swallow hard, trying to push the image of his deft fingers moving up to his collar, slowly unbuttoning his shirt out of my head.

Sin and sex appeal drip from this man, and I know the DILF jokes are going to be strong with this one.

A tour of the school is next, and I'm once again left with my mouth hanging open in shock from how nice everything is.

29

After we've been shown around, the kids are welcome to go into one the classrooms to play. I can tell this is a big deal by the way everyone is acting, and when we get into the classroom, I can see why.

The kids are off playing, giving the parents time to measure each other up. I'm not always the best at reading people, wanting to give them all the benefit of the doubt. And as a sufferer myself of Resting Bitch Face, I try not to judge based off of looks.

But dammit, so many of these moms look like they have sticks up their asses. They're all put together, wearing heels and carrying designer purses. BMW Asshole stands near the door of the classroom, on his phone again.

I slink back, moving out of direct line of sight from a group of moms who make the Stepford Wives look like party animals.

"Hey," a strawberry blonde woman says, walking over. "You're new here, aren't you?"

"Uh, yeah. Yeah, I am." I press my lips together in a tight smile.

"I thought so. I didn't remember seeing you at the open house this summer. Not like I'm creepy and remember everyone, but I'm a fellow twin-mom so you kind of stood out to me." She smiles, showing perfect white teeth. Her lips are perfectly full, probably from injections, and her strawberry blonde hair falls in perfect curls over her shoulders.

"I'm Rose."

"Harper. Nice to meet you." I look out at the kids playing. "Which ones are yours?"

Rose turns, looking for a few seconds to locate her children. I didn't see any other identical twins, but sometimes all it takes is different hairstyles to make my own look like two different people.

"Mason is in the blue shirt with the sloth on it, and Madison is the one picking her nose in the corner." She lets out a sigh and shakes her head. "Your girls are darling."

"Thanks. Your kids are too, nose picking aside. Mine went

through that stage a few months ago. They've either stopped or learned to do it when I'm not looking."

Rose laughs and the knot in my chest loosens a bit. Maybe I'll make a mom-friend here after all.

"How many volunteer spots are you going to sign up for?" Rose asks. "I feel like one or two a month is good enough, but you know how they are." She looks at the Stepford Wives and rolls her eyes. "They're here every day. Like, what's the point of sending the kids to school if you're going to be here with them every day, right? Though it is kind of nice to get out of the house and feel like you have a purpose."

"I, um, work, so I don't know how much I'll be able to do here at the school. But coming in once a month does sound nice, just to help out and see how the girls are doing."

"Oh, what do you do?"

I can't look at Rose as I'm lying, though I'm really not lying. Just fluffing the truth. "I work in public relations at a marketing firm. It's boring, I promise."

"I'm sure it's interesting. What about your husband?"

"It's, uh, just me." I smile as I look at my girls, playing with a dollhouse that probably cost as much as a month's rent for our little apartment. "Just me and the girls."

"Well, kudos to you. You're obviously doing something right."

"Thank you," I say, turning my face up to look at Rose. Her words mean more to me than I expected, and I have to work hard not to get emotional. I cry easily, and while Tessa thinks it's cute and endearing, it annoys me to no end. "I try."

"Being a mom is hard. Jack wants another, but I'm just not ready. You know how it is being pregnant with multiples. There were times I was certain my skin was going to rip right in half, and they were just going to spill out onto the floor."

I laugh and nod my head in agreement. "Wait, your husband's name is Jack?"

"Yes, Jack and Rose, I know, I know. He reminds me almost daily there was room for two on that door."

We both laugh and the knot loosens even more. I like Rose. She's talkative, but nice and much more down to earth than what I expected for someone so insanely gorgeous.

"Hey," I say, lowering my voice. "Who's that guy?"

"The hottie in the suit?" Rose narrows her eyes, taking a few seconds to check BMW Asshole out. "I'm not sure. Do you know which kid he brought?"

"That dark-haired boy by the blocks. He told us his name was Henry."

"Oh, Henry Ortiz. Yeah…I'm not sure who that guy is. It's not his father and he's definitely not the manny." She tips her head. "I know Nicole, Henry's mother. She's not the have-a-public-affair kind and that is not her husband." Tearing her eyes away from BMW Asshole, she looks back at me. "Why are you asking? Hoping he's single too?"

"Oh, God no. I'm just—"

"Madison!" Rose scolds and hurries forward right as Madison pulls a big booger out of her nose and sticks it in her mouth. Rich or poor, five-year-olds are all the same, it turns out.

Playtime goes on for ten more minutes, and the girls are sad to leave, which makes me happy to see that they're liking it here and have made a few new friends already. They talk about everything they did as we go to the car, and I'm smiling the whole way.

As I'm slowly driving down the row of cars in the little parking lot, a car starts to back out of its spot right in front of me. I slam on my brakes and hit the horn.

"Oh for fuck's sake," I mutter under my breath. It's BMW Asshole, and I swear he waited until I was right here to start backing out. I beep the horn again, and he responds by rolling down his window and flipping me off.

"What's going on, Mommy?" Penny asks.

"Nothing, sweetheart." I turn around and give them a reassuring smile. "I'm so glad you guys had fun. Tell me again what you liked best."

"The dollhouse," they say at the same time. Twisting back in my seat, I watch the taillights from the BMW move away from us.

Thank God I never have to see that asshole ever again.

CHAPTER 5

ALEX

"Good morning, Mr. Harding."

"Morning." I step into the elevator next to a man who has to be an intern. His shirt is a size too big, he's clutching a large stack of files, and he's scared shitless to be in this close proximity to me.

A few more people get in with us, and one annoyingly holds the door for someone who's coming in from the lobby. I look down at my watch, able to see the intern out of the corner of my eye. He keeps leaning forward, opening his mouth as if he wants to say something but then chickening out. A ballsy move isn't enough for me to grant anyone a promotion, but it's enough to get my attention.

This intern could be shit at the job. Or he could be good.

The elevator doors shut with a ding, and I turn my head up. There's a woman standing near the doors. Long, dark hair falls down her back in waves, and she's wearing a tight gray skirt that hugs her perfect ass. Long legs end in black heels, and I look her up and down once more.

Her back is to me. She could be anyone. But I'm pretty sure I'd remember an ass like that. Staring straight ahead, she adjusts her purse on her shoulder every few seconds. Her shoulders are tense and the way she shifts her weight back and forth between her heels and the balls of her feet let me know she's nervous about something.

The elevator stops at the next floor up, and a few more people try to cram in. I'm not afraid of elevators, per se, but I'd be really fucking pissed if we got stuck like this, with barely enough space to breathe, let alone move.

The woman in the tight skirt steps to the side, making room. She turns slightly, and her hair moves over her shoulder, covering half her face. Still, there's something familiar about her. If she works in this building, then I've seen her before.

She rides all the way up to the fourteenth floor with the intern and me. If she worked on my floor, I'd definitely remember her. I'll find out who she is soon enough, though when the elevator door open, she dodges out and hurries down the hall toward the restrooms.

The sight of her fuckable ass made my cock stir in my pants, but she's out of my mind when I step foot into the office. Since I left early yesterday, I have a lot of work to catch up on. My new assistant better be on time this morning.

I set my shit down at my desk and look at my watch again. The workday officially starts in two minutes. Where the fuck is my assistant? Punctuality is important to me, and not being on time makes it hard to get the job done.

And I want coffee.

Grumbling, I walk out of my office. My father is standing near the front desk, talking to the woman in the tight skirt. She's laughing at whatever he said, and the fucker is eating it up.

You're too old for her, Pops. Give it up before you embarrass yourself.

"Ah, good, Alex," Dad says, holding out his hand. "Perfect timing." He motions for me to come over, and the woman, whose ass looks even better from this angle, flips her hair back over her shoulder, and it's like everything moves in slow motion.

Her full red lips have been painted red and are currently pulled up in a brilliant smile that lights up the whole fucking room. Long lashes come together when she blinks, and deep emerald-colored eyes sparkle even though we're inside, standing beneath fluorescent lights.

She's gorgeous, and I know I've never laid eyes on her before, yet she looks so damn familiar it's driving me crazy.

Suddenly, her smile disappears, and her eyes widen. I blink and realize she's the holier-than-thou, tired-looking mom that yelled at me from last night. I don't normally snap like that to complete strangers, but she was way out of line. I didn't see that she had her signal on. I was distracted, I'll admit, but I'm not that big of an asshole to zoom in and take someone's spot.

What. The. Actual. Fuck.

She looks worlds different than she did last night. Her hair isn't pulled up in a messy bun. Instead, it's hanging loose, framing her pretty face. I don't even remember what she was wearing before, but it sure as hell wasn't this sexy librarian get up. All she needs is a pair of fake glasses to take off so she can chew on the ends when she tells me I have an overdue book.

Perky round breasts are hidden beneath her blouse, and the top button has come undone, or she left it that way on purpose. Her skirt is tight around her slender waist, and she looks much too young to be the mother of the two children I saw her with last night. Her beauty struck me then as well, and I mistook her to be the nanny at first. Then I saw the way she looked at her children and knew she was their mother. Only a mom could be that annoyed and frustrated yet still look at her children with nothing but love in her eyes.

I usually don't hire anyone I'm physically attracted to. Mixing business with pleasure is just as bad as shitting where you eat, and it's something I never do. This woman is definitely attractive, but I think I'm safe from being tempted to woo her into my bedroom.

I know how much of a pain in the ass she is.

And now she's here, standing in my office, talking and laughing with my father.

"You," she rushes out, slowly shaking her head back and forth. The color drains from her face and her lips part.

"What are you doing here?" I ask and close the distance between us.

Dad looks from the woman to me and back again. "Do you two know each other? This is Harper, your new assistant."

"Wait," Harper says, looking even more horrified than before. "I thought I was working for you. I was told I'd be working with Mr. Harding."

"I am Mr. Harding," I spit, annoyed to be shadowed by my father. Yes, he started this company, but I'm the one who brought it to the high-earning level it is today.

Harper stands there like a deer in headlights, emerald eyes wide. Her cheeks flush, and the redness creeps down her neck and over her chest.

"Is there going to be a problem?" Dad asks slowly, eyes flitting between Harper and me.

"No," Harper says quickly. Too quickly. "There won't be." She forces a smile and directs her attention to me. "I look forward to working with you, Mr. Harding."

"Yeah, I'm sure you do." I'm not one for pointless small talk or sugarcoating anything.

She extends her hand for me to shake. "Where are my manners? I'm Harper Watson, and it's so nice to meet you."

I take her hand and am taken aback by how soft and warm she feels. Her fingers are slender, and her touch is gentle at first, but then her grip tightens into a firm handshake.

Her eyes are still wide with shock and fear, reflecting back an innocence I've never personally known. It makes the strangest

EMILY GOODWIN

feeling flash through me, and I find myself wanting to protect this innocence inside of her almost as much as I want to take it.

There's a chance I'll be doing both by firing her by the end of the day. I can't imagine someone who yells at strangers over something as trivial as a parking spot is going to be a good fit for me.

"Likewise." I let go of her hand and miss her soft, smooth skin already. "Follow me to my office. I have a lot to do today."

She gives me a curt nod, puts another fake-ass smile on her pretty face, and turns her attention back to my father. Her smile turns genuine and Dad takes her small hand in both of his own.

"It was an honor to meet you," Harper tells him. "Ever since I read that Forbes article about you and the company, I just knew I had to work here."

Dad beams and inches his fingers up her wrist. Harper tenses. Sorry, lady. Your idol is a fucking creep. Who. Is. Married.

"Work hard and prove yourself and you'll never know where you'll end up." Dad gives her a wink and Harper flushes again.

"Thank you, sir." She pulls her hand back and presses it against her thigh. Looking uncomfortable, and looks at me. I motion for her to follow me into my office.

"Listen," I start and do my best not to check her out. It's strange, actually, having a female assistant. When I first started here, Dad wouldn't allow it out of fear I'd end up sleeping with them. Back then, I would have. Now I know better.

This career means too much to me.

Dan Swanson was my first assistant. He's a few years older than me and had more education and experience under his belt than I did at the time, but sometimes it's more about *who* you know. Now Dan is one of our best publicists who I consider a personal friend.

It's not that I think Harper will do a bad job because she's a woman. Our top agent is a woman, and I strongly advocate for all our female employees here to be treated fairly and receive equal pay. It's different, that's all, and I can't see her being too thrilled about having a lunch meeting at *Tommy's*, a tavern-style restaurant famous for their waitresses. More specifically, the tight white shirts and short plaid skirts they wear.

And for sure there are many women who are fine with that and even into that, but Harper? Miss Uptight-mom? No fucking way.

"We were both surprised at this. Clearly there's been some sort of mistake due to a lack of communication. I can make sure you get your previous job—"

"No," she blurts. "It's fine with me, I mean...if it's fine with you." The color comes back to her cheeks and she nervously pushes her hair back. "I really need this job and won't disappoint you. And...and I'm sorry about last night even though you were wrong to steal my spot." Swallowing hard, she looks at me, really looks at me.

I stare at her for a few seconds, not even sure what to fucking do. She's been here all of thirty seconds and she's already vastly different from the assistants I've had in the past. She said she needs this job but isn't groveling at my feet like most interns and assistants do. It's refreshing, really.

"I don't care about last night," I tell her. "What I care about is getting my job done, and getting it done well. I need someone who can jump right in. I don't have time to hold anyone's hand."

Her hand isn't the only thing I'd like to hold...

"I'm a fast learner," she tells me, taking a tentative step forward. "I'm smart and I'm capable and will be able to do whatever you need me to do. Well, not whatever. I won't murder anyone. Or do anything illegal, just to cover my bases. Maybe some illegal things, I don't want to cross them off the list. I suppose it depends on what illegal activity you'd want me to be doing, like breaking into a morgue to steal files about a suspicious death that may or may not have been caused by vampires,

I'd be all in. But steal computer files from a competitor, count me out."

I blink. Once. Twice. Three times.

"What?"

She takes a breath and looks me right in the eye. "I can handle the job and will get started right away. Your previous assistant is supposed to call and talk me through things too."

"Good. Start by getting me a coffee, please."

She nods. "How do you like your coffee?"

"Black."

"Okay. I'll, uh, be right back." She disappears out of the office, and it hits me that she has no idea where anything is on this floor. I go to my desk and open up my emails. There are over a dozen junk emails in my inbox, which pisses me off. How the fuck does my work email address even end up on these mailing lists? Jason would have had these deleted by now, and I've responded to two clients before Harper comes back with my coffee.

Today is going to be a long, fucking day, and I can't promise Harper will still be my assistant by the end of it.

CHAPTER 6

HARPER

I cannot believe I yelled at my boss.

Technically, he wasn't my boss yet—wait, yes he was. *Oh my God.* I signed all the paperwork before I left the office yesterday. I just didn't know he was my boss, and he didn't know I was his assistant.

Such a good way to start a job, I know. I don't expect to be friends with my boss and it's not like I want to hang out with him after work either. But people usually like me, and Alexander Harding definitely does not.

It's my first day on the job and my boss already hates me.

And I think I hate him a little too. He's pompous, entitled, and rude. I'm going to hate working for him and having to bring him coffee every morning and do a million other little tedious things he's more than capable of doing himself.

This job is temporary, and I won't be here forever. If it were a big bag of lemons, then I hit the lemonade jackpot. What tastes sour today can be sweet tomorrow, and it will pay off in the end.

I'll just have to remind myself of that every day. Probably twice a day. I'll drink my lemonade...but first I need to figure out where to get Alexander his coffee.

Mind whirling, I walk a few feet forward only to slow and look around again.

"Harper, right?" someone calls. I turn around to see a young man leaning over a desk at the entrance to the office. I nod and he waves me over. "I'm Marcus."

"I'm Harper, but you, um, already know that. It's nice to meet you."

"You look a little lost."

"That would be because I am."

He gives me a sympathetic smile and comes around the desk. "Let me give you the two-minute tour."

"Thank you."

"Bathrooms are down the hall by the elevator," he starts, pointing to the doors that lead into the main office area. "And then we have the interns." He waves his hand at the open area behind the large secretary's desk. There are a dozen or so desks filled with bright-eyed, hopeful-looking interns hoping to move up and get a permanent job at the firm.

We walk through them, pausing at the hallway that takes us to Alexander's office. He shows me the two conference rooms, more offices, and finally, the break room.

And holy shit, it's nice.

Huge.

Fancy.

And the snacks are free.

I'm going to gain ten pounds my first week.

"Thank you again," I tell Marcus, spotting the coffee pot. It's next to an espresso machine, which looks way too complicated for me to use. Thank goodness Alexander just wants a black coffee.

Two men in fitted suits are seated at a table near the windows, talking about how they could bounce quarters off of the ass of some dancer at a club last night. I slip into the room, going right for the coffee. I assume there are mugs or paper cups in the cabinet.

"...and her big tits, hmmm, I'm telling you, man—" One of the men looks up, cutting off as soon as he sees me. "Oh, shit. Sorry."

The other turns and does a double-take, checking me out. He wants me to know he finds me attractive, and I'm not sure how I feel about that. It's flattering on one hand, and a little creepy on the other.

I'm not a piece of meat, though it is nice to know mama's still got it.

"I don't think we've met," the guy talking about big tits stands and buttons his suit jacket. "I'm Dan Swanson, and we're not always this vulgar."

Heels click on the hard floor behind me. "Don't bullshit her," a woman says. "They're usually worse." She steps into the room and extends her hand for me to shake. She's tall, thin, with the smoothest blonde hair I've ever seen. "Clarissa Lewis, nice to meet you."

"Harper," I say and shake her hand. "Nice to meet you too."

She goes to the fancy espresso machine and I wonder if I can nonchalantly stand back and watch her use it so I can figure it out. If not, I'll be writing down the make and model and watching Youtube videos on it later.

"I didn't know we hired new interns."

"I'm, um, not a temp. I'm Mr. Harding's new assistant."

"You're replacing Jason?" Clarissa looks away from the espresso machine and eyes me up and down. "I would not have expected that."

"Is that a good thing?" I ask with a nervous laugh. I've already forgotten the sequence of buttons she's pressed on that damn machine.

"Give me a week and I'll get back to you on that." She fills up her coffee and turns to leave. "Good luck. You'll need it."

"Will I really need luck?" I ask Dan once Clarissa is out of the break room. I open the same cabinet she did and grab a white mug.

"Nah," Dan waves his hand in the air. "Alex isn't so bad when you get to know him." He gives me a reassuring smile, but his eyes can't hide the lie.

I'm going to need all the luck in the world to get through this.

~

"Shit!" I blink my eyes, hoping I'm just reading the time wrong. Nope. "Shit, shit, shit!" I throw the covers back and slide my arm out from underneath Penny. She came into my bed this morning, just a minute before my alarm went off.

She told me she had a bad dream and wanted to snuggle until she felt better. I turned off my alarm, telling myself we'd just lay here for five minutes and then get up. Well, twenty minutes have passed and now we're running late.

Still grumbling, I fly out of bed, trip over my clothes that I stripped out of and left on the ground, and hurry into the bathroom. I'm not a morning person in the least, and both girls have inherited my night-owl gene. It's a struggle to get them up and out of the house every morning, even though we've been getting up and going to daycare for most of their lives now.

It's strange when I stop and think about it—which isn't going to happen this morning. I'm in too much of a rush—but I'd give anything to stay home with my babies now instead of working that dream job. They're going into kindergarten on Monday and I feel like I've worked more than I've played with them, which is normal, I know.

But it doesn't make me like it.

I wash my face, brush out my hair, which is thankfully holding a wave thanks to yesterday's loose curls. Tapping the screen of my phone to see the time, I have a few seconds of mental panic where I'm not sure what to do or how the hell I'm going to make it to work on time this morning.

Racing out of the bathroom, I go into the kitchen and open the pantry. We're really low on groceries, and my bank account is really low on funds. Not a good combination.

"Mommy," Violet calls from her bedroom. "Where are you?"

"Kitchen," I reply, not having to talk louder than my normal "inside voice". The apartment is small, consisting of a small living room that flows into an even smaller kitchenette. We have one tiny bathroom with a sink, tub, and toilet crammed into a space smaller than a walk-in closet, and then the two bedrooms. Horses have bigger stalls than the rooms we sleep in, but hey, at least we have a roof over our heads and a safe place to stay, right? Though if I were to look up the crime stats for this neighborhood, I'd start sleeping with a knife under my pillow again.

"Morning, baby," I tell Violet when she slowly walks to the table. She reminds me of a zombie with slow, jerky movements and messy hair. That girl wakes up with impressive bedhead. The girls both have heads of gorgeous, thick, dark brown hair, which they got from me.

Their perfect natural curls...those they had to get from their father, as well as their hazel eyes. Because their father had hazel eyes too...I think. We weren't in a relationship when I got pregnant. We weren't even casually dating.

I went to a party with Tessa, needing a distraction from the worst week of my life. In my last year of college, I needed to make up for lost time when it came to partying. I preferred to spend my nights in my dorm with a book where Tessa liked to go out and get drunk. I can't remember how many nights I held her hair back, keeping it from dipping into the dirty co-ed toilets as she puked up half a bottle of vodka.

Despite the puking that was always paired with crying and empty promises that she'd "never drink again", Tessa always went back out and raved about how much fun said parties were. We're opposite in a lot of ways, which is probably why we make such good friends.

And the one time Tessa got me to go out with her, the one time I needed a break and a drink and to just forget about how unfair the world was, it only proved to me that it doesn't matter if you're a good or bad person.

Things just happen.

Bad things.

Good things.

Unfair things.

They just happen randomly.

Or maybe it wasn't random at all. I'd lost everything only to be given two precious daughters who I love more than life itself. Who have me waking up every morning wanting to do better.

For them.

"Can we have breakfast?" Violet asks, rubbing her eyes. "I hungry."

"I'm hungry," I correct. "And yes, we have to speed eat without choking this morning." I open a cabinet and pull out crackers and peanut butter. Getting out two plates, I give each girl four crackers and smear peanut butter on them, and then grab an apple from the back of the fridge. After cutting off all the bruised spots, I have enough left over to give each girl three slices.

I really need to do better.

The lump in my throat comes back, and I have to swallow hard to make it go away. I've gotten a pay raise from the new job, and I'm going to go crazy at the grocery store once the money comes through.

Okay, not *crazy*-crazy, but I'm getting fresh fruit and veggies. And bacon. So much bacon. Again, not really. Just one package, but a girl can dream.

"Eat, sweetheart. I'm going to get your sister up." Violet nods and rests her head on the table. I feel bad making them get up early so I can drop them off at daycare, but we're going to have to get used to getting up and leaving even earlier once school starts. The girls have to be there by eight-thirty, and need to be picked up by two-thirty. Thank God Tessa is willing to take them either home with her or over to Dad's apartment.

"Penny," I say softly and go back into my room. I pull up the blinds to let in the little bit of light this cloudy day has to offer. The outside of the window is in serious need of cleaning, but there's a better chance of me winning the lottery, meeting a prince in disguise who falls madly in love with me, and finally getting my letter to Hogwarts—on the same day—than there is that the super would hire someone to clean the windows of this apartment complex.

We didn't move in here for the glitz and the glamour, luckily.

"It's time to get up, sweetheart."

Penny slits her eyes open and groans, pulling the blankets back over her face.

"I know," I tell her and flop down on the bed. "I want to go back to sleep too, but I have to take you guys to daycare so I can work."

"No daycare. No daycare," she groans, voice edging on whining. Only my kids can wake up and whine, I swear. It grates my nerves if I'm being honest, and my patience is shortened when I'm tired.

Which I always am.

"It's Friday!" I scoop her up in my arms and sit her up. "That means we get to sleep in tomorrow and watch movies and go to the park if it's nice."

"Can we do spa day?"

"What's a spa day?" I ask, hoping she doesn't mean go to an actual spa. Even if I could afford it, I think I'd draw the line at taking five-year-olds. It would be the opposite of relaxing.

"We do face masks and paint nails. I saw it on Babydoll."

Babydoll is what they call watching YouTube Kids. I'm not sure why that name stuck, but it did.

"That sounds fun! I'll see what I can find for face masks. I have nail polish and I still have that bath bomb Aunt Tessa gave me for my birthday to use. That sounds like something you'd do a spa too, doesn't it?"

Penny perks up, smiling and nodding.

"But we can't have a spa day if I don't go to work. So come on, get up and eat and I'll pick out clothes for today."

"Can I match sissy?"

"I'll see what I can do," I tell her with a smile. The girls have similar clothes, but since ninety-nine percent of what they own came secondhand, it's not like I was able to buy sets of anything.

Ten minutes later, I'm still rushing around to get ready. Penny started the day slow, and now Violet is taking a turn having a meltdown and won't sit still as I try to brush her hair.

"I'm not doing your hair," I tell her and let go of the handful of thick locks I was holding. "You are old enough to sit still while I put your hair in a ponytail. You can wear it down now."

Violet flops from the couch to the floor, crying. "I want my hair up. Please, Mommy!"

I close my eyes, knowing that I shouldn't give in. She's whining because she knows I end up feeling bad, but it's hot and humid out and they go outside at daycare. She really should have her hair up, but she should also sit still for thirty seconds and not turn her head back and forth just to test me.

"No. We tried three times and you didn't listen." I set the hairbrush down and get up, grabbing my cosmetic bag. I don't wear a lot of makeup, mostly because I don't have time and good makeup is expensive. But I want to make an effort for at least the first month at my new job.

And as much as I hate admitting it, everyone on floor fourteen looks so put together. Like they're actually in charge of their lives and aren't rushing around with two minutes to spare while a five-year-old is rolling around on the floor crying.

I risk losing a minute of precious time to go to the bathroom, but there's never a promise I won't get stuck in traffic on my way into the city, and having to pee while sitting still on the highway is awful. When I come out of the bathroom, Penny is on the floor too, hugging her sister.

I'm an only child, so I don't quite get the bond between siblings. These two are sisters but so much more. They have their own personalities. Penny is a bit more easygoing and Violet is much more of a daredevil, but they are so alike in many other ways, and not just in how they look.

"Ready?" I ask and they both look up.

"Can you do my sister's hair, Mommy?" Penny asks. "I told her to *sit still*." She emphasizes the last words and it's so dang cute.

"Yes, but we need to hurry. Get your shoes on while I put her hair up, please."

Penny nods and Violet sits up. I quickly pull her hair into a ponytail, brushing it smooth. I add big white bows to both girls' hair, grab our stuff, and speed out the door.

We make it to daycare right on time, and I'm not the last one in the car line. The line moves slowly, and when we're two cars away from the door, I put my new fancy Lexus in park and turn around in my seat so I can undo the girls' car seat straps.

Violet jumps right out of her seat and looks out the window, thinking it's cool she actually has leg room to stand in this car. Penny doesn't move, but rests her head against her seat.

"What's wrong, baby?" I ask, turning back around. The line inches forward.

"I don't wanna go to daycare."

"I know, but you have to."

"Why can't I stay with you?"

Oh, my heart. "Because I have to go to work."

"Stay home," she begs, eyes filling with tears. "I'll miss you."

Violet looks at her sister with wide eyes, and I know what's about to happen. She loves school, like Penny usually does, but

49

now thinks that she should be sad and crying because her sister is.

"I'll pick you up as soon as I can and then we'll have the whole weekend to spend together. You'll have fun once you're in. You love your friends!"

"I want to stay home."

"We're already in the car. I'm not going home."

"Then go to work with you," she tries.

"Yeah!" Violet agrees. "Can we go to work with you, Mommy?"

"No, my loves, I'm sorry but you can't. They don't let kids in the building," I lie, hoping it will help. Though I can't imagine Alexander would ever allow children in the office. He's so cold and stuffy…and incredibly good-looking.

Which isn't fair, by the way. He's such an asshole. Why can't someone kind and caring who likes to volunteer and snuggle puppies have his looks?

I drive up to the doors, and Miss Amy, one of the daycare workers, opens our car door.

"Oh, Miss Watson. I didn't know this was you. New car?" she asks and helps Violet jump down.

"Hah, I wish. It's my boss's," I say, feeling it's easier to leave it at that. Saying I have a "company car" sounds too fancy, and explaining that I was given a reliable car to drive around so I can be at Alexander Harding's beck and call is too degrading.

Miss Amy holds out her hand for Penny, who wraps her arms around herself and shakes her head.

"What's wrong Penny-lenny?" Miss Amy asks. She's so good with the kids and most of the time they love her. It's one of the few things that make me feel better about dropping them off here every morning.

"I miss Mommy."

Miss Amy leans farther into the car. "I have an idea, but you can't tell Mommy, okay?" she whisper-talks. "I just opened a brand-new box of crayons. How about you draw a super special picture for Mommy?"

Penny sniffles. "Okay."

"Thank you," I tell Miss Amy, blinking away my own tears. I give each girl and extra hug and kiss before driving off. I'm so upset that I don't realize I'm running late until I pull into the parking garage at work. My old car is still sitting in my same reserved spot, and I pull into a much closer one reserved for Mr. Harding's assistant.

I quite literally run to the elevator to take me to the building, and walk as fast as I can across the lobby and into another elevator. It's eight fifty-four and it takes about a minute to go up to the fourteenth floor, well, as long as we don't stop at every single floor.

Which is what happens. Okay, not *every* floor, but we stop at floor number five. And seven. And ten. And twelve. I practically shove my way off the elevator when we get to my floor and burst into the office, not letting out my breath until the doors shut behind me.

It's eight fifty-seven. I'm not late.

"Hey, girl," Marcus says when I breeze past.

"Hey, how are you?"

"Good. It's Friday. Got big plans for the weekend?"

I shake my head. "I'm hanging out with my kids. So nothing crazy eventful, but I'm looking forward to it."

"You have kids?" He raises his eyebrows. "You're so young. No offense or anything, I just assumed we were like the same age."

"We probably are. I'm twenty-five and have five-year-old twin girls."

"Twins? You look amazing for giving birth to freaking twins."

"It was five years ago," I laugh, not adding that the stress of being a single mom and not being able to buy groceries for myself helped me lose the baby weight. Though I think the whole construct of "baby weight" is utterly ridiculous. Women grow human beings inside of them. Who the fuck cares if we put on a few pounds, get stretch marks, or have loose skin on our bellies?

Let me say that again: women grow humans inside of them. It's nothing less than a miracle, and physical appearance pales in comparison. I've been told over and over how lucky I am not to have gotten stretch marks, and I'm proud of my C-section scar. Not one, but *two* tiny humans came out of me.

It's fucking awesome.

"Well, you look amazing nonetheless."

"Thank you," I say with a smile. That compliment was just what I needed to lessen the ache in my heart over dropping the girls off at daycare. I head to my desk, drop off my purse, and peer inside Mr. Harding's office.

He's on the phone, and holy hell, Alexander is looking fine today in a dark grey fitted suit. It's strange, really, how most of his body is covered up yet I find him to be dripping with sex appeal. He looks up and catches my eye. I give a small wave and a smile and then head into the break room to get a mug of black coffee in case Alexander wants some again this morning.

The break room is full of food this morning, enough so I stop, blink, and make sure I'm not imagining it. There's a chef in a white coat standing behind a hot buffet, and I'm pretty sure those flute glasses are full of actual Champagne.

Why didn't I start working here sooner?

"Morning," a twenty-something-year-old guy says, coming into the room. "I'm Taylor, Dan's assistant. You're Harper, right?"

"I am," I say, not looking away from the coffee. I don't want to spill a drop. "Nice to meet you. Have you been here long?"

"Not too long. Only seven months." He picks up a glass of orange juice. "The guys all hassle me and say this is a chick drink, but I love a good mimosa. Want one?"

Thank goodness he said something, or I would have chugged the thing before I tasted the alcohol.

"Maybe later. I don't drink often, and I haven't had breakfast."

"Get one before they're gone."

"So you guys do this often? Eat bacon and eggs while drinking?"

He nods and holds out a plate for the chef to start filling. "Every Friday. And the first Monday of the month we get massages. Well, *they* do. We can too if there's time." He laughs like the thought of having free time is hilarious. "I better get out there. Good to meet you, Harper."

I take a lingering look at the hot breakfast and force myself away. Hopefully I can give Alexander his coffee and then sneak back in for a plate for myself.

He's still on the phone, so I set his coffee on my desk and sit down, looking over the calendar for the day. A few minutes tick by, and I look up every thirty seconds or so to see if Alexander is still on the phone.

He is.

Finally, the door opens, and he stands in the threshold. I go right into story-writing mode and imagine him tearing off his shirt and throwing someone—who just happens to look like me —into a hidden office closet to make passionate love to.

But then I can feel his anger coming off him in waves.

"Good morning, Mr. Harding." I stand up and pick up the coffee.

"What are you doing?" he asks.

"Giving you coffee," I say slowly, aware that more than one intern is staring at us. "What does it look like I'm doing?" I ask with a slight laugh and a smile. I have a nice smile. Mom used to say it was infectious and I could turn any frown upside down. Maybe that worked when I was a cute five-year-old, but right now, it's pissing Alexander off even more for some reason.

"If you don't take this job seriously then maybe I should find someone else who does."

What? No. I can't lose this job. I won't even get severance pay.

I haven't been here long enough. "I do take it seriously. I promise."

"But you were late."

"I got here at eight fifty-seven. I'm supposed to be here at nine."

"Your day starts at nine. That means you need to be here and ready before then. You are my *assistant*. You're supposed to assist me. It's not very helpful when you're not here on time, is it?"

"I...I..." I fumble over my words, and Alexander turns and marches back into his office like an overgrown, entitled toddler. Who's still good-looking. *Dammit*. I sink back down into my chair and try to pretend half the office didn't just see me get yelled at on my second day.

I'm running on so little sleep, still shaken from the outburst that happened at drop-off. The mom-guilt is sitting heavy on my heart, and I can't help but think this was a mistake.

This job isn't worth the stress and I should have stayed with my old one.

God, I feel like a failure for thinking that. It's only the morning of day two and I'm already wanting to quit. Mom would be so disappointed in me. Tears well in my eyes at the thought of her. She was my friend as well as my mother, even during those rocky teenage years when I wanted nothing to do with either of my parents.

But Mom just had that way about her. A way of making you like her no matter how hard you tried not to. She was kind and understanding and had more patience than I ever will. Though, she was only raising one little hellion, not two.

All at once, it hits me again how she'll never meet her grand-daughters, and how the twins will never know just how amazing their grandmother was. I only hope I can share her inspiration through stories about her, and keep her memory alive for years to come.

I turn away from Alexander, looking down at the calendar on

my desk. Thank the fucking stars he's in meetings for the rest of the day. I'll bring him his coffee—and try my damnedest not to spit in it—and then stay out of his way. His first meeting is at ten, so I only have to suffer through one more hour with him breathing down my neck.

Everything about him annoys me, and I don't like that. I try hard not to be a judgy person and not let men like him get under my skin. Men who think they are God's gift to humanity. Who think they are better than everyone because they are rich.

Fuck you, Alexander Harding. And fuck your insane good looks and your chiseled jaw that's somehow already covered in the perfect five o'clock shadow even though it's nine in the morning. Fuck your designer suit and your watch that cost more than a year's worth of my rent.

And most of all, fuck you for filling me with so much negativity. Because as much as I'm trying not to, I know one thing is for certain: I hate Alexander Harding.

CHAPTER 7

If there's anything that makes me uncomfortable, it's someone crying. Maybe it's because there were many times in my life when I wanted to cry but wouldn't allow myself. Each and every time I felt the wrath of Dad's fists. Every bruise, every busted lip. Every lie on how it happened.

Every night when Mom would cry herself to sleep, when Nicole would sneak into my room and hide under the covers of my bed, afraid our father would come in, drunk and tired and ranting about work.

But I never let myself. *Boys don't cry,* Mom would tell me. *Don't let your father see you like that*, she'd say when tears would fill my eyes and the pain of being abused got to be too much.

So I didn't.

I still hate myself for seeking his approval. As a child, I could excuse it. Maybe if he liked me, he'd stop taking his anger out on me. Maybe if he were proud, he'd let me join him for Sunday brunch when he'd meet with investors, explaining to them why they should trust in his brand-new company.

I respected him, no matter how much I wish I didn't. He was my dad, after all, and as the years went on, I saw him in a new light. Not just the abusive asshole who made my life a living hell, but an abusive asshole who was smart, cunning, and established himself in the cut-throat business world in Chicago.

Our lives changed, but Dad didn't, and it wasn't until I was sixteen and bigger and taller than him that he stopped. He hit me for the last time when I hit him back, breaking his nose and staining one of his designer shirts with blood.

It's fucked up, I know, how that was the turn of events, but the next weekend, I went to brunch with him and members of the board. If I'd known then what I know now, I would never have gone to lunch with him. I was still young, still a kid with stars in my eyes who believed in second chances and had high hopes.

I made excuses for him. He made a lot of money, and this was a high-stress job. He made a lot of money and was always under pressure. He made a lot of money, so it was okay to be an ass.

No matter what, it always came down to one thing: money.

Don't get me wrong, I like my comfortable lifestyle. I like my penthouse and my cars. My designer clothes, latest technology, and hiring a service to get me through daily life. But in the end, things are just that...things.

And sitting here, watching Harper blot at the fat tears that are pooling in her eyes, reminds me of just how frail life is, and how *things* don't matter in the end. I could die alone in my multi-million-dollar penthouse, surrounded by all the *things* in the world, and none of it would matter.

A most unwelcome feeling settles heavily in my chest, and I fight against the urge to want to comfort Harper. To dry her eyes and make her smile. I don't know her, yet I can sense something inside of her, something rare and precious. It's a light I don't want to snuff out, and having these feelings is unsettling.

I shouldn't have been so harsh. I didn't mean to, and I'm finding it hard to keep things professional with her when my mind keeps drifting to some very *nonprofessional* thoughts about her.

I take my job seriously, and I need Harper to as well. But I didn't have to come down so hard, though I know it had everything to do with hoping she'd take me up on the offer and go back to her old job on the floor below, where I wouldn't have to see her pretty face or full lips.

I'm not really an asshole, and I don't want to be. I grew up with one and saw the devastation it put on our family. It's easier to close off my heart and pretend I'm immune to emotion. It works for a while but then everything I've repressed usually comes flooding back at night, right as I'm laying down to sleep.

It's suffocating, reminding me how very alone I am, how the people who call themselves my friends don't know me at all. It's no fault of their own since I'm the one who wears the mask. Who hides the pain with drinking and partying and making it look like I'm living my best fucking life every day of the week.

There's a reason Harper gets under my skin so much, and it's not only because I find her insanely attractive. She has the perfect *girl next door* vibe, but I think in her case, she's honestly oblivious to it. And the other reason…it's right there, screaming at me from the back of my mind but I refuse to listen.

I'm not ready yet.

And even if I did, so what? She's my assistant. Off limits. I don't date in general, and I'm not getting involved with someone from work.

I place my hands on my desk, prepared to push myself up and go over to her, but I don't know what I'd say. Being comforting and showing emotion isn't my thing, but it's killing me sitting here doing nothing. I stand right as the phone rings. Harper sniffles, shakes herself, and answers the phone, putting on a big smile.

The person on the phone obviously can't see her smile, yet she needs to convince herself she's okay. I have the feeling that's something she's used to doing, and I find myself curious about her all over again. She has twins, who look like mini versions of her. Briar Prep isn't cheap, and maybe it's stereotypical of me to assume that if she's sending her children there, she's married to someone who makes more money than an assistant with no experience under her belt.

Yet she's not wearing a ring, though that doesn't mean much nowadays. Many people don't want the binary label of love or marriage, but there was desperation in her eyes yesterday when she said she needed this job, and I don't think the thought of upsetting me and risking a promotion put her on the verge of tears. She's afraid of losing her job, because without it, she—and those girls—would be screwed.

I blink, tearing my eyes away from her, and look back at my computer. I have back-to-back meetings today and don't have time to waste thinking about Harper. She's my assistant. She'll work here for a year, if she even makes it that long, and then will move on to something else. I keep my personal life separate from work for a reason. Work consumes most of my life, I don't want to think about it in any way when I'm finally home and trying to unwind and relax.

And Harper...Harper seems like the opposite of relaxing. She's too bubbly. Too talkative and chipper even though she looks like she could use a long nap and a big glass of wine. I wonder what she—goddammit. I need to stop.

She laughs at whatever someone on the phone says, and her smile lights up her whole face. She rests her elbow on her desk and leans forward as she jots something down on a notepad. She removed the pink sweater she had on over her black dress, and one of the thin straps falls off her shoulder. She's a maelstrom of things that shouldn't be paired together, yet are. Soft and delicate while being weird and quirky. Serious yet emotional.

Desirable yet unobtainable.

I'm still looking at her, watching that childish-looking lemon charm dangle off her neck when she looks up. Our eyes meet and she freezes again, still holding the phone against her ear. I tear my eyes away, looking back at my computer.

She laughs again, but her face doesn't match the humor. She's playing along with whoever is on the phone, and is doing a damn good job at it. A few seconds later she hangs up. Out of the corner of my eye I can see her looking at me, hesitating before getting up.

She pauses at the open door and softly knocks. "Mr. Harding?"

"Call me Alex," I tell her. "And come in. I'm, uh, sorry I snapped earlier. I'm not a morning person."

Harper gives me a small smile. "Neither am I. That was Jerry Harold's assistant who just called. Jerry wants to know if you can reschedule the meeting you were supposed to have today for next week."

Dammit. That's the third time he's rescheduled. Jerry is co-owner of the largest toy company in the United States. They just bought out another toy company last year and are one of our biggest clients. *Reach PR* has been poaching our clients for months, and despite their stupid name, have been able to steal a few of our biggest.

I won't lose to them again, and I'm sure Harold's constant rescheduling has to do with that other fucking PR firm. He's been with us for years, though, and was one of my father's first big clients. Their last ad campaign we put together for them increased their revenue at a record-setting percentage, and we've never run into any issues. Why hesitate now?

"Did he give a time that would work for him?"

"No, he wanted me to check your schedule first and you're pretty busy all next week."

"Arrange another meeting, and move anything you have to in order to meet with Harold. He's a big client and is top priority."

"I'll do that. Do you, um, still want your coffee? I can reheat it for you."

"I'll take it, and reheating isn't necessary. It's usually cold by the time I can get to it anyway," I say, offering a slight smile, in which she returns with a full grin.

"I know the feeling. If I can't find my coffee it's usually because I put it in the microwave and forgot about it." Her eyes linger on mine for another few seconds. "I'll call Francine back and let her know to reschedule as soon as possible."

"Thank you," I tell her, finding the light that's returned to her eyes much more attractive than I like. She turns to leave. "Harper," I call.

"Yes?"

"You seemed pretty friendly on the phone with...with Francine, was it?"

"I suppose. Am I not supposed to be?"

"No, you can, and it's good, actually. Don't be obvious, but if you can, find out why Harold has rescheduled."

"Okay. I'll try. And, um, you do want that coffee, right?"

"Yes."

With a nod, she hurries out of my office and grabs the white mug from her desk.

"Thank you," I say and take the mug from her. She leaves the office and I get back to work, reading over a client file, until Harper knocks on the door again.

"Mr. Harding? Sorry, I mean, Alex?"

"Yes?" I save what I'm working on and turn away from the computer. Harper is standing in the doorway again, fiddling with that little yellow lemon charm hanging around her neck.

"I, um, talked to Francine."

I wait a beat, but she doesn't go on. "And?"

"She, um...she thinks Harold might be wanting to, um...to go with another PR firm." Color creeps up her chest, spreading up her neck and to her cheeks.

"Did she say why?"

She pulls on her necklace and looks at me sympathetically.

61

"She thinks it might have to do with that article about you and the models a few weeks ago, but I swear I don't know what she's talking about and I won't go back to my desk and Google it."

She reminds me of a toddler, telling on herself before she even does anything bad. It's so irritatingly adorable her words don't fully register for a few seconds.

And then it hits me.

Shit. I know exactly what article she's talking about. It was supposed to be focusing on the business, and how I'm one of the younger CEOs in the city, but instead took a different direction and highlighted a recent trip to Vegas that involved me, a party bus full of lingerie models, and the copious amounts of liquor consumed that weekend.

I regretted it almost instantly. Not the sex—the sex was great. But the part where I tried to convince myself it was enough to fill the void inside my chest. It wasn't, and it was then I realized that if an elaborate, crazy weekend filled with hot models, enough alcohol to kill an elephant, and expensive dinners and hotel rooms couldn't soothe the hurt…nothing will.

CHAPTER 8

HARPER

Tessa hands me a glass of pink Moscato. "Cheers to surviving your first week at the new job!"

I gently clink my glass against hers. "It was two days, but still felt like a feat. Though, really, it's not too bad. Well, besides my boss being a very sexy ass. I sat by a few of the interns today during the whole seven and a half minutes I got for a lunch break and they said that it's considered a compliment if Alex walks by and *doesn't* criticize what they're working on."

"Sounds like a lovely guy."

"Right? Though all of the interns were excited to be there. They said putting that experience on a resume makes it almost a guarantee they'll get a job. I can't imagine being that coldhearted all the time, though. Do you think he has some tragic backstory or something?"

"Don't do that thing you do where you make up stories for people," Tessa warns. "Some people are just assholes and there's no real reason why. I mean, just look at your boss. Like, literally look at him." She gets her phone, does a quick internet search, and pulls up his photo. Or maybe it's an advertisement for that Gucci suit he's wearing because holy shit, he's got dark and

63

brooding down to a science. "He was raised with a silver spoon in his mouth and became one of the youngest CEOs in the city because his daddy owns the company. And he looks like this. Even I find him attractive and I'm gay."

"I still think something had to happen to make him so callous. Oh! Maybe he fell madly in love with a woman only for her to go and break his heart by sleeping with his best friend. No, his father! And the twist is, she's his father's secretary and he's forced to see them together every single day, happy and in love."

"Now that's a romance novel I'd read, but I'd want him to seek out revenge. I love a good dark twist to my romance. Bonus points if someone dies."

"Who, the father or the cheating secretary?"

Tessa shrugs. "Maybe both in a fiery car crash."

"Orrrr maybe they get in a car crash, but she gets amnesia and doesn't remember leaving him for his father, so she wakes up thinking she's still in love with Alex."

"And then they hook up only to realize she's pregnant, but they don't know who is the father!"

We both start laughing, and Tessa pours more wine into both our glasses. "If there ever was a sign we watched too many telenovelas as kids, this is it."

"Yeah, we did," I say, mind drifting back. My mom got us hooked on telenovelas, and ever since I was old enough to remember, I can recall her watching them at night, back when she'd record them on VHS tapes so she could fast forward through commercials.

"I swear that's the reason I passed Spanish," Tessa laughs. "You and your mom translating things for me taught me better than all the classes I took."

"I don't speak Spanish around the girls," I say as it hits me all at once. I always intended to have my children know how to speak Spanish, just like how I did. My mother was born and raised in Mexico, and illegally crossed the border when she was eighteen.

She and my father met after she'd only been in the country for a few months, and it was love at first sight. Fate. Destiny. The best love story you could write.

Just like something out of a telenovela.

Until she died of cancer six years ago. Her parents still live there, and we went to visit them as often as we could until Mom got sick. There's no way I could afford to take the girls to see their great-grandparents anytime soon. Thinking about it still pains me, and I blink rapidly to keep the tears at bay.

"So, chances are Alex isn't in a weird love triangle involving his father, but I still want to believe he has some sort of tragic past. It makes me not hate him so much, which I really don't want to do. Hating the man I work for sucks."

"It would. I hated the old principal we had, remember? She made work a living hell. We threw a party the day she left."

"I do remember that. You said you were going to bring me cake and then ate it all before you got to my house."

"You're never going to let that go, are you?" she laughs.

"Not until I get cake," I tease and look down the hall. The girls are fast asleep, snuggled up together in the same bed. When they finally outgrew their toddler beds, I was able to afford one pretty decent twin-sized mattress. They prefer to sleep together, which is good because only one bed is going to fit into that tiny room. We don't have much, but we have each other.

"And, speaking of his father—love triangle aside—it's just weird between them. His father works just a few doors down from him and they hardly speak. They don't even acknowledge each other when they pass by in the halls. I guess it's only been two days and maybe they're busy and trying to be professional, but can you imagine if my dad worked with me?"

"You'd never get a single thing done," Tessa laughs. "Between the dad-jokes and him constantly asking if you want him to make you a snack."

"Right?" I laugh. "I don't know..." I trail off and shake my head. "I guess really, I'd rather believe there's a reason he's so closed off than to face the fact that you're right and there are just assholes in this world for no rhyme or reason."

"You're too good of a person, Harp. And I highly doubt Alex is upset about the lack of relationship he has with his father when he's sleeping naked on a bed of money." Tessa cocks an eyebrow.

"Do you think people actually do that?" I bring my wine to my lips. "Sleep on money, I mean. Money is gross and you do not want to see it under a blacklight."

"It's a figure of speech, dummy," Tessa laughs. "It would stick to crevices and not be comfortable."

"Only if you're sleeping naked."

"Right." She slowly shakes her head. "I forget you're a freak and wear clothes to bed."

"Sleeping naked is way more comfortable, but when two five-year-olds climb in bed with you randomly throughout the night, it's nice having at least one layer of clothes on before I get my nipples steamrolled."

Tessa laughs. "Steamrolled?"

"It's what I call it when they snuggle up and accidentally pin my poor nips between their body and the mattress."

"I sleep naked with other people all the time. I can't believe I haven't had that happen."

"I swear it's something only children can do. They're able to inflict pain like you've never imagined," I say with a straight face. "Childbirth is just the beginning."

Tessa laughs again. "You're making it really easy to stick with my decision not to have children. The twins and my constant ebb and flow of students is more than enough for me."

"You're more than welcome to babysit anytime you want," I say with a wink.

"Oh, I will. When you go out on a date."

I purse my lips and bring my wine to my mouth again. "I was hoping you'd forget about that," I grumble.

"I'll never forget about trying to get you out there again. You love love, my friend. You're a hopeless romantic and I want you to be happy."

"I am happy," I press. "Stressed, anxious, and so nervous I can't sleep at night, but I'm happy."

"Harp," she starts.

"I'm joking! This new job is going to alleviate a lot of the stress. I was actually thinking about selling my old clunker for parts for the extra cash and using the company car for as long as I can before they figure it out."

"Isn't that the point of the car? To use it?"

"Yeah, but personal use was never clearly explained, and I didn't want to ask." I take another drink of the wine Tessa brought over.

"If the school gave me a car, I'd drive the fucking wheels off."

"I don't want to do anything to mess things up. This job can really turn things around for us. I'm getting paid double what I made before, which is still low and just goes to show how pathetic the pay is for entry-level jobs."

"The whole *you need experience* thing pisses me off," she says, gently swirling the wine around in her glass. "And it's almost the opposite with teaching. A teacher with tons of experience will have a hard time finding a new job because they're more expensive to hire than a new grad. Fucking bullshit."

"It is!"

"So, you think you'll get promoted in time?"

I look at the pink liquid in my glass. "I don't have my degree, so no. But maybe…just maybe I'll be able to take a night class here or there and can finish the last credits I need."

"You'll get back to it, I know. You're smart, Harps." She drains

EMILY GOODWIN

the wine and sets the glass down. "Are the girls excited for school on Monday?"

"They are. I think they're still under the assumption it's going to be like daycare, where it's pretty much a free-for-all play day with lunch and a nap peppered in between."

"The first week or two are filled with a lot of playtime. I probably shouldn't say this since it's my job, but it's fucking nuts to expect five and six-year-olds to behave five days a week in a classroom."

"It makes me sad to think their childhood is basically over."

"Don't be so dramatic." Tess rolls her eyes. "We do play a lot in between lessons. Though by the end of the year, I'll have parents asking me what Ivy League college I think their child will get into. Like seriously. It's fucking kindergarten."

"You're joking."

"I wish. Some of these parents are already mapping out their children's academic futures, which translates into figuring out ways to make sure they go into business and make lots of money just like dear old dad. And mom, which I'm seeing more and more of now, which is fucking amazing."

"That is. Were you able to find out who Henry is to Alexander and why he was there?"

"I did! Henry's mom—Alexander's sister—is a surgeon and was preforming surgery during the open house. Alexander took Henry for her."

"That's nice."

"It is. And see, he has family. He's not that lonely."

"Fine, but I'm still going to pretend he has some sort of trauma in the past and once he experiences true love, he'll turn into the nicest man in the world."

Tessa laughs and shakes her head. "Just change his name when you write about him in that super-secret journal you have."

I let out a dramatic gasp. "You're not supposed to know about that!"

"Please, I've known about it for years and I used to read it in college. You could seriously be a writer. Those stories were really engaging."

"I can't believe you read it!"

"You left it out on your bed more often than not. I think it was your subconscious way of wanting someone to read it and tell you it's good."

"I've always thought it was good."

"Maybe you should pick one and roll with it. Write out the whole book and try to get it in the hands of an agent."

"You say it like it's easy."

"Oh, trust me, I know it's not. But it's worth trying, isn't it?"

I used to entertain the thought of being an author, but it seemed so far-fetched, like one of those one-in-a-million chances that you had to get really lucky to stumble upon.

"Maybe," I tell her, not wanting to totally brush it off. "One job at a time, though."

"Fair enough." She sets her phone down on the coffee table. "You have me wanting to watch a telenovela now. Ready for a crazy Friday night? Wine, Latin drama, and I'm thinking I might order us a pizza."

"I'm liking this plan." I take another drink of wine and get up to get the TV remote. I had to cut cable and all streaming services, but Tessa lets us use her Netflix account.

We spend a minute searching for something good to watch, and we're halfway through the first episode when the pizza arrives. We eat half of it, and I put the rest in the fridge, excited to surprise the girls with pizza for lunch tomorrow.

Tessa hangs out for another hour or so, and then leaves to meet a date at a bar downtown. Going out and being social has always been her thing, and while most nights I'd choose to stay in with a book or a binge-worthy TV show, sometimes I feel a little down that I don't even have the option to go out.

Which, of course, makes me feel bad. I'm not able to go out

because I have two wonderful children who I love more than life itself. It's not selfish to want a night off every once in a while, and I think, really, it would make me a better mom if I got a break.

I've been too physically tired or just mentally spent to play with the girls more often than not, and I feel like I'm always rushing around trying to get things done. Dad and Tessa help as much as they can, but they both work as well.

I wouldn't have been able to get through this without them, and finding out I was a pregnant really showed me who my true friends were. I was no social butterfly, that's for sure, but I hung out with people and had a handful of friends at school.

They hung around long enough to come to my baby shower, but after that, I stopped getting invited out because they thought I'd just say no anyway, which was true most times, but still hurt. All of that was going on just months after we lost Mom.

It was a dark time in my life for sure. But as Mom told me over and over, *make lemonade*.

For the next year, the lemonade was sour. Hardly drinkable. But I learned to tolerate it, and eventually, things got better.

Sweeter.

I pull my t-shirt over my head and walk to the bathroom for a shower. I turn on the water and strip out of the rest of my clothes. My phone rings right as I step in, and I scramble like mad and end up slipping on the laminate floor as I get out.

No one calls me after ten PM unless it's an emergency. My mind races with the million and one things that could be wrong right now: Dad was in an accident at work. He got mugged. Robbed. Shot. Tessa's date turned out to be a murderer and the police are calling me because I was the last person she called.

But it's not Dad or Tessa.

It's Alexander Harding.

"What?" I mumble and reach for the towel hanging on the hook near the shower. I step back onto the bathmat and clumsily wrap the towel around me with one hand while I answer the phone with the other.

"Hello?"

"Harper. It's Alex."

"Yeah, I, um, saved your number. Is everything okay?" I rush out. Maybe he got into a heated passion-fueled fight because I was right about the love triangle and needs to be bailed out of jail.

"Yes, why wouldn't it be?"

"You're calling me at ten-thirty on a Friday."

"Oh, right. I didn't realize it was late. Sorry if I interrupted anything."

"You didn't. I was in the shower but panicked when I heard the phone ring, so now I'm naked and dripping water all over my bathroom floor."

Alex laughs and my face turns bright red. This is why I shouldn't drink. Half a bottle of wine and I have no filter.

"Well, then I'm sorry I startled you."

"Are you still at the office?" I ask and shut the bathroom door. I leave it open when I shower so I can listen for the girls getting up, but I don't want to wake them by talking.

"Yes, I'm wrapping up a project. That's why I'm calling."

"Oh. You don't need me to come in, do you?"

"No, but if you could check your email, that would be great."

"Sure. Are you looking for anything in particular?"

"An email from one of the interns who was working on the Jenkins project."

"Okay." I pull my phone away from my ear and open my email. I got the option to have a work phone to use for calls and emails, but I have a hard enough time keeping track of things as it is. One phone is plenty for me. I log into the work folder and see a lot of emails.

Alexander prefers people to email me first and then I can read through them and forward anything he needs to see. I find the email from the intern and forward that on over.

"Sent."

"Thank you, Harper," he says, and that weird feeling of sorrow comes back. Working this late on Friday is kind of sad, isn't it? Maybe it's the wine talking again. I also get a tad emotional when I drink. I remind myself what Tessa said. I'm sure Alex is working late so he can make gobs more money.

"So do you work this late on Fridays a lot?" I ask.

"If I need to. I prefer not to be at the office, but I have weekend plans and don't want to be bothered."

"That makes sense. I wouldn't want to think about work either." Oh, shit. I just told my boss I don't want to think about work, eluding to me not liking my job. "Not that I don't like my job or anything. I do, really, even though it's only been—"

"It's okay, Harper," he laughs and that feeling of sorrow starts to turn into something else. Warmth, perhaps? That's the first time I've heard him laugh.

"Well, I hope you have a good weekend. It'll be more eventful than mine, I'm sure."

"You don't have plans?"

"Nothing more than hanging out with my kids. I'll probably just watch *Harry Potter* before I crash tonight too. Or *End Game* if I feel like crying. That scene with Captain Marvel when the other woman says, 'she's got help,' gets me very time."

"I haven't seen *End Game* yet."

"What? How you not seen it? Did you watch *Infinity War*?"

"I have, and I enjoyed it.

I blink in disbelief. "Then how did you not die waiting for *End Game* to come out?"

He laughs again. "I suppose part of me isn't ready to watch it. I know who dies. I might have looked up spoilers."

"Really?" Now I'm laughing.

"Really, and I don't know if I can bring myself to watch it," he admits.

I'm smiling, finding this all sort of cute. "I never would have taken you for a Marvel fan."

"You either."

"Oh, I'm a huge nerd. Comics, fantasy, science fiction…I love it all."

"Movies or books?"

"Both!" I exclaim and lean back, still smiling. "I love to read but don't have much time. I feel old admitting that when I sit in bed to read at night, I end up falling asleep."

"I like audio books," he tells me. "I listen to them when I'm driving."

"That's a good idea, actually. I'll have to try it sometime."

"Yeah, you should."

A few seconds of silence tick by. "I'll let you get back to the shower," Alex says.

"Good. I'm getting cold since I'm still naked." I squeeze my eyes closed. Why did I just say that? "I'll, um, see you at the office Monday."

"Yes. Monday. At the office. Have a good night."

"You too. Bye."

I set my phone on the bathroom counter and put my head in my hands. If there was an award for being awkward, weird, and borderline inappropriate, I've won it.

Monday morning is going to be fun.

Though, really…I'm not dreading it. Because that short conversation with Alex made him seem more like a real person and less like a coldhearted robot of a human.

It makes him—dare I say it—almost likable.

CHAPTER 9

ALEX

"Uncle Alex!" Henry leaps off the swing, landing and falling on his knees. He pops right up, unscathed, but I can't say the same for his pants, which are now sporting bright green grass stains. Nicole, who's fussing over red and blue balloons, just lets out a sigh and shakes her head.

Henry runs through the yard at full speed, coming danger-ously close to the edge of the in-ground pool. It makes me nervous, and I rush forward, ready to jump in and get him if need be. He's been taking swimming lessons, but has inherited his mother's athletic ability, which is none.

Henry jumps into my arms and I pick him up, giving him a tight hug before setting him back down.

"It's almost my party!" He's so excited he can't stand still. "Look at the decorations!"

"It looks good, buddy," I say and look around the lawn. "How much longer do you have to wait?"

"Too long," he whines dramatically, throwing his head back, making me laugh. "Are you staying for the party?"

"I wish I could," I tell him. "But I need to catch a plane and go up north to Michigan."

"What's out there that's so important?"

"Work."

Seemingly giving up on the balloons, Nicole comes over. Her hair is all done up and she's wearing a pink dress. Henry's sixth birthday is on Tuesday, and his birthday party is today. I'm not in on the parent-loop, but Nicole mentioned before that there is a lot of social pressure to put on a big, elaborate, and perfect kid party.

Seems ridiculous to me, since all this show is for the parents to one-up each other with. The kids just want pizza, cake, and a bounce-house. Nicole has really gone all out with this Marvel-themed party. I look at a big cutout of Captain American and think of Harper.

And how she said she was naked and wet.

An image of her conjures in my mind right away. Beads of water slowly dripped down her long, dark hair, falling to her chest, rolling along the gently slope of her breasts. Her cheeks were flushed from the hot water, and skin warm to the touch.

Fuck, I can't think about that now. Or ever. She works for me. I can't think about her like that. Instead of thinking how oddly easy it was to talk to her, I need to focus on how annoyingly chipper she is. How she's a little scattered though she tries hard to cover it up.

"Wanna open your present now?" I ask Henry, rustling his hair.

"Yes! Can I, Mom? Can I?" He jumps up and down.

Nicole glares at me. "Well, I can't really say no now and sound like a bad guy, can I? Let's go inside."

Henry runs ahead and Nicole and I follow behind. She's a few years older than me, and while we had our fair share of fights over the years, we've always been close. Nothing brings siblings together like an abusive father and a negligent mother, I suppose. She told me once before, after she had one too many cocktails at a Fourth of July party, that taking care of my injuries caused by Dad's fists is what made her want to be a doctor.

Mom never wanted anyone to know what went on behind closed doors, and often downplayed the pain I'd feel each and every time Dad took a swing at me. Nicole never did, and though she's my older sister, I'm fiercely protective of her. If any man ever laid a finger on her, I'd fuck them up so bad they'd be lucky to be able to walk after.

"You better not have gotten him anything crazy," Nicole steps into the house. "We're trying to teach him to be more of a minimalist in terms of material possessions."

I turn and sweep my hand in the direction of the backyard we just came from. "Good job with the minimalism. It was so *minimal* I hardly even noticed you were having a party."

"Hilarious as always." She rolls her eyes. "And I mean it! I told you not to go crazy with gifts this year."

"So, do you consider keys to the four-wheeler he was asking for crazy?"

Nicole whips around, eyes wide. "You better be joking or you're the one who's going to tell him he can't have it! There's nowhere to ride it here!"

"I didn't really get him his own."

"His own? Alex," she scolds "What did you get him?"

"The crystal growing set he asked for—seriously, your kid is a nerd—and passes to go ride go-carts at an indoor track."

Nicole smiles. "He'd really like that. I know our schedules suck and we're both really busy, but he soaks up every minute he can get with you."

"I like spending time with him too."

"Calvin and I were just talking about taking a family vacation. His sister wants to join, and it would be fun if you did too…and if you brought someone."

"Don't start," I warn, tone coming out harsher than I meant. For the last three years, Nicole has been irritatingly persistent that I change my playboy ways and settle down and have babies of my own. I love my nephew, but one of my favorite things about him is getting to give him back.

I open my mouth to tell her that I like being single, going out, and not having any strings attached. I'm a free agent and can do what, or whoever, I want.

But lying is too much effort, and that's exactly what it is: a lie.

"There is a very pretty and very single nurse on my surgical team," she goes on, totally ignoring my request for her to drop it. "I can set you guys up. I think you'd really like her."

"Sure. Set us up. And arrange for a hotel room for the night too."

"Gross." She makes a face and rolls her eyes. She calls Calvin, her husband, down and we all go find Henry in the living room, not-so-patiently waiting to open his gift from me.

He loved it, of course.

"Well, buddy," I start, looking at the time on my watch. "Happy early birthday."

"Don't leave, Uncle Alex. Stay for my party!"

"Uncle Alex has to leave," Calvin reminds Henry. "He has to get on a plane and claim to work by drinking whiskey and touring a distillery." He looks at me and laughs. "Sounds like a terrible day at the office."

"I've had worse," I laugh. "Though it's going to be a quick in-and-out trip. Nothing *too* relaxing."

"Bring me back some booze," Nicole adds with a smile. "You can say it's a marketing move. If I like it, I'll buy more."

"Trust me, she will," Calvin whisper-talks, snaking his arm around Nicole, who erupts into giggles. Calvin squeezes her side and leans in for a kiss.

"Gross." Henry wrinkles his nose.

"I'm right there with you," I tell him with a wink. "Have a good party, okay? Don't eat too much cake." He gives me a hug goodbye and Nicole walks me to the door.

"Thanks for stopping by," she says, stepping onto the covered brick porch. "It really does mean a lot to Henry. With Cal traveling so much for work lately, I think Henry wants any sort of male role model in his life."

"Wait. Back up. Call the presses. You just called me a role model."

"I didn't say you were a good one," she laughs.

"I didn't either, so don't hold it against me."

Nicole gives me a quick hug. "Have a safe flight. Where are you flying out of again? And what's your flight number?"

"Nicole," I say sternly. She's always been a nervous flyer, and when she was on a plane with engine failure a few years ago, it took her nerves into a full-blown fear. "I'll be fine. You know I'm more likely to die on my way to the airport than I am to get in a plane crash."

"That's supposed to help me feel better about my baby brother going off all on his own?"

"If anything, worry about my liver. I'm sure it's going to be working overtime this weekend with all the whiskey I'll be consuming. For work."

She shakes her head and tries to look at me like I'm a patient she's about to lecture about taking their health more seriously.

"Be careful with that too. There are bears and coyotes and occasionally a wolverine in the UP."

"I'm not going to the Canadian border, and it's still summer. The wolverines are hibernating, I'll be fine. And when I get back, I'll figure out a time to hang out with Henry."

Nicole beams. "He'd really like that."

I smile back. "I would too."

CHAPTER 10

HARPER

"**H**old still," I say for the hundredth time this morning. I'm working hard to keep my cool, but my patience is already wearing thin and we've only been up for twenty minutes.

Which is exactly why I'm about to run out of patience completely.

Violet was too excited for school and couldn't fall asleep last night. So naturally, she kept her sister up, and I finally had to separate them around ten thirty. I put Penny in my bed and kept Vi in their room. It took them each about twenty minutes to settle down and finally fall asleep...which put me really behind on everything that I was already behind on.

The laundry didn't get folded or even sorted. The dishes have been in the sink for so long now it's going to take boiling hot water and commercial-grade degreaser to get the hard and dried food off them at this point.

And then I made the mistake—or maybe saving grace—of looking at my work email right before dinner, and holy shit. There's no way I can really take a full weekend off and still be on top of things. I feel like I need an assistant just to be Alexander's assistant.

I don't know how Jason did it, and that one day of phone training was not nearly enough. He made it sound so simple, and I suppose at its core it is. I *assist* Alex in doing his job.

I answer emails, get him coffee, run errands, handle his phone calls, and schedule appointments and meetings. I'm lucky he keeps his private life totally private or I'd be feeling like Anne Hathaway in *The Devil Wears Prada*.

I spent three hours answering the emails I could and forwarding the others to Alex or the interns handling the particular project and cross-referencing a few files that Alex will need for his meeting in the morning.

"Penny," I say through gritted teeth. "This shouldn't be an issue every time I do your hair. You are old enough to know how to sit still." Man, do I feel like a broken record.

"I am sitting still!" she whines right back. "I'm just moving my eyes, Mom."

"Kid, you are not just moving your eyes." I set the brush down and grab the hairspray. "Now close your eyes." Waiting a beat, I spray the top of her head with hairspray and smooth back her ponytail. Tessa brought over big pink bows, saying a lot of the girls at the school wear them. They're oversized but ridiculously cute, and since everyone wears the same uniform, the colorful bows are a good way to sneak in a little personality.

"Am I done now?" Penny throws her head back dramatically right as I'm putting the bow in, causing a big section of her hair to snag and pull up from the ponytail.

"Well, you were." I close my eyes and grit my teeth. It's the first day of kindergarten. We're having a good, stress-free morning even if it kills me. "Please, for the love of all things holy in this house. Sit. Still."

I pull the band out of her hair and start again. The second time around works, and then I move on to Violet. The universe threw me a bone, and she sat perfectly still as Penny showed off her new flossing dance skills.

"All right, my little kindergarteners," I say with tears in my eyes. "Grab your chalkboards and please don't smudge them until after I've gotten a few pictures."

Dad got me plain, square chalkboards from the dollar store, and after I spent hours doing work, I spent another hour trying to make Pinterest-worthy designs for the "first day of school" chalkboards the girls are going to hold for a picture.

I pose then against the front door and turn on every light in this tiny apartment. We have a window behind our table, and one in each bedroom. I'm not sure if that's up to code for fire escapes or not, but one thing is for sure: it hardly lets in any light.

"Smile!" I tell the girls and go through a sequence of awkward and forced smiles before I get a photo that's good enough. I text one to Dad and email a few to my grandparents in Mexico, who only check their email a few times a month.

I take a few more photos and then realize the time. "Oh shit."

"Mommy said shit! Mommy said shit," Penny chants while Violet laughs hysterically. I just roll my eyes and fly over to the table, grab my purse, and shove my feet into shoes.

Along with bringing the bows yesterday, Tessa brought over a ton of shoes and clothes she bought—mostly while drunk and browsing Amazon, she said—but can't wear to school since they have a strict dress code for teachers.

As a researcher, I had to dress "nicely" but didn't have to put as much effort into my appearance as I do now. Today, I'm wearing a silky dress that I dare say looks rather good on me. I put on the one and only push-up bra I own this morning, and the amount of cleavage I'm showing borders right along the lines of *she's got boobs and can't help it* and *trying too hard.* I've always been well-endowed, and when I attempted to breastfeed the twins, my cup size doubled. I was able to last three months, which I'm still pretty proud of, and after my milk dried up, the increased size of my bust didn't go away.

Tessa and I have been the same shoe size since we met, which

81

made for lots of shoe-sharing over our years of friendship. Her weakness has always been high-heeled shoes, and I honestly don't know how she made it through the day wearing some of these shoes. Commanding a room full of kindergarteners is hard enough on its own, let alone in four-inch heels.

The red heels I put on go perfectly with the dress, and I slept with my hair in braids so it would be wavy this morning, giving me the illusion of having actually put time and effort into styling it. I *want* to do my hair and makeup every morning before work, but dammit, I'm so tired.

I give the girls a hug and a kiss and then head out, locking the apartment door behind us. The hallway leading from our apartment to the main doors always smells like pot and pee. I take each girl's hand and quickly walk through it, not stopping or allowing myself to look when we pass by an open door.

There could be a dead body in that apartment for all we know, or more likely, someone passed out naked from drinking too much last night. I cannot wait to get the girls out of here, to live somewhere that doesn't make me want to hold my breath as I run from my house to the street.

We get to the car and get buckled into car seats in record time. The girls are big enough to be in booster seats and out of their five-point harnesses, but I'm not ready. The harness seems so much safer, and both my girls can be such shits I don't trust them not to unbuckle while I'm driving.

"Are you excited for school?" I ask as I pull out of the apartment's tiny parking lot.

"You already asked us that, Mom," Violet says, voice void of emotion.

I laugh. "Well, I'm asking again. Are you?"

"Yes," they say in unison.

"And Aunt Tessa is going to be your teacher."

"I know, Mom," Penny reminds me. "You told us already."

"I'm allowed to repeat myself." I take my eyes off the road and turn around just long enough to look at each beautiful girl. "I'm old."

They laugh, and I smile despite the hectic morning and the little sleep I'm running on.

"You have money in your lunch accounts," I tell them—also for the millionth time. "Aunt Tessa said the food is really, really good and you can pick whatever you want from the line!"

"How will I know where to go?" Violet asks, a little nervous.

"Someone will show you. Either your teacher, the people who serve you lunch, or an older student." Tessa told me fifth graders come down to the kindergarten room as a surprise and "adopt" a kindergartener for the first week.

"But what if I get lost?"

"You won't," I assure her.

"I'll find you, sissy," Penny says and reaches over, taking her sister's hand. My heart melts and my smile comes back to my face, along with tears I try to blink back. I promised myself I wouldn't cry, and it's not like this is the first time my girls are going to be away from me.

I *did* sob uncontrollably when I dropped them off at all-day daycare for the first time. It was a kind of hurt no one could have prepared me for. Both for missing my girls so, so much, and for realizing that I'd changed from a career-driven woman to a mom.

A mom who'd give anything to stay home and take care of her babies.

A mom who was going to quite possibly miss her girls' first words and first steps.

I steal another glance at the girls in the rearview mirror. Life didn't turn out the way I thought…not at all. It's not perfect. Hell, it's hard sometimes, really fucking hard. But things don't have to be perfect to be good.

~

"HARPER!" ROSE RAISES HER HAND IN THE AIR AND WAVES ME OVER. Her makeup is on point today, and it doesn't seem too far-fetched to believe she has a personal stylist at home because those braids in her strawberry blonde hair are Daenerys Targaryen level complicated.

"Hey," I say back and wipe a tear from my eye, hoping I didn't smudge my mascara. A shorter woman with a bob cut stands next to Rose. I remember seeing her at orientation, but can't place her name or which kid she came here with.

I just dropped off the girls and left the school. My heart is heavy and full of joy at the same time. My babies are growing up, and time really is going so fucking fast, just like everyone said it would.

"Look at you," Rose says when I get to her side. She looks me up and down and wiggles her eyebrows. "Damn, girl."

I laugh. "Please. Have you looked in a mirror?"

The brunette with the bob-cut laughs. "Right? I tell her all the time she could get back into her modeling career with no issues."

"You used to model?" My eyebrows go up. "Not that I'm surprised. You're gorgeous."

Rose waves her hand in the air, dismissing us. "It was either that or get a real job, and I've never been one for work. Besides. I have stretch marks on stretch marks after carrying twins."

"I have stretch marks from carrying one baby," the brunette laughs. "Though if I'm being honest, I had them before I even got pregnant." She has a slight southern accent and has a certain energy about her that's a bit magnetic, like she'll invite you over for sweet tea and cookies and it'll be the best damn sweet tea and cookies you'll ever have.

"Harper, this is Kate. Kate, Harper," Rose introduces. She leans in close to me, lips brushing against my ear as she talks. "She's one of the good ones."

"It's so nice to meet you," Kate tells me and takes my hand in hers. "Rose said you're the mother of those adorable identical twins."

"I am. And I'm sorry, but I can't place you from orientation."

"Oh, honey, it's fine. I'm terrible at putting faces with names and just remembering names in general. Heather is my girl. About yea high—" She holds her hand up to her hip—"and has black, curly hair, just like her daddy."

"And she's in Miss Miller's class too?"

"She is! And we're just thrilled about it. Everyone wants Miss Miller."

I smile, making a mental note to tell Tessa about that later. She'll love hearing how everyone wants her to be the teacher of their children.

"We're going to get brunch and cry into our mimosas," Rose starts. "You have to join us, and I won't take no for an answer."

"I'd love to," I tell her, and feel a little crushed that I'm actually making mom-friends for the first time but can't hang out. "But I have to go to work."

A group of three other moms—the ones who made the Stepford Wives look like off-the-chain party animals—is standing nearby. One who's wearing a powder blue pantsuit turns and looks me up and down.

"You work?" she questions. Her blonde hair is styled up around her head in a way that makes me think she takes *the higher the hair, the closer to God* literally.

"Yeah, I do," I tell her, and she raises her eyebrows, gaze going to my left hand. It's something I'm used to, sadly. People look for a wedding ring once they find out I have children. "Don't you?"

"My *husband* makes more than enough for the both of us." She gives me a tight smile and turns back to her group of friends.

"Well, I would have guessed she worked in broadcasting," Kate starts, voice a low whisper. "And today was *dress like your favorite newswoman from the early eighties* day."

Rose and I both start laughing, and the heat of embarrassment

85

I'd usually feel from being openly judged doesn't even have a chance to hit me.

"Right?" Rose shakes her head. "And that hair? Let's hope she doesn't walk past an open flame because that much hairspray will go up in smoke." She smiles. "Let's plan for something on Saturday. Bring the kids over to our place and force them to be friends so I can hang out with moms I actually like."

I laugh again. "I like that plan, and Saturday should work."

"It will for us too," Kate tells us. "I'll bring Champagne so you can get that mimosa after all," she adds, giving me a wink.

"Now I really like this plan," I say.

"What's your number?" Rose pulls out her phone. "I'll text you Saturday morning." We exchange numbers, and then it's time for me to leave before I'm late for work.

I walk past the group of uptight moms, and actually feel sorry for them. Try as they might, nothing they say will get to me.

I'm a single mom who has to work to survive, and I'm damn proud of how far we've come.

CHAPTER 11

ALEX

"Good morning, Mr. Harding." Harper's voice floats through my office, soft and gentle, soothing as it is sexy. All she said were four little words, and my mind immediately goes to our phone conversation Friday night. She's funny in a way I didn't expect, and talking to her came easily.

"Please, call me—" I save the project I'm working on and turn toward Harper. Holy shit, she looks amazing today. "Alex." My voice dies in my throat, and it takes everything I have not to do a double-take.

Red is definitely her color. It brings out the vibrance of her eyes, and almost matches her red lipstick. There's a slight flush to her cheeks again. I can't tell if it's makeup or natural, and the fact that she so obviously wears her emotions on her face is endearing.

"Good morning, Alex." Her full lips pull up into a smile. "How was your weekend? Did you destress from work on your trip?"

God, she's gorgeous. "A little, but it was a work trip."

"I assumed so since it was on your calendar," she laughs and crosses the office. Her breasts bounce slightly with each step as she comes over to my desk, setting a mug of coffee on the corner. "Was it a good trip, at least?"

"Overall, yes. There are worse ways to spend the weekend other than sampling whiskey."

"Oh, that does sound like fun. And if you need a second opinion, I'm your girl." Her smile is back, and she gives me a wink. There's something about her, something I can't quite put my finger on. She's different than the women I usually surround myself with, and instead of being off-putting, it's the exact opposite.

Harper is someone I can see myself spending a long night with, without the mask of alcohol or having to flaunt my wealth in order to feel worthy. No, it'd just be us, maybe enjoying a quiet dinner and a walk along the lake once the sun has gone down. There's something genuine about her, something that makes me think the money, job title, and all my possessions would be lost on her.

She'd see me, the broken boy who put all the jagged pieces of himself back into place and grew into a fractured man.

It's a ridiculous thought to entertain. I don't know Harper at all. And most importantly, I'm her boss. Work relationships aren't against company policy, but it's against my personal policy.

Don't shit where you eat.

What if Harper and I go at it hot and heavy and then sizzle out? She'll still have to be my assistant. How fucking weird would it be if either of us started dating someone else? It risks too many problems, and this job is way too fucking important to me to be jeopardized by a woman.

Even a woman as gorgeous and quirky as Harper. Let me rephrase that: *especially* a woman as gorgeous and quirky as Harper.

I look at her, eyes lingering a moment too long on her pretty face. She acts so oblivious to her own beauty, but at the same time I find it hard to believe she's unaware exactly how good her tits look in that dress. How they push against the material every time she breathes, as if they're testing the strength of the buttons. It won't take much for the top one to pop off, splitting the V of her neckline farther down, teasing me even more.

The air shifts, and despite the warmth coming off of Harper, I feel a draft. I look past her and see my father walking down the hall. Ah, makes sense now. I cannot wait for that fucker to retire and get out of here for good. He's always preaching about how important it is to adapt and change but he's been stuck in his old ways long enough and once I fully take over, I'm going to take this company to the next level.

I've already been in contact with a smaller, yet quickly up-and-coming marketing company in New York about working together. We have the experience, the clout, the long list of satisfied clients. And they're new and fresh—a bit too hipster for my personal liking, but that doesn't matter—and are able to attract a different demographic than we could here.

If Dad got on board with it, he'd want to take credit, and I'm tired of living in his shadow. This was my idea and I'll be the one putting in the work. I'm not going to breathe one word to him until he's officially signed all the paperwork handing everything over to me.

He looks up and into my office, meeting my eyes, and for a split second, he hesitates, making me think he's going to come in here. That is not how I want to start a Monday.

"I have work to do," I snap, and Harper actually leans back from the harshness in my voice. It wasn't directed at her, but I can't very well go about explaining my distain for my father to her.

"Right, of, um, course you do." She blinks rapidly and pushes her hair back behind her ear. "I'll go back to my desk." She takes a step back. "Unless you need anything."

"I'm good for now, thank you," I say and tell myself I shouldn't feel bad. She's my employee, not my friend, and she certainly will never be anything more.

Harper goes back to her desk, and I go back to work. We start each week with a meeting, catching up on company news and going over the different client projects. The meeting starts in half an hour, and I go over a proposal for a long-standing client of ours until then.

Harper doesn't turn around when I step out of the office. She's on her knees, bent over the bottom drawer of her desk. My eyes go right to her ass, and when I snap my gaze away, I notice two of the interns standing off to the side, staring at her ass too.

Their heads are together, no doubt commenting on just how fucking good she looks. Then one holds out his hands a few inches away from his waist and makes a crude gesture, like he's fucking some invisible woman from behind. Like he's fucking *Harper* from behind.

My blood instantly boils.

"Break time already?" I ask, voice startling them.

"Sorry, sir," the one who was air-humping Harper says. He lowers his eyes and hurries to his desk. Shaking my head, I look back at Harper, wondering what the heck she's doing bent over like that, and find her scowling at me.

Right. It looks like I just came out here and snapped at those interns. If only she knew what they were doing at her expense.

"Need any help with that?" I ask her, not allowing myself to think about the fact that twice within an hour I made myself look like an ass to her.

"No, but thank you. There's a pen stuck under this drawer and it catches when I pull it open. It's not a big deal, but it's kind of annoying to have to wiggle it back and forth before it comes out."

I nod. "That would be. I'll have maintenance come up and fix it."

"Nah, there's no need to bother them. I'm sure they're busy

enough. And I can open the drawer. Though for all we know, this pen could have a super secret message rolled up and hidden inside."

I smile. "Well, if there's even a chance, we should find out. It could be a message from the future warning us about humanity's demise."

"Right? It's like it's my mission to get this pen out."

"Can you do it later?" I ask, smile still on my face. I'm aware half the interns, whose desks are in a large open area of the office right next to us, are looking at us. Is it really that rare that I joke around with people at the office?

Yes, yes it probably is.

"Sure." She stands up, smoothing her hands over her skirt, and looks at me like she's waiting for me to give her a task. Right. She's had very little training and is doing well considering.

"We have meetings every Monday and you come sit in on them with me to take notes.

"Oh, okay. Makes sense." She shoves the drawer back in place and I can hear the pen rolling under the drawer. Grabbing a pen and a notebook, Harper follows me into the conference room.

"What do I take notes on?" she asks apprehensively. "Everything? Like record minutes?"

"No, just note any changes so I can remember to follow up on things. I'm kind of forgetful, but don't tell anyone," I say with a smile.

Harper smiles back. "Your secret is safe with me."

It's just the two of us in here until the others arrive, and the air is tense. If I can feel it, she can too. I sit at the head of the table and motion for Harper to sit next to me. She opens her notebook and writes today's date at the top in big, loopy letters.

A few more seconds tick by, and if I don't do something about this tension in the air, I'm going to need a knife to cut through it. It's so thick it's tangible, and I'm on the brink of a mental war with myself.

I don't want Harper to think I'm a bad guy. I'm not. Or at least, I don't want to be. That has to count for something, right? But on the other hand, it doesn't matter. I'm not here to be her friend. As long as we can work professionally together, I shouldn't give a shit what she thinks about me.

But, fuck, I do.

"The view is amazing up here." Harper's voice comes out so soft I'm not sure if she's talking to me or herself.

"It is," I agree. "I like when it storms. You can see the clouds gathering over the lake before it hits, and then it's as if I'm up there with it, inside the storm as it rages down on the city below."

"I was terrified the first time it stormed," she starts, still looking out the window. "I mean when I was in the high-rise." She turns, and warmth rushes through me when her eyes meet mine. It goes right to the tip of my cock, and I'm thinking about her slowly undoing those buttons again. "I'd never been in a storm twelve-stories up until I worked here. I thought the building would sway like crazy and the windows would give out. Then I realized it's not much different than being on the ground."

She swivels her chair around and looks out the window again. "It's a good perspective, isn't it? No matter where you are, it storms just the same. You can be high up or down low, and you still feel the wind and the rain, you still hear the same thunder and see the same flashes of lightning."

"I never thought about it that way."

She reaches up and touches the little lemon charm hanging around her neck. "That's because you've always thought you were above the storm," she says, voice barely louder than a whisper. Before I have time to react to her statement, Dan, Clarissa, and a few interns come in.

Puzzled by what Harper said, and trying to figure out if it was supposed to be an insult, I'm slow to get the meeting started. Harper is doodling in the notebook, and five minutes into our weekend catchup, I realize she's sketched out an impressive start to the skyline right outside the window.

My father joins us halfway through the meeting. He's only there to watch me and will no doubt find something to pick apart and criticize me for later…which he does.

Of fucking course.

"My office," he says stiffly as he leaves the meeting half an hour later. I'm a little surprised he relayed the message himself this time instead of making his own assistant do it.

I respond with a curt nod and go on as usual, hoping no one else caught on to the condescending ways he looked at me during the meeting. He of all people should know the damage instilling mistrust in me would do to the company. Though it honestly wouldn't surprise me if he hoped I'd fail once he left the company.

Watching everything he built burn to the ground would be worth it just to tell me *I told you so.*

My employees filter out of the conference room, and I wonder what type of relationship they have with their parents. Happy families only exist in movies, I'm sure of it, and another reason to why I'm in no rush settling down is because I don't want to be an asshole father. My own was…I don't want to be damned to follow in his footsteps.

～

"Close the door." My father doesn't look up from the book open on his desk. Clenching my jaw, I remind myself his retirement is approaching…just not fast enough.

"Yes?"

"Sit down." He sweeps his hand out at the chairs in front of his desk but still hasn't looked up.

"What do you want, Father? I have a conference call in—" I look at my watch "—seven minutes."

"I saw you looking at your assistant during that meeting."

"Okay?" I don't miss a beat. "I was looking at everyone."

"It wasn't just that you were looking at her, but the way you were looking at her. You can't think with your cock if you're going to take over. I wouldn't have hired such a pretty, young woman if I'd known you'd have trouble keeping it in your pants."

I grit my teeth, knowing if I open my mouth a big ol' *fuck you* will come tumbling out. Once that's free, I might grab something off the old bastard's desk and throw it. But, fuck, I can't do anything that would make him slow down the already slow-as-molasses process of finally getting the fuck out of the business.

And, it's true.

I'm attracted to Harper. Very attracted to her. She's hot for obvious reasons, but there's something else about her that draws me in.

"You have nothing to worry about. Mrs. Watson and I have a professional relationship and nothing more."

"Miss," Father hisses. "Didn't you look over her file at all?"

I didn't, and when I thought of taking a peek last night, I felt like too much of a creep. She's already hired, HR is processing the paperwork. There's no need to go back and look at her file.

"Is that all?" I put my hands on the arms of the chair, ready to push myself up.

"Yes." He finally looks up. "This job is demanding. It can be lonely and finding temptation right here in front of you might seem like a good idea at the time, but you will regret it."

"The thing is," I stand, "I'm not married with two children at home. Sleeping with anyone in this whole fucking office won't break a marriage the way you sleeping with your assistant did."

With that, I turn and storm out of the office. I'm raging and need to calm down. I'll feel better once I'm back in my office and space has been put between me and that asshole.

Back in my own office, I heft down in my chair and open up an internet search. I've been on-and-off searching for a classic car in the area over the last few months. Everything I have is new, and looking through old cars for sale calms my nerves and makes me have tunnel vision to what's going on around me.

All I think about is the car. On finding flaws. On making sure the VINs are legit. I start looking locally, don't find anything impressive, and expand my search to the whole Midwest. An overwhelming amount of people have posted old cars, and the thought of driving an hour away just to test drive this 1970 Corvette is exactly the distraction I need.

Harper softly knocks on the office door and steps inside.

"I typed up and printed the notes. My handwriting isn't the neatest."

"I'm sure it's better than mine," I laugh without thinking. Looking up, I see Harper's pretty face and feel that same rush go through me. She comes closer and sets the notes on my desk. "So I was thinking, and I still can't believe you haven't seen *End Game*. But now I'm curious if you've seen the other movies leading up to it. I'll admit I was late to see the Ant Man movies, but I tried to watch all the others first to avoid spoilers."

Nodding, I pick up the notes she set on my desk and quickly look them over. She was very thorough and is well-organized. She's still adjusting to her new schedule but is doing a damn good job.

"I don't know if *End Game* is available to stream anywhere, but I'm sure you can rent a digital copy online no problem. If you need something to do during lunch, you should totally watch it so then we can talk about it."

I hardly have time to breathe during my lunch breaks, and if I leave the office for lunch it's because I'm meeting a client. Calling Harper in here, turning my monitor around, and watching a movie together, even for a brief twenty or thirty minutes, sounds really fucking nice.

I twist in my chair, finding Harper standing close to my desk.

My eyes slowly trail over her, and I'm again taken aback by not only her looks but her personality. She's so vibrant in every way.

My eyes land on that little lemon charm. She's worn it every day she's been here, and it's either the only piece of jewelry she owns or has some sort of significance to her.

Fuck. My mind *is* drifting. Drifting away from work and the conference call that'll be coming in any second now. Harper needs to be at her desk, ready to answer and patch the calls through to my office, not in here, looking hot as hell and talking movies with me.

"I'm sorry, Harper," I start, seeing my father's face flash before my eyes when I blink. "I have work to do. It's best we don't discuss movies at work."

Her name feels too good coming off my lips. I want to moan it while I pull her hair to the side, lips grazing against her skin, the touch so soft it sends shivers up and down her spine, wetting her pussy and making her want me as much as I want her.

But I can't have her. Not now…not ever.

CHAPTER 12

HARPER

And they say women are complicated.

I click the seatbelt into place and fire up the engine of my company-issued Lexus. Letting out a breath, I put the car in reverse and slowly back out of my parking spot. It's weird looking at the backup camera and not actually turning and looking behind me. It's like I'm doing something wrong.

The car beeps at me, letting me know I'm close to the SUV next to me. It makes me slam on the brakes, thinking I'm close enough to hit it. Will I ever get used to driving a so-called smart car? I felt fancy in my old Honda because it had power windows.

I drive past Alexander's spot on my way out and shake my head at his Tesla. I almost got whiplash from him today. We had a friendly chat on Friday night. He was nice and talkative this morning, and then he was back to being cold and uptight.

And then I thought I caught him looking at me with lust in his eyes. It surprised me at first, because someone like Alex doesn't go for someone like me, a broke single mom of twins. But I knew what I saw, and I can't deny the spark I felt when we talked. It was almost as if he let his guard down for a split second and I saw the real him.

I try to tell myself it doesn't matter. I need this job, and I'm good at it. Give me another week or two to get used to the way the office works and I'll be the best assistant he's ever had.

Still, I stew over it on my way to Tessa's. She brought the girls home with her after school and I'm dying to see them and ask how their first day was.

Tessa lives in a small but nice condo not too far from the school. She has two Yorkies that I try to love but just can't stand. They've peed on my shoes one too many times for that. And I think I'm just a cat person at heart.

I park as close as I can and hurry down the block, making a mental note to bring a pair of running shoes to keep in the car tomorrow so I can change out of these high heels. I'm ready to sprint if it means seeing my girls faster.

Someone is going into the apartment right as I get to the lobby doors, and I sneak in right behind them. They go to check their mail and I get into an elevator. Pressing the button for the fourth floor, I practically bounce up and down with excitement.

I miss my babies every single day I'm away from them…but then I come home to screaming, bickering, and being asked a million times to *make the Barbies talk, Mommy*, and want a few hours alone to enjoy the peace and quiet.

It's a vicious cycle, being a mother, where I'm always trying to find that balance between *I want to spend every second with my sweet girls* and *leave me the fuck alone before I lose my goddamn mind*. I've heard that wine helps. Once I get my next paycheck, I'm going to get myself a nice bottle of something sweet to enjoy a glass or two of before bed.

The elevator dings and I'm out before the doors are fully open. I jog down the hall, only twisting my ankle once, and stop outside Tessa's apartment door. I try the knob first, ready to yell at her for not keeping the door locked, especially when the kids are here. It is locked this time. Hopefully me running through the list of every single reason why she *should* keep the door locked swayed her mind. She lives in a better part of town than I do, but it's still Chicago.

I knock, and it takes way too long for Tessa to open the door. Thirty seconds is painful to wait.

"Hey, hey!" she tells me, opening the door and stepping aside. "Damn, I'm almost jealous that red top looks that good on you. I knew I lacked the boobs for it, yet I ordered it anyway."

I stick my chest out and shake it, making us both laugh. "They're not all they're cracked up to be, you know."

"Oh, puh-lease. Like you'd trade your perky D's for anything but."

"If they were perky, then no, I wouldn't trade." I look past her and into the living room. "Where are the children?"

"Oh no!" Tessa gasps loudly. "I must have left them at school!"

"Oh no!" I play along. "I guess I should go back and look for them, then."

"Mommy!" they scream in unison and throw a blanket off their heads. The biggest smile breaks out on my face, and my heart couldn't be fuller.

"My sweet girls!" I drop my purse on the ground and open my arms. Penny and Violet jump off the couch and come running.

"Mommy!" they say in unison. I sink onto my knees when they get to me, hugging them as tight as I can. I kiss them each twice and hug them for another good thirty seconds before straightening up.

"How was school today, my little loves?"

"Okay," Penny tells me.

"Just okay?" I laugh. "Did you learn anything?"

"No," Violet answers.

I look up at Tessa, holding back my laughter. "Well, that's a shame."

"To be fair," Tessa starts, holding up her finger. "They probably didn't. The first day is pretty much chaos. But I think I have

99

a great class this year, and we're going to have so much fun, aren't we, girls?"

"Yes!" they cry out together, and I pull them in for another hug.

"Can we finish this episode?" Penny asks, attention leaving me for the TV.

"I'm sure Aunt Tessa wants to relax sans children for a while."

"But she ordered pizza and I'm starving," Violet complains. "Please, Mommy?"

"I did order pizza," Tessa says. "I was all set for eating healthy this school year, but I need comfort food after the first day."

"You don't mind us staying?"

"Please do. If you don't, you'll be leaving me alone with an extra-large pepperoni, deep-dish pizza."

"Well, when you put it that way…" I stand, smiling again when I look at my girls. Letting out a sigh, I shift my gaze to Tessa. "So you had a rough first day?"

"Nah, it wasn't anything unusual. And I really do think I have a good bunch this year. I usually have one or two difficult students, but the real kicker is always the parents." She rolls her eyes. "There are two moms in particular I have my doubts on."

"The Stepford Wives," I say and grab my purse, moving it out of the way of Jelly Bean and Goose, the two Yorkies. I don't trust them as far as I can throw them. Which I'd never do, by the way. Though if I did, I don't think they'd go far. I've always lacked athletic ability.

Tessa laughs. "I know exactly who you're talking about, and yes, them. One of their kids really shouldn't be in kindergarten this year, but God forbid I suggest they un-enroll him and let him go to preschool another year." She rolls her eyes. "The sad thing with private schools is administration really don't give a shit since they're getting money, and that particular family donates a lot."

"Ugh. That doesn't sound fun. I'm sorry."

She waves her hand in the air, dismissing me. "It's fine. We'll all be in a good routine in a week or two and I'll have parents giving me Coach purses and gift cards for swanky salon massages for Christmas."

"I should have been a teacher."

Tessa lets out a snort of laughter. "I promise you public school teachers would not agree with that statement. I'm lucky."

"You are."

"Enough about school...how was your day?"

"Ugh." I toss my head back and follow Tessa in through the entry way. We dodge in front of the girls and go into her kitchen. It's white and bright and I love it. "I think I hate my boss. Like really hate him."

"You actually hate someone?" She raises both eyebrows. "What happened to him being really involved in a super taboo love affair or something?"

"Or something is more like it," I huff and roll my eyes. "I think you might have been right about him being an ass—an A-S-S-hole," I say, spelling out the bad word and hoping the girls don't pick up on it.

"Did something happen?"

"He called me Friday night after you left to see if one of the interns had emailed me something about a project—which they did."

"He called you on a Friday night?"

"He said he didn't realize how late it had gotten and I believe him. We talked, like friendly talked, and I was thinking like hey, maybe he isn't so bad after all. But then when I get to the office, he's all like *'Harper, don't talk about movies at work,'*" I say, doing a terrible job at mocking Alexander's voice. "*"Harper, keep it professional. Harper...Harper..."*" I grit my teeth. "Just the way he says my name is like nails on a chalkboard. And you should hear the way he talks to the interns! I don't get it. We talked for a decent while

Friday, and if I hadn't told him I was naked, we probably would have talked longer."

"Wait, back up." Tessa holds up her hand. "You told him you were naked?"

"I mentioned that I'd just gotten in the shower and then heard my phone ring and got scared it was someone calling with bad news."

"I still don't see how that equates you to telling him you're naked. Were you hoping he'd take his clothes off too?"

"If he did, I wouldn't know. Next time I'll make sure to request to FaceTime instead of calling him." I let out a heavy sigh. "He's confusing, and I don't like it. Because I don't like him."

"You sound like you're all hot and bothered by this guy."

I make a face and shake my head.

"Mommy?" Penny calls. "What does hot and bothered mean?"

I narrow my eyes at Tessa, and she stifles a laugh. "It means the temperature outside is hot and it bothers me," I blurt.

Tessa opens her fridge and pulls out a bottle of red wine. "Well, you are rather upset."

"Of course I am. He's a grade-A you-know-what."

"And it has nothing to do with your want for everyone to like you?" She sets the bottle of wine down on her small island counter and looks right into my eyes.

"I don't want everyone to like me."

Tessa cocks one eyebrow and purses her lips. "Mh-hm."

"Fine, it makes me happy to know people like me. I'm a rather likable person, if I do say so myself. So it makes no sense why Alex doesn't like me. What did I ever do to him?"

"Honey, calm your tits. That guy is an asshole. No ifs, ands, or buts about it. There's no backstory, no reason behind him snapping and being cold."

"Maybe you're right." I let out a defeated sigh, not sure if I'm ready to believe that yet. "This is a good job. I'm making more than I was before, I'm getting benefits, and I have a sweet car to drive. Alex can hate me all he wants, and I'm going to hate him right back."

Tessa laughs. "Okay. That's a mature response to this situation."

"Thank you." I tip my chin up, trying to look smug. "I'm super mature. But really...I'm going to do my job. We don't need to be friends and he can dislike me all he wants. I'm a good assistant, so I'll just focus on work and nothing else."

"Good idea. This is temporary," she reminds me. "Want any wine?"

"Like less than half a glass since I'm driving."

She pours the wine and we go into the living room. I take a small sip and set my glass on the coffee table. I wedge myself in between Penny and Violet, taking one in each arm. Someday they're going to be too old to snuggle with me like this, and I want to soak up these moments, no matter how small, for as long as I can.

"Tell me about your day," I try again.

"It was fun," Violet says, which gets a smile out of Tessa. "We have centers!"

"Oh, that does sound fun! What are your centers?"

"I don't remember them all, but the iPad center is my favorite!"

"Of course it is," I laugh and kiss the top of her head. Penny goes on to tell me about a girl named Heather in their class that they played with at recess, and how much fun sitting in the cafeteria was.

"Do most kids buy lunch every day?" I ask Tessa. I want to make sure my kids are taught not to worry about going with the crowd and are confident on their own two feet. But I also recognize how important fitting in is with school-aged children.

"Yes," she assures me. "The food is good. Really good. Most teachers buy everyday too."

"What, is it prepared by some famous chef?" I joke.

"Yes," she answers seriously.

"Dang. I need to come eat lunch with you girls some time and try out the food."

They both think that would be the coolest thing in the world, and I give them both kisses. The pizza comes not long after that, and we pretty much have to eat and leave.

As expected, the girls protest, and it's a bit of a battle to get them out. I eventually have to carry Penny out as she cries, and Violet is watching her sister, tempted to start throwing a fit as well. I give her my best *mom glare*, daring her to start. She decides its best not to tempt me, thank goodness. It's been a long fucking day.

I DO MY BEST TO AVOID ANYTHING REMOTELY NON-WORK RELATED with Alex the next day. Other than asking what kind of dressing he wants on the salad he ordered for lunch, the only other words we exchanged were related to projects going on in the office, when his next appointment was, and who was calling on the phone.

I finished my work right on time and left the office at 5:03 PM, almost on time. Alex was still in the office with his door closed, and I get the feeling he stays late at work most nights, even though he said he didn't.

But it doesn't matter.

He's not avoiding a tragic home life by burying himself in work. He doesn't have a long-lost lover or anything remotely interesting. He's just my cocky boss, and day one of treating him as nothing more was a success.

Dad picked up the girls from school today and brought them back to our place. Dinner was in the oven when I stepped inside, and we had a nice, low-key family meal. He made Mom's famous taco salad, and we talked about her throughout our meal.

The girls might not have met their grandma in person, but they sure know a lot about her from the stories we tell.

Wednesday was similar, and it was wash-rinse-repeat on Thursday. Get up at the crack of dawn, stumble around the apartment getting myself ready, make breakfast for the girls, and fight with them to get out of bed.

Drop them off at school, wave and say a hurried hello to Rose and Kate, and then rush off to work where I avoid Alex's gaze as much as possible. A few times I could feel him staring at me, and when I looked up, I swear there was sadness reflected in his eyes.

Which doesn't matter.

I'm so ready for the weekend. I was up late again sorting through emails and trying to fix a file that one of the interns messed up. It was simple data input, something I'm used to doing from my days as a researcher. The mistakes are easy to fix, but very tedious.

I climb into bed at one AM, sleep for a glorious forty-five minutes, and wake up to Violet poking me in the face, saying she couldn't sleep. I tuck her in with me, fall asleep again, and wake up to Penny screaming because she woke up alone.

I finally fall back asleep a whole three hours before my alarm went off, and I am just dragging. My only saving grace is knowing I can have a plate full of bacon when I get to the office.

And probably a mimosa, because why the hell not?

"You know what tomorrow is?" I ask the girls as we pull up to the school. There's a drop-off carline, but it moves slow and it's actually faster to park, get out, and walk them to the front doors. Rose and Kate do that too, and it's nice being able to at the very least smile and wave at them.

"What?" they ask in unison.

"Saturday! Which means we get to sleep in, and you don't have school!"

"Yay!" they cheer.

"Can we go see a movie? Heather's mom is taking her to see a movie."

"We'll see," I tell them. I get my first paycheck from the new job today, as well as one from my previous. It'll only be half of what I usually got, but the way the pay periods fell is going to feel like I won the lottery. If we can swing a matinée, maybe we could see a movie. I could bring our own drinks, hidden in my purse, and we'd be able to split one small bag of popcorn. "We get to go grocery shopping tomorrow too."

"Good. I'm tired of eating eggs all the time," Violet mumbles. I'm sick of them too, but it's the cheapest semi-nutritious thing I can make for them, and eggs were on sale for forty cents a carton a while back. I stocked up and have been trying to get creative with them.

We've done the standard: scrambled, fried, sunny side up. For a while "egg toast" was a hit, which was simply tearing out the middle of a piece of bread and plopping an egg down in it, frying it up that way. Hard-boiled eggs with salt worked for a good while as well, but even I'm having a hard time forcing them down.

Someday…someday this won't be an issue.

"Eggs are high in protein and low in carbs," I tell them, but I'm not sure if that's even true at all. "But yes, we'll look for some other healthy options." I've worked hard to try to hide my money problems from the girls. I don't want them to ever worry. Not when they're this little.

I park and get the girls out of the car. Holding each of their hands, we start toward the school. I walk them to the front and stop right outside the main entrance. I hug them each twice and kiss their foreheads before sending them off.

"Harper!"

I stand and turn to see Rose near the curb. She's wearing a light pink dress. It's low-cut and flowy around her feet. There seems to be a perpetual breeze blowing back her thick hair, and bad lighting doesn't exist when she's around.

"Hey," I call back to her with a smile. We didn't hit the normal amount of traffic lights on the way here and I have about five extra minutes before I need to rush off to work. "You look amazing."

Rose pulls me into a hug. "You say that like you don't."

I let out a snort of laughter as I lean back. "Take a closer look at the bags under my eyes."

"You're a single mom who works. Of course you're tired." It's not an insult but just a fact. There's no judgement in her voice at all. "And I'm guessing you haven't had any work done?"

"No, I'd love some Botox on my forehead, though."

"This," she starts, and motions to her face. "Is an ongoing work in progress. I was in the beauty industry long enough to appreciate natural beauty when I see it."

"Thank you, but I'm just a mess today."

"Women have a tendency to do that, you know."

"Do what?" I pull my heavy purse off my shoulder. I don't know what I have in there that makes it so damn heavy.

"Deflect compliments. You're hot, Harper. All on your own with no cosmetic interventions. Own that shit."

My lips curve up in a smile. "I'll try to."

Kate jogs up to the curb, clutching her daughter's hand. The girl looks like a mini version of her mother, right down to the way they walk. She gives her a quick kiss and sends her off.

"Rough morning?" Rose asks Kate when she huffs her way over.

"Oh, you don't know the half of it." Kate's brows are furrowed and she has a coffee stain on the front of her shirt. "Of all the days for the nanny to get food poisoning. I'm meeting a potential donor for breakfast right after this but look." She points to the brown stain on her ivory-colored blouse. "I didn't bring a change of clothes, and what is even open in this area to shop at right now?"

"A donor?" I echo, mind going to a sperm-donor.

Kate nods. "I try to convince people or companies to donate to nonprofit organizations, and Mr. Heely seemed on board for a really big donation, but if I show up looking like this..." She lets out a sigh and shakes her head. "He's not going to take me seriously. The guy already is hesitant to work with a woman. Fuck," she mutters and pulls out her phone. "It's so early and literally nothing is close by."

"I can trade you shirts," I offer. The black v-neck top I have on would match her pants. "I'm a bit taller than you, but your boobs are big enough to fill out the shirt more and make up for the difference."

Kate looks at me, eyes wide, and I think she's about to bust out laughing at the thought of wearing my clothes, which cost a fraction of what hers do.

"You'd really do that?"

"Yeah. It's always cold in the office and I wear a sweater most of the day. No one will even see the stain."

"You're a lifesaver! Thank you!"

"No problem." I look toward the school. "Can we go in to change? They're tight on security."

"There's a Starbucks across the street," Rose points out.

"Oh, right." Kate closes her eyes in a long blink and lets out a breath of relief. "Thank you again, Harper. I'll buy you a coffee too. You are saving me such a headache."

"You don't have to. We have pretty good coffee at work."

Kate smiles. "You're a saint."

"If you're getting coffee, then I'm coming," Rose tells us. "I'll drive. Parking is a bitch over there." We hurry to her Range Rover. Kate sits up front and I climb over a booster seat to sit in the middle of the back row.

"Getting donations and grants for nonprofits is a really neat job," I tell Kate. "I went to school for PR hoping I could so something similar."

"We're always looking to hire new faces. Send your resume through and I'll put in a good word."

"I never finished my degree," I admit and fight hard not to feel embarrassment or shame. "I got pregnant with the twins my senior year in college."

"Oh, well, do you think you'll finish your degree now that they're older?"

I shake my head and look out the window. "No, it's just us at home. I don't see how that'd be possible."

"Their dad isn't involved at all?" Rose asks and I shake my head again. "What an asshole."

"Maybe," I start and twist my hands around in my lap. "But in his defense, I don't think he knows he's a father."

"I'm curious now." Rose looks at me in the rearview mirror. "Sorry. I don't want to trigger anything."

"No, you're fine. It's not like that." I flick my eyes up and meet Rose's gaze for half a second. If these women are going to be my friends, my real friends, then they should know the truth. "I had a really, really, *really* bad week and thought getting drunk and having a one-night stand would be the perfect distraction. Well, it was distracting all right."

"I've had a few of those weeks where everything is shit and you just need a fucking break. Like right now." Kate turns around. "What happened that week?"

"My mom died." The words come out so easily, and I hate it. I blink rapidly, trying to keep the tears at bay. It's been over five years and still hurts.

"Oh my God, I am so, so sorry." Kate reaches around and pats my hand.

"Thanks. It wasn't just that, though. My grandparents—her parents—live in Mexico, and even though they had all the paperwork they needed to come here for the funeral, they got detained in immigration and it was a terrible battle to get them out. The whole thing was such a big cluster-fuck of a mess…" I close my eyes and shake my head, not wanting to think about it. "Things got sorted, but after…after all that, I went out with a friend to what was only like my second college party ever."

"Oh, honey." Kate's southern accent comes out a little stronger.

"I got all dolled up, pre-gamed, and decided to put on this stupid persona, which made sense at the time. I called myself Antoinette and said I was visiting from California."

Rose slows to a stop at the light and turns around, waiting for me to continue.

"The girls' father is a man named Michael, or at least that's the name he gave me. I told him a fake name, so who knows on his end. It started out like an obvious hookup, but we actually ended up talking for hours about just the most random things. I'd already kept up the fake name and didn't want to tell him the truth at that point, afraid he'd get mad and leave."

"So you had a connection?"

I nod, thinking back to that night. I told him about everything that happened, burst into tears a few times, and he just held me as I cried. Then he told me about his brother who died in the line of duty only two years prior. We bonded over grief that night, and I never ever expected to form a deep connection with a guy I was hoping would fuck me into oblivion, giving me just a small reprieve from the real world.

"We really did."

"You never saw each other again?"

I shake my head. I was heartsick over him even before I found out I was pregnant. Tessa and I spent hours searching the internet for him, but it was like the guy was a ghost. And I might have actually believed he was one until I started puking my guts out about a month later.

"I was never able to find him. Someone from the party

thought his last name was Cooper and lived in Hyde Park, so I looked up every Michael Cooper in the entire city and sent them letters on pink paper like a crazy person. But none ever contacted me back, so they either weren't him or he didn't want anything to do with some random chick he knocked up. So, it's just been me and the girls ever since."

"Wow." Kate slowly shakes her head. "You've come so far. That's incredible."

"I don't feel that incredible. I'm just doing what any mother would do for her children." I remember what Rose said about deflecting compliments. It's true. I do it all the time because I feel weird accepting praise.

"I don't think I could make it through a week without the nanny," Kate confesses. "You're badass, Harper."

Rose meets my eyes again in the mirror and gives me a reassuring smile.

"Yeah," I say, smiling as well. "I guess I am."

CHAPTER 13

HARPER

I lied.

The office isn't cold. But I do have a sweater, which I'm definitely wearing. Not because I care about the coffee stain, but because this shirt is loose in the top and I'm at risk for a nip-slip at any moment. And though it's stained, it's the most expensive thing I've ever worn, I'm sure.

I pull the pink sweater out of the bottom drawer of my desk. I have to yank on it pretty hard this time. That pen is really driving me nuts, but I have no idea how to get it out without taking the whole drawer off...which I don't know how to do.

Pulling the sweater on, I walk back to the break room and fill a plate with bacon, two pancakes, and a bagel with cream cheese. I get Alex's coffee, and walk back, setting the plate at my desk and then taking Alex his coffee.

He's sitting at his desk, looking fine as hell once again. Today, he's wearing a navy suit with a pale pink button-up shirt underneath. The color is the last thing I expected but looks so damn good on him. I pause for a split second, waiting to see if he's busy or on the phone or something.

He looks up, and when his eyes meet mine, my heart skips a

beat, and I have to remind myself there's not going to be a hot kiss in an elevator like the one from a particular favorite movie of mine.

"Good morning, Harper." His voice is deep and cuts right through me, warming me. Hearing him say my name is border-line erotic. *You hate him, remember?*

"Good morning. Here's your coffee." I set the mug down on his desk, smelling his cologne as I draw near. "You have a meeting with Justin Perry at nine-thirty today, and there was a message from Mr. Harold asking to reschedule."

"Again?" Alex lets his eyes fall shut as he reaches for his coffee, blindly wrapping his long fingers around the handle of the mug.

"Would you like me to try and find another time to meet with him?"

Alex takes a drink of coffee and shakes his head. "No, it's clear they don't want to do business with us anymore, though I'm not sure why. It has to be more than that stupid fucking article. Pardon my language."

"It doesn't offend me," I assure him. "I swear one of my kids' first words was *fuck* because I said it so often."

He laughs and the stress on his face goes away, just for a moment. It's strange, how I can sense that he's holding up this façade, that he's not really a bad guy under all the armor he's wearing. Or maybe I just want that to be true. "Do you still talk to Harold's assistant?"

"Not really, but she did send me a friend request on Facebook. Do you want me to try and talk to her or something?"

"No, I can't ask that." He brings his hand to his head and plows his fingers through his hair. I never fully realized until right now just how thick it is. How good it would feel for me to run my own fingers through it.

Oh. My. God.

I need to stop.

Alex is my boss, and more importantly, he can't seem to stand me half the time I'm around.

"I'll try to stay friendly," I say before turning to leave. I know losing this client bothers Alex, and though I've only been here a week now, I'm starting to learn a few ins and outs of this business.

Reach PR is our biggest rival, and they've been stealing clients left and right. It's a shitty tactic, and it hurts us. Did Mr. Harold decide to go with them? If he did, Alex will be pissed, for sure.

Alex doesn't say anything else, so I turn to leave.

"Harper?"

"Yes?" I turn around, and his eyes meet mine. It's like he's searching for something he doesn't think he'll ever find, and behind the cocky attitude, the fancy suit, and that smirk that looks so good on his handsome face, I see a glimpse of him, the real him again.

"You know what, never mind. I can handle it."

Giving him another nod, I turn again, and this time make it back to my desk. Since his meeting today has been canceled, I update the multiple calendars I work with. One is a big desk calendar, and the rest of the month is mapped out thanks to Jason. The other is a traditional planner, and the third is a shared calendar online.

I add important dates for the next week into my phone, setting alarms and reminders to make sure I don't forget anything, which in turn would be Alex forgetting something.

Since the planner is something I take home with me, I add my own personal to-dos to it as well. Parent night at the school is on Monday. It starts at 5:30, and Tessa is keeping the kids with her at school until I get there after work.

I—again—feel bad for them. No five-year-old should have to be at school that long, but what am I going to do? Dad works that evening and Tessa will be at school all day, leaving later than we will. I'll pack them extra snacks to get them through the evening, and might send a bag of Barbies and comfy clothes to change into. Thank God Tessa is my best friend. I don't know what I'd do if we didn't have her.

Public schools offer some sort of kid-care, either at the school or by providing transportation to a safe place for kids to hang out while they wait for their parents to get off work. But this fancy Briar Prep would scoff at the idea of daycare. I know I'm the only single parent with students attending the school.

I close the planner and finish my breakfast. Looking in through the open door, I see Alex sitting at his desk, typing up an email that he'll probably have me proofread before he sends.

My phone vibrates with a text. It's Kate, saying she got the donation and thanking me again for the shirt. Kate comes from a rich family and married a rich guy. Rose's upbringing was more or less normal, hailing from a middle-class family with four older brothers. She got into modeling in high school and met her first husband at a fashion show. He turned out to be an abusive asshole, and she ended up falling for her divorce lawyer, who's her current husband and father of her children.

Smiling, I unlock my phone.

Me: I knew you'd get it! And that top is killer ;-)

Kate: Hah! Right? I'm sure it sealed the deal.

Me: Oh, no doubt!

Kate: Heather just adores your girls. Are we still on for a playdate tomorrow?

Me: Yes! The girls will be excited when I tell them.

Smiling, I set my phone down only to pick it back up again. My paychecks should be hitting my bank account right about now, and I need to look at see how much I actually got. Neither paycheck is from a full pay term, and my credit card statement is due in two days.

Rent is due soon as well.

And I'd love to be able to surprise the girls with something other than eggs and off-brand Pop Tarts for breakfast next week.

My stomach hurts thinking about it, and my throat gets that closed-up, tight feeling all over again. Dammit. The little bit of joy I felt from scheduling a playdate is gone. Vanished. Zapped away by the stress of real life.

"Are you all right?" Alex's voice startles me. I didn't hear him come out of the office.

I look up, realizing just how tense I am, and force a smile. I shouldn't hate him for being born rich. I hate him for being a dick of a human being. Yet feeling the stress of not knowing how to make ends meet, no matter how hard I try, and then looking at him...it's not fucking fair.

"Yes," I flat-out lie. Though really...I'm not lying. Because I will be all right, and it could be worse.

"You look upset."

"I am, but it's nothing work-related."

"Oh...okay. That's good, I suppose." He takes a few steps forward only to freeze and take one big step back. "If there's anything we can do around here to help, please don't hesitate to let HR know."

HR isn't going to give me the five grand I need to cover rent, pay down my credit card debt, and buy groceries, get the girls new clothes, shoes, and sheets that aren't "scratchy" as they say, and give me enough to put to the side for "oh shit" money.

"Thank you," I tell him. "I'll be fine. I learned long ago how to make lemonade."

He gives me a quizzical look but doesn't question me. Instead, he keeps walking, going into one of the senior agent's offices. I reach up, taking solace in the way that little metal lemon feels against my fingers.

I can make the best damn batch of lemonade you've ever tasted...but it's damn near impossible to do so when I can't even afford the fucking lemons.

CHAPTER 14

ALEX

"How was your weekend?" Harper's voice floats through the office. She's not talking to me, but I look up anyway. She's wearing a black wrap dress today, that hugs her curves wonderfully. Her hair is pulled to the side in a braid, and she's wearing those bright red shoes again that match her lipstick.

The intern she's talking to has her back to me, making it impossible to hear what she's saying. Whatever it is makes Harper laugh, and her entire face lights up when she smiles. I don't know how Harper's weekend was, and she's not going to ask how mine was either.

She's a talkative and bubbly person, and having her not fill the silence with awkward small talk is actually more awkward. She's been a perfect assistant and I have no complaints. She's organized, which in turn keeps me organized. She stays on top of things and keeps my calendar updated, informing me of appointments, schedule changes, and managing the projects the interns have turned in for approval.

But that's it.

She hasn't asked me about movies, hasn't rambled on and on about something random. It's efficient this way, and as long as we're getting our jobs done, that's how it should be. Yet I can't help but be bothered by the way she looks at me, like I'm the money-hungry dictator of the office.

I've never cared much for being liked. I'm the boss, not a buddy, and I firmly believe the quality of work goes down when my employees think they can get away with shit because "we're friends". I'm no slave-driver, and I don't want people to hate coming to work. That can fuck up productivity and quality just as badly.

I feel like I've found a good balance. I hold this company and everyone working here in high standards, and they know it. It puts the right amount of pressure on everyone, where they'll work hard and give it their all, but not so much they crack and jump off a fire escape on their lunch break.

Laughing again, Harper walks off with the intern, returning just a minute or two later with coffee.

"Good morning, Alex," she says, setting the coffee on my desk. She flicks her eyes to me and smiles. "Should I prepare the conference room for today's meeting or do you need anything first?"

"No, I don't. Thank you." One of our senior interns is giving a mock presentation today. He's a bright kid who I think can go far, and I'd like to hire him once his internship is up. He's got a very persuasive personality and can sell just about anything. I let him take the lead on one of our smaller projects, and if his presentation goes well today, he'll be able to present again to the client.

Ten minutes later, I join Harper in the conference room. Jay, the intern presenting today, is there as well, and I can tell he's nervous as fuck.

"Breathe," I tell him. "This is a trial run, and if it doesn't go smoothly, this is the time to fix it."

"Thank you." Jay lets out a deep breath.

"You're going to do great. I looked over the proposal and was really impressed."

Jay flashes the biggest smile and opens his laptop. I catch Harper watching me out of the corner of my eye, and when I turn, she smiles. But it's not one of her forced, fake smiles. This one is genuine.

"I was in your shoes once," I tell Jay. "But it was worse since my father was watching. He's much harsher to family than he is to anyone else."

Jay laughs. "Right. My own father is a big fan of *tough love*."

I smile and nod. Dad left the *love* out of *tough love*. He was just tough, and I don't remember a time in my life when he wasn't that way. All the way back to some of my first memories, he was always like that.

An asshole.

Then it hits me hard, like a sucker punch to the gut, why it bothers me so much to see Harper looking at me like I'm a jerk. The look of distain in her eyes is the same look I have when I see my father.

$\approx$

I PRESS THE INTERCOM BUTTON ON MY PHONE. "YES?"

"Your sister is on the phone," Harper tells me. "She said it's urgent."

"Thank you." I let go of the button and pick up my phone. "Nicole? Is everything okay?"

"It will be if you want to do me a huge favor again."

"Depends on what it is. I learned years ago not to agree to anything with you until I get full details."

"It's parent night at Briar Prep and Calvin was supposed to go with Henry. I have a scheduled gall bladder removal at that time, so Cal had it covered."

"And he doesn't now?"

"He was flying in from Denver this morning and his plane got delayed. There's a chance he'll still make it, but it'll be cutting it really close. I feel like I'm failing as a parent." Nicole's voice breaks. "I miss orientation and now parent night…" She sniffles.

"You're not a bad parent. Not at all." I open my calendar to double-check my schedule for the rest of the afternoon. I have a phone conference at 4:15 that shouldn't take more than half an hour. I have paperwork, like always, but I can take it home with me like I usually do anyway, or come back to the office. "What time is parent night?"

"It starts at 5:30. It's nothing all that formal. You'll get to talk to Henry's teachers and see how he interacts with his classmates."

"Teachers? He has more than one?"

"He has several. Kindergarten isn't playtime like it was when we were in school, you know. They have art, music, P.E., science, library, computer lab, and social studies throughout the week."

"What the hell do they teach kindergarteners about in social studies?"

She laughs. "I don't know. Maybe about the state or something."

"Glad we went to kindergarten when we did."

"I know, right? Looking at his schedule reminded me of med school," she jokes and then lets out a sigh of relief. "Thank you, Alex. I've been sick over this all morning and have been obsessively watching for flight updates. Assuming the traffic from O'Hare isn't bad—hah, I know—Calvin should be able to get there right around six."

I lean back in my chair, glad I'm able to help my sister. My eyes go to Harper. She'll be at parent night too.

This won't be awkward at all.

"We'll hang out at the school until he gets there. Please tell me kids are still allowed to play on playground equipment."

"They are, but a group of moms is trying to get the slides taken away because they think they're too dangerous. And another mom is worried someone is going to get strangled on the swings."

"No wonder people are growing up to be such entitled pussies."

"I know, right? I need to go prep for surgery. Thank you again, Alex. So much. I'll take you out to dinner or something to thank you. But I get to choose the restaurant. I'm not going to a strip club."

"Fair enough. Though *Tommy's* isn't a strip club. The waitresses all just happen to be busty and wear tight white shirts and short skirts."

"You're disgusting," she deadpans, and I laugh.

"Don't be jealous."

"You know what I am jealous of? One of the night nurses here dances on her time off and makes so much money. Why did I spend years of my life studying medicine when I could be up there on a stage shaking my ass for over five hundred bucks a night?"

"You went to medical school because you like to slice people open and play with their insides," I remind her.

"Oh right. And it's only acceptable to do that when you're preforming surgery. It's such a shame being a serial killer is frowned upon," she says seriously. We have a weird sense of humor between us, which can quickly take a morbid turn. I think it helped up get through our shitty childhood. "And I'm pretty sure a respiratory therapist just overheard me," she laughs. "I'll see you later. Thank you again, Al."

"You're welcome. I'm glad I can help."

CHAPTER 15

ALEX

I set the armload of files down on my large island counter. It's ridiculous to have a kitchen as big and fancy as this when I hardly ever use it, I know. My pantry is well-stocked, my fridge is always full, and once a week the housekeepers go through and throw away all the wasted food.

My penthouse is large, and when I moved in six years ago, I slightly entertained the thought that maybe I wouldn't always be living here alone. The closest I came to sharing my home was the summer Michelle Smith stayed with me. She was the epitome of a blonde bombshell, and I fell hard.

Or so I thought.

Turns out, she'd internet stalked me for a few months, finding out my favorite TV shows, where I like to eat, and even how I like my coffee. What I thought was fate turned out to be a professional stalker hoping she could cash in on the money I've worked hard to earn. The moment I mentioned a prenup would be a must before I ever got married, she packed her bags and got out of here.

So I know better now.

I walk through my large kitchen and into the living room.

Flicking on the TV, I take off my suit jacket and loosen my tie. I left work a little earlier than normal today, so I'd have a few minutes to come home and sit down before going to the school.

I relax on the couch and watch a whole five minutes of TV before getting up and making a protein shake that I drink while I change from my work clothes into jeans and a t-shirt.

Then I head out, picking up Henry from his house, and go to the school. It's busy tonight, much busier than the kindergarten open house night. We park on the street a good ways down, and I give Henry a piggyback ride up to the school.

I have to sign in as soon as we step foot inside, and Henry runs up to the woman in the polka-dot blue dress and gives her a hug.

"Uncle Alex, this is my teacher Miss Tessa!"

Miss Tessa pats Henry's back and looks at me for a good few seconds before smiling and holding out her hand. "Nice to meet you. Again. You were here on the open house night as well, weren't you?"

"Yes. Nicole wasn't able to make it again."

"She emailed me. I think it's great that Henry has a family member so willing to come in and help. We don't see that too often," she tells me.

"He's my family." I put my hand on Henry's head and mess up his hair. He laughs and protests at the same time. "He's one of the troublemakers, isn't he?"

"Hey!" Henry laughs. "I'm a good kid!"

"You?" I raise my eyebrows incredulously. "No way. You're probably the biggest troublemaker in the class, right, Miss Tessa?"

She laughs. "Henry is a joy to have in class. He's sweet and always listens."

Henry puts both hands on his hips. "See?"

Miss Tessa and I both laugh. "If there's any crucial information, I'll pass it along to my sister." I look at my watch. "Though there's still a chance Henry's dad will make it before tonight ends."

"You can tell her she has nothing to worry about," Miss Tessa says quietly, leaning in. "It's so early in the year, but I see no signs of any sort of behavior problem at this point."

"Good. Though I didn't really expect any."

"Told you, I'm good." Henry takes my hand. "I want to show you my classroom!"

Miss Tessa looks behind me, and for some reason, I know exactly who she's looking at.

Harper.

I turn and see her walking through the doors. Wind blows her hair back away from her face. It's out of the tight braid she had it in at work today, and it's hanging in loose waves over her shoulder. Every time I see her, I'm taken aback by her beauty.

Her eyes meet mine and she comes to a halt, shocked to see me. Blinking, she recovers fast and looks past me at Tessa—the teacher. They exchange a look that's lost on me, and Henry tugs on my hand again. I give him my attention and let him pull me to his classroom.

He shows me his desk, his cubby, where he sits on the floor when everyone gathers around the whiteboard, where the bathroom is, where his friend Mason sits, where Mason's cubby is, where Mason sits on the floor when everyone gathers around the whiteboard…

Several moms wearing pantsuits come in, and I overhear them talking about how the room is too colorful and how they should write in anonymous suggestions to have the classroom be themed in warm beige tones. They must be the same moms who want to get rid of the slides and swings on the playground.

I lean against the counter at the back of my room and pull out my phone and look up football pregame scores to pass the time.

"Hey, stranger."

I don't have to look up to know whose voice that belongs to. "Harper. Hi."

"Filling in for your sister again?"

"I am. How'd you know my sister is Henry's mom?"

Red rushes to her cheeks. "Henry mentioned something to my girls." She turns and motions to her twins. "That's them."

"They look just like you."

"You think?" She scrunches up her nose and it's so damn cute. "People say that, but I don't always see it. Maybe because I want them to look like me."

"They're like carbon copies."

Harper beams. "Good." She watches her kids play with a doll-house for a few seconds before looking back at me. "Well, I'm going to go mingle. It's what we're supposed to do at these things, right?"

"You're asking the wrong person," I laugh. "I'm still hoping Henry's dad makes it in time. His parents...they're really involved. It was bad timing both nights that neither could be here."

"Oh, I don't doubt them at all. I'm a single mom, trust me when I say I get bad timing. My girls love Henry. They think he's cute but don't tell them I told you. So, your sister and her husband are doing something right with him."

"She'll be happy to know that."

Harper smiles once more and walks over, talking to a pretty redhead. The uptight moms move about the classroom, pointing out more things that should be changed. One of them even has a clipboard. I'm surprised that they have children, because the thought of having sex with them is so fucking off-putting. I can't imagine living with someone that anal and obsessive.

I look back down at my phone as they come closer, not wanting to accidentally make eye contact and risk a conversation.

"That one," one of the moms whisper-talks. "Rumor has it they live in the south side."

"The south side?" another echoes. "Is it safe to have them here? Those children could be violent. What about their father? Where is he?"

"Jail?" another suggests. "Or maybe he was deported. I over-heard their mother speaking with one of the groundskeepers. In fluent Spanish."

"If she's really from the south side we should get her and those bastard children out of here. We just need to prove that's where she's from."

I've never once claimed to be a saint, but I know an asshole when I see one. And those three women are the crust around an unwashed asshole. I look up and see the ringleader pointing a boney finger at Harper's back.

What in the actual fuck?

I'm so shocked I'm at a loss for words...and this is the first time that's ever happened. Harper gives the pretty redhead a hug, and the redhead runs her hands down Harper's back, fingers inching down to her supple ass. I've never been more jealous of a single person in my whole entire life.

"Ugh, of course she's friends with that slut."

"They're the *twin moms*," another scoffs, rolling her eyes. "Like they're better than us because they carried two babies at once. They didn't even give birth. They had those babies sliced out of them effortlessly."

I know there are shitty people in the world. I expect it, really. In politics. In corporate America. But in a fucking kindergarten room?

Again...what in the actual fuck? I don't know in what world major surgery is considered effortless. Are these women for real?

"Come see the gym!" Henry tells me, running back over. "Mason might be there."

I blink, tearing my eyes away from the walking, talking

garbage in designer shoes standing just a few feet from me. "Sure. Let's go see the gym."

My stomach starts to feel unsettled as Henry skips along ahead of me. I should have said something, but what? *Go fuck yourself* is the only thing that comes to mind, and I get the feeling that won't go over well.

Henry shows me the gym, and then we go into the art room. The art teacher is in there, talking about the projects the kids will be working on throughout the year. My phone rings when we're walking out. It's Calvin.

"Hello?"

"I'm pulling in as we speak," he says.

"I hope you mean into a parking spot."

He laughs. "If not, this would be weird."

"We're past weird. I've told everyone I'm Henry's *other father* and his biological daddy is on his way. Better pat my ass a few times to seal the deal."

"Hilarious," Calvin replies dryly.

"I know. I'm a comedian. Really, though, I'll get Henry and meet you up front."

"Thank you again, Alex, for covering for us twice now."

"Of course," I tell him. Calvin is a good guy. A huge nerd, with a receding hairline and the perfect *dad bod*, but a good guy. I don't think there's a single person on this earth who's good enough for my sister, but Calvin comes in a close second. "You're family."

"Henry's lucky to have you."

"He is," I chuckle. "We'll meet you up front." I end the call and find Henry, telling him his dad is here. Henry jumps and up down with excitement and races to me, ready to meet up with his father.

Harper is up front, standing against a wall and looking really uncomfortable as some sleaze in a suit talks to her. The butt-crust moms are a few yards away, watching.

They're setting her up, and while I have no idea what it is, I'm going to stop it.

"No thanks," Harper tells the guy. He shifts his gaze from Harper to the group of moms, and it's then I notice one of them has a cell phone out, recording the interaction.

"A single lady like yourself...it's not safe to be out alone at night. Add in the children...I'd love to escort you home."

"That's really not necessary." Harper sets her jaw and stares the guy dead in the eye. It unnerves him and he leans back. *That's my girl.* "I can handle myself, trust me. And my boyfriend wouldn't be happy about some random man following me home. He's a bit possessive." She makes a face and sucks in a breath. "The last guy who got too close...well, I'll just say it's a good thing my boyfriend was able to afford such a good lawyer to keep him out of jail."

The guy's face pales, and he pushes away. Harper shudders and rolls her eyes. She seems more annoyed than anything else, which makes me think she's dealt with assholes like this before. It's not surprising. She's drop dead gorgeous and that unfortunately seems to attract guys just like that sleaze-ball.

Henry spots Calvin, and my attention is redirected once again to my brother-in-law. He gives me a one-armed hug, thanking me again, and then is pulled away by Henry, who's excited to show him the million and twelve things he showed me in his classroom.

I can't see Harper, and I assume she left. But then I spot her girls, running around with a few other kids near the cafeteria doors. I scan the room and see Harper bent over a table with a big PTO sign behind it.

Needing to get home and get started on the work I brought from the office, I plan to tell her a cordial goodbye and then head out.

"That particular event is usually reserved for fathers," one of the PTO moms tells Harper. "But I'd love to see more women showing up. I mean, we do most of the prepping, packing, and set-up anyway. If you sign up, other moms might too. Usually it just takes someone being the first to put their name on the list to get others to join."

"Well, I'll gladly sign up. It's just me with my girls so we're used to doing things together in man-centered actives."

"Great!" the PTO mom exclaims as Harper finishes writing her name down. She straightens up and turns with a smile on her face. We lock eyes again, and my heart does that weird fluttering thing. I'm in good shape. I work out and eat healthily most of the time. Maybe I should see a cardiologist and have them check out the weird flutterings I feel whenever Harper is around.

"Harper, is it?" one of the crumbling pieces of shit says, stopping Harper by holding up her hand.

"Yes. I'm Harper. Nice to meet you." She extends her hand to shake the other mother's hand. She looks at Harper's outstretched hand and flares her nostrils, looking away. "Did I just overhear you saying you're a single mom?"

"You did. Because I am."

"But you also just said you have a boyfriend."

Harper's brows furrow and she looks from the asshole mom to the guy who was hitting on her. He's standing next to another pantsuit-wearing, shit eater, and it's clear now that he's not into Harper.

Though I'm sure if he was given the choice, he'd choose Harper a hundred times over.

"You can still be a single mom with a boyfriend, you know."

"So he's not the father of your girls?"

"Nope," she says quickly. Her shoulders tense and she's growing more and more uncomfortable as the seconds tick by. And so am I.

"How nice someone cares about both you and your girls."

"Yeah, so rare to find someone who wants to date anyone with a kid," Harper snaps back.

"So this boyfriend…what does he do for a living?"

Harper blinks rapidly. "He, um…he works downtown with people. Clients. With clients."

"Lovely. What's his name?"

"His name?" Harper swallows hard. "It's… it's…"

"You don't really have a boyfriend, do you?" the asshole mom asks in a condescending voice.

Color takes over her face as she realizes what's going on. Harper doesn't have a boyfriend, and I can't stand here and do nothing. I don't think. I just act.

"Yeah," I say, striding over, stopping just inches from Harper. She traded her heels for flats, and my six-foot, four-inch frame towers over her. I swallow my pounding heart and put my arm around her slender waist. "She does have a boyfriend."

CHAPTER 16

HARPER

"He's your boyfriend?" Mindy's pencil-thin eyebrows go up so high they disappear beneath her thick, blunt-cut bangs.

My mouth hangs open and I don't know to say. Or do. Falling onto the floor and melting into a puddle of liquid goo sounds like a good idea.

Because Alex is pretending to be my boyfriend.

Part of me wants to play along with it. Show that fucking stick-up-the ass Mindy that yeah, I can get a guy. A hot guy with bulging biceps and a bulging, well, bulge in his pants. An educated man who runs his own company. And quite possibly, he's a miserable asshole who'd probably be happy hanging out with the likes of you, Mindy.

But another part is proud of being single and raising my girls on my own. It's been damn hard and I'm so fucking tired, but I did it. Alone. And I'm perfectly capable of continuing to do things myself.

My breath leaves me, and I'm suddenly all too aware of Alex's hand resting on my side. The heat of his skin comes off his palm in waves, and standing here, tucked up against him, feels so right.

It doesn't make sense.

I can't stand this guy.

He's a grade-A meanie…so why is he being nice to me? Or is his niceness actually not nice at all and he's being so condescending I'm mistaking it for helping me out of an awkward situation?

I don't overthink things or anything.

Without thinking of what I'm going to say, I inhale and open my mouth. "Yeah. He is."

Mindy eyes Alex up and down. He's dressed casually right now, and it's the first time I've seen him out of a suit and tie. The formal look is amazing on him, but this t-shirt and jeans look… I'm digging it too.

"I saw you at the kindergarten orientation and you weren't together then," Mindy says, sticking her nose up in the air like she just solved a fifty-year-old cold case.

"We like to keep things private," Alex says, looking down at me with a smile. "Don't we, babe?"

"It's a new thing," I say and bring my hand up to Alex's chest. I splay my fingers over his pec and oh my God, I've never felt a chest more firm than this. I can only imagine what he looks like without a shirt on.

Heat rushes between my legs, and my body moves on its own accord, angling my hips toward Alex's.

"And like my sweetheart said," I go on. "We like to keep our private life private." Smiling, I look up at Alex. I can play pretend like the best of them, but when I meet his eyes, my heart flutters and the heat intensifies. Dammit. Why does he have to be so attractive?

Alex feels it too and tenses, but his tension causes him to tighten his hold on me. I'm squished to his side, hand pressing against his impossibly firm chest.

I need to step away from Alex. Take my hand off his pec. Move out of his embrace.

He's. My. Boss.

"Harper, hey!" Kate calls, holding up her hand in a wave. Heather, her daughter, is holding her other hand and has a sour look on her face. She slows and tugs on Kate's hand, trying to break away. Kate tips her head down and gives her the dreaded *mom glare*, and it works. My glare is starting to lose its power, and I'll cry the day the girls ignore it completely.

"Kate, hi." I smile and am still fully aware of Alex's body right up next to mine. I should step away but it's like I suddenly don't remember how to get my brain to tell my feet to move.

His shirt is so damn soft. He smells good. He's warm. Fuck, it's been so long since anyone has held me, even innocently like this.

The twins see Heather and come running over. The frown on Heather's face turns upside down, and Kate lets go of her hand to let her go talk to my girls.

"She's the reason I drink," Kate huffs and Mindy gives her a judgmental stare. "I don't know how you do it with two." Her eyes go to Alex. "And who is this?"

"This is Alex," I say and finally break out of his embrace. I miss it the moment his arm leaves me. It's like someone ripping warm blankets off you too early in the morning.

"You never told me you were dating a total hottie." Kate leans in and gives Alex a nod of approval. "Or anyone at all. When did this happen?"

For the second time in a five-minute span, I freeze. I'm not a good liar, and more importantly, I don't like to lie. It feels yucky when I lie, and I know it's only a matter of time before I either blow my cover or someone busts me for it.

"Recently," Alex answers for me.

"You look familiar," Kate tells him. "I feel like I've seen you before."

"You did. At orientation night."

"Right! You're Henry's...dad?"

"Uncle. My sister got stuck in surgery that day and couldn't make it."

"Surgery?" Kate's hand flies to her heart. "Is she okay?"

"She's a surgeon," Alex laughs. "I forget how that sounds."

"Oh good." Kate reaches out and puts her hand on my arm. "You landed a good one here." She winks at me.

"I did, didn't I?" Alex is smiling down at me again, and I have no idea how he's able to sell this so convincingly.

"He's a lucky one," I laugh and pat his chest.

"We should double date sometime," Kate says. "Ditch the kids and go out for drinks."

"That sounds wonderful," I blurt without thinking. Mindy scowls at us. She probably desperately needs a break from her home life for just an hour or two but would never admit it, and her refusal to let herself unwind makes her scoff at anyone who does. It's like reverse-jealousy. "But we're, uh, really busy and usually have opposite schedules." I look up at Alex, hoping he'll just agree with me.

"We'll figure out details later," Kate says.

"Sounds good."

"See you in the morning, hun! And it was great to meet you, Alex."

I force a smile and suck in my breath, waiting for Kate to take a few steps away to breathe. The girls are still sitting on the floor in the corner, laughing at whatever they're watching on Heather's iPad. I take Alex's hand, repress the shiver that wants to make its way through me when my fingers lace with his, and pull him to the back of the lobby.

"What the hell?" I whisper-yell. "Kate is my friend!"

"Are you mad because she said I was a hottie?"

I can't tell if he's joking or not. Wide-eyed, I just shake my head. "I lied to her. You're not my boyfriend. You're not even my friend," I spit and see the tiniest bit of hurt flash across Alex's face. "You're my boss."

"I'm sorry." He runs his hand over his hair, messing it up. Only he could get even better looking with messy hair. "I overheard that stuck-up bitch drilling you and thought you'd appreciate the cover."

"I do. I think." I close my eyes and let out a breath. No one has ever socially saved me before, and the feminist in me is having a mental debate on feeling relief, in seeing him like a knight in shining armor, coming to my rescue, or being annoyed that he didn't think I could handle it on my own.

"I had it handled," I say, deciding to go with the latter.

"Really? You didn't seem like it," he counters. "Quick, tell me what name you would have given your fake boyfriend."

"Maybe Jimmy Dean isn't fake."

"Jimmy Dean? Like the sausage?" He chuckles.

"Yes, it was the first thing that came to mind." I shrug. "I like sausage."

Humor glints in his eyes and his lips part as if he's going to tell a dirty joke. He stops himself and takes a deep breath. "I'm sorry if that caused you trouble with your friend. Tell her we broke up and it'll be done and over with."

"But it's still a lie."

"Not really."

"Not really?" I raise my eyebrows. "In what alternate universe do you live in where not telling the truth isn't considered lying?"

"There's a difference between withholding the truth and a lie."

"I know, and this isn't withholding the truth." My heart is racing, and I can feel the blood rushing to my cheeks. "This is straight-up lying."

"Then tell her the truth." Alex shrugs. "She'll probably think it's funny."

"She probably will. And yeah…I will." I force myself to take another calming breath. "So…thank you. I can't stand Mindy or her stupid pink pantsuit."

"It is pretty awful," Alex laughs and redirects his gaze to

Mindy. "If Umbridge and a dementor had a love-child, that's what it would look like."

My jaw falls open. I'm too stunned to laugh. "You're a Harry Potter fan?"

"I am. Why, you find that surprising?"

"Yeah, I do. I didn't think you were into that sort of thing."

"There are a lot of things I'm into that you have no idea about." His voice deepens, all gravely and seductive and my mind immediately goes to the gutter. I'm left there gaping at him, feeling like a schoolgirl standing before the lead singer of her favorite boyband.

And Alex knows it.

"I'll see you at the office in the morning. Have a good night, Harper."

He lets his eyes wander over me, making no attempt to cover up that he's checking me out before turning to leave. I watch him walk out the door, not sure if this actually happened. Maybe I fell and hit my head. Or I'm dreaming.

I look at the clock on the wall above the doors leading into the offices. The second hand moves, and I count the beats.

One.

Two.

Three.

Four.

Five.

Nope. Not dreaming. Time doesn't move in my dreams. I flatten my hands against my thighs, realizing they're all sweaty and clammy. Feeling disoriented, I have to look around the lobby three times before I find the girls to go home.

"How was your day?" I ask them when we get into the car. It's the first chance I've had to actually talk to them.

"Long," Penny sighs, sounding so grown up it makes me laugh. "I'm tired."

"Me too, kid." I turn around and look at her pretty face. "Me too."

"Can we not go to school tomorrow?" Violet asks.

"You have no reason to stay home," I tell them both. "You're gonna learn sooner or later that you're going to be tired more often than you're not." Though if I were to let them play hooky, that means I'd stay home from work too. I can pretend we all got a sudden case of the flu or something.

Anything to avoid Alex.

Because I saw a different side of him tonight and the Jekyll and Hyde thing is fucking with my head. He's funny. Likes Harry Potter. And saved me from a world of embarrassment.

Maybe he's not such an asshole after all.

CHAPTER 17

HARPER

I stand outside Alex's office, coffee in hand, and push my shoulders back. I've been thinking about him nonstop since last night, and I still can't decide if I'm grateful or annoyed.

It was pure chaos when we got home last night, starting with finding out the A/C units in the entire building had pooped out during the day. It wouldn't be that big of a deal if it wasn't humid, and if humidity didn't make that weird musty smell in the hallways ten times worse.

Max, a neighbor on the floor below, knocked on the door right after I got the girls in bed. He's always had a bit of a crush on me, and over the last year, it's gone from innocent to making me a little uncomfortable.

After seeing it was him through the peephole, I kept the chain on the door and cracked it open. He said he had a spare box fan if we needed it, since the air hadn't come back on yet. I would have loved the fan but declined it anyway. The one fan we do have is in the girls' room. I'd rather them be comfortable than me.

A cold shower and a glass of ice water later, I felt much better, but then I thought I heard someone outside the front door. I pushed the couch in front of it and moved the girls—and the fan

—into my room since there's a straight drop-off under my window, making it harder for someone to climb up and break in.

I need to get us out of that shitty apartment before something really does happen. I've lost count of the number of gunshots we've heard since moving in. I don't feel safe there, and the girls are old enough now to recognize my fear and start feeling it themselves. It kills me to know we're not safe in our own home.

It's a bit of a miracle the nice Lexus hasn't been stolen yet, though I think my saving grace might be people thinking it belongs to one of the drug dealers that lives on the floor above us. Everyone knows not to mess with their shit.

My hair is to the side in a braid today since it's too hot to wear it down, but I might have spent a little extra time on my makeup this morning. I'm wearing another one of Tessa's too-sexy-for-school-yet-still-office-appropriate outfits today. It's a dress, and the deep red color isn't something I'd normally choose, but I loved it the second I put it on.

We leave in a mad rush for drop-off, and I get into the office with five minutes to spare.

"You have got to be fucking kidding me," Alex grumbles, shaking his head as he looks at his computer. "Dammit!"

"Is now a bad time?" I ask, finally forcing myself to step inside. The office has glass walls and the door is usually open. Alex can see me standing outside and delaying the inevitable will only make things more awkward.

"It's fine."

Nodding, I go to his desk and set the coffee down. "Everything okay?"

"Yes," he says but doesn't sound like he believes it. "I think we might have lost one of our biggest clients to our rival, though."

"Jerry Harold?"

"Yep. That's the one."

"Oh. I'm sorry."

Alex shakes his head and leans back in his leather chair. He looks so different from last night. He's in a suit like normal. His hair isn't messy, and I don't think I'll see that handsome face crack even a half-smile today.

"Do you think you could win them back?"

"If I could talk to Jerry, yes. But he keeps rescheduling meetings so that's probably not likely." Alex takes a drink of coffee and sets the mug back down. Then he looks at me—really looks at me—and it's like his hand is on my waist and the heat of his skin is soaking in through the thin fabric of my dress.

"If there's anything I can do to help, let me know."

"I will. Thank you, Harper."

"It's my job. And I wanted to thank you again." I shuffle closer. It's probably a good thing there is a desk between us right now. I'm tired and still freaked out from last night and am craving to have someone—anyone—put their arm around me again.

That's all.

I'm not starting to like Alex or anything.

"For last night," I go on. "I don't think I seemed as grateful as I was. The whole thing kind of shocked me, if I'm being honest."

"You are welcome, and that woman—Mindy, right?—and her friends didn't have nice things to say about you. I feel like you should know that. It pissed me off to hear them talk like that."

"I know they talk. It's not a secret I don't really fit in at that school." I divert my eyes to the ground. "And I don't really give a shit what they think about me, but I don't want my girls to be treated differently just because some of the kids have royal assholes for parents. I know I'm biased since I'm their mother, but I think my girls are turning out pretty okay."

"I do too." He takes another drink of coffee. I doubt his night was anywhere near the one I had, but he does look tired. And while he's still making millions, losing one of the firm's biggest clients has to feel really fucking terrible.

There's a knock at the office door, and I turn to see Mr. Harding Senior standing in the threshold. His face is sullen, and I swear an icy breeze just blew through the room. No one needs to say anything for me to know it's time to get the hell out of here.

I'm barely through the door when it's closed behind me. I slip back into my desk chair and open up the calendar, making sure nothing has changed since last night.

It hasn't.

I spend a minute straightening up my desk, which is already straightened. It's funny, considering how unorganized and messy my house is yet I'm on top of shit at work. I suppose if I could only be organized in one area of my life, the area that pays me is the way to go.

Stealing another look at the office, I see Alex sitting, stern-faced, in his desk chair, staring at his father with a mixture of hatred and fear. Maybe my love triangle theory wasn't so out there after all.

"It's so awkward when this happens," Tiffany, one of the interns says as she passes by my desk. She flicks her eyes to Alex's office.

"You mean when his father comes in and talks to him?"

She nods and motions for me to come with her into the break room. I didn't get a chance to eat breakfast this morning, and a bagel with an ungodly amount of cream cheese sounds wonderful right now.

"So this is totally off the record," she starts, voice low. She flicks on the electric tea kettle to heat up water for her own tea.

"Of course."

Opening the box of tea bags, she looks around to make sure no one can hear us. "No one really knows why they don't get along, but it's always been tense. I've been here for a year and a half now and the only times I see them together outside of company-wide meetings are when something's gone wrong. And then the rest of the day Alexander is so quiet and in a worse mood than usual."

"That's kind of sad. I have a great relationship with my dad. I can't imagine not having that but having him be a jerk to me on top of it."

"Right? My folks are back in Texas, but we talk weekly. I wouldn't really say we're close, but they'd never yell at me at work."

I grab a bagel out of the warming drawer. Yes, a freaking *warming drawer*. I get a raisin-cinnamon bagel today and go with a raspberry cream cheese.

A few others come into the break room, and we stop talking about Alex. I take my bagel and a glass of ice-cold orange juice back to my desk. Mr. Harding Senior is still in Alex's office, and Alex has a *please shoot me* look on his face.

It's hard for me to imagine life being difficult when you have that much money. I believe the saying that "money can't buy happiness" but it can sure make your life easy.

Taking a bite of my bagel, I think back to last night and how quickly Alex stepped in to help me out. I'm sure his father is unhappy about losing that client...which would be Alex's fault and has to do with that article the assistant mentioned.

Speaking of said assistant...I break off a piece of my bagel and pull my phone from my purse. Francine sent me a friend request on Facebook. She's an over-sharer and I unfollowed the day after accepting the request. She's a stalker's dream, checking-in and posting almost hourly updates of what she's doing.

Alex said all he needed was a chance to talk to Jerry Harold. I go to Francine's Facebook profile. She's just posted a photo of a cup of coffee with the caption "#secondcupalready".

Right. It's early. I'll keep checking throughout the day...which is exactly what I do. At ten-thirty she posts a selfie of herself by the lake with the hashtag "workperks". It looks like she's picking up coffee and pastries.

She shares a funny cat meme at eleven. Then another photo of her third coffee of the day. She comments on someone's political rant a few minutes later, which reminds me exactly why I unfollowed her in the first place.

Finally, at noon, she posts something I could use. I read her status and jump up, moving so fast I hit my knee on the corner of my desk. I rub it while I walk, not knocking on the office door before I go in.

"Are you all right?" Alex asks, seeing me limp in

"I am. I'm good. You're good too. Or you will be. Hopefully. Maybe."

"What are you talking about, Harper?" He stands and moves around his desk.

"You said you wanted a chance to talk to that Jerry guy, right?"

"Yeah, I did. Did he call and reschedule?"

I shake my head. "No, but I know where he's eating lunch."

Alex responds with a blank stare. "Okay?" he finally says.

"You should go. Just happen to go to the same place for lunch and run into him."

"You mean stalk him."

"Stalking is a harsh word for obsessively checking his assistant's social media accounts in hopes for an update that could let me know where her boss will be at any moment during the day."

"That sounds exactly like stalking."

"Yeah, but only slightly."

Alex blinks. Once. Twice. Then he smiles. "Okay. But you're coming with me."

≈

"Stick to the plan," Alex tells me for the third time.

"Right. We go in, head to the bar and hope to get a reservation."

"We will get one," Alex presses, also for the third time. It's lunchtime and this place is super popular, yet Alex is insistent he'll be able to get us a table. He's going to do that move I see in movies where he slips the host a hundred-dollar bill, I'm sure.

"We got this," I tell him with a smile as the car pulls to the curb. We're in the back of some fancy town car, being dropped off in front of an expensive restaurant. Alex gets out first and holds his hand out for me to take. I'm wearing a dress and heels again and could use the help to quickly get out of the car, but the second his fingers touch mine, I want to recoil.

Because it feels so good.

So warm.

So familiar, which doesn't make sense. He had his hand on me for all of two minutes yesterday. It was all an act to fool that living, breathing, piece of shit, Mindy. He's my boss, and until yesterday, I was certain I hated every fiber of this man's being.

I get out of the car and blink in the bright sun. I leave my sunglasses in the car on purpose. If they're not safely tucked inside the center console, then they'll be lost and I'll be back to squinting or driving with one eye closed as I try to block out of the glare of the sun.

"Have you been here before?"

"Once or twice," he tells me and leads the way inside. I'm busy looking around, admiring the subtle European theming this place has going on when Alex bypasses the line of people waiting to check in and gets us in.

Damn. It must be nice to be rich.

All the tables are full, but we'll get the next one. The hostess leads us to the bar to order a drink while we wait for the table to clear up.

"Do you see him?" I ask Alex once we're seated and have ordered glasses of wine.

"Not yet. I'll do a sweep," he tells me and gets up, acting like he's just going to the bathroom but is really looking out across the restaurant for Jerry. I pull out my phone, entertaining myself by scrolling through Instagram.

Our wine comes, and I slowly sip mine as I wait for Alex to come back. This glass cost fifty-two dollars. Alex is paying, of course, and in all honestly, it's not *that* much better than the ten-dollar bottle of pinot Grigio Tessa had at her place the other night.

Another few minutes pass, and Alex isn't back. He's either still in the bathroom or got kidnapped and is being held for ransom. After one more minute, I turn in my seat and look for him. There are tables behind the bar, blocked off by a half-wall and fancy artwork.

"Excuse me, miss," the hostess says, coming up to me. My first thought is she knows I can't afford any of this and is going to ask me to leave.

"Yes?"

"Your date joined another party and has requested I bring you over."

"Oh, um, okay." I stick my phone in my purse follow the hostess, who carries our drinks, to a table near the back of the restaurant. Alex is sitting at a table with Jerry Harold and a woman with short, brunette hair. She sees me before either of the guys do, and stands up with a big smile on her face.

"Harper!"

"Kate," I exclaim, blinking to make sure I'm seeing everything correctly. "Hey. What are you...what...I mean...you're eating lunch." I look at Alex in question. His eyes meet mine, silently pleading for me to go along with him.

"Of course," Kate laughs and gives me a hug. "I thought I saw you two walking in but wasn't sure. Then I saw your boyfriend walk by and it turns out Daddy used to work with him, and I just had to ask you two to join us! Such a small world, right?"

Daddy? Oh my God. Kate's father is Jerry Harold. I knew she came from money, but I had no idea. And—oh shit—she still thinks Alex is my boyfriend. We never had a chance to talk last night.

"Daddy, this is Harper." Kate takes her seat again, and I'm left standing there, too stunned to move.

"It's nice to finally meet you," Jerry says and motions to the empty chair next to him. "Kate's told me all about you."

"Hopefully all good things," I laugh, brain going on autopilot as I slide into the chair. I'm right across from Alex, and I try to give him a *what the fuck* look without being too obvious. He knows I don't want to lie to Kate.

"Only good things. You've really impressed my daughter, and that's not something that's easy to do." He shifts his gaze to Alex. "And it makes me wonder if I misjudged you."

"Misjudged me?" Alex echoes.

"The news isn't always true," Jerry goes on. "But you know what they say about the internet. You can't put anything not true on there," he laughs with a wink. "Harper here has made quite an impression on my Kate. And seeing how you two are together, then I do apologize for believing what I've read online."

Alex give me a loving look, trying to really sell the fact that he's not the playboy that article made him out to be. I broke down and Googled it, too curious not to know what it said about him.

"Our company prides itself on being family-friendly in all areas," Jerry starts, and Kate shakes her head.

"Daddy," Kate says sternly. "You promised no talking about work."

Jerry holds up his hands. "Right, my darling. I did. No more work talk, but I will have my assistant call your assistant and set up another meeting."

CHAPTER 18

HARPER

"More wine?" the waitress asks.

"Yes, please," I say and hold up my glass. I've been sitting here lying to my new friend for the last half-hour. She thinks I'm dating Alex, and that lie is what got her father to reconsider working with Alex.

I'm happy my idea worked, and Alex is getting his second chance, but now I feel like I'm stuck with the lie and I hate it. If I come clean and tell Kate, she'll no doubt tell her father and then what? Will he go back to thinking Alex is just some playboy and not want to work with him again?

I take a big sip the second my glass is full. I've been so busy stewing over what to do, I didn't fully let myself appreciate how good the food here was, even though the portions were tiny.

The second glass of wine starts to hit me, and the knot in my chest starts to loosen. Yeah, I'm in a bit of a hard place right now, but I'll figure it out. We order dessert and the cheesecake is to die for. I'd pick up my plate and lick it if it wasn't frowned upon.

I polish off my wine and get up to use the bathroom. I'm tipsy, realizing just how hard that wine is hitting me now that I'm up. Kate comes with me to the bathroom, and I debate the whole time I'm sitting in the stall peeing if I should just blurt out the truth or not.

Dammit, I don't want to blow this chance for Alex. I'll wait until after Jerry has signed a contract or something, which feels so sleazy of me. Fuck. I need more wine.

"I had no idea Alex was *the Alex* as in Alexander Harding. That guy was named one of the city's most eligible bachelors two years ago." Kate fixes her hair in the mirror.

I squirt lavender-scented soap onto my hands and stick them under the water. "Oh, right. I forgot about that."

"Rumor has it—or had it, I should say—he's as total playboy too. And look at you, snagging a man like that." She playfully bumps her hip into mine. Yep, definitely need more wine. "How is he with your kids?"

"Ummmm…" My mind races. I can't say they haven't met because he was at the school with me just yesterday. And more so, I don't want to keep lying. "They, um, really don't know him as my boyfriend yet. I didn't want to introduce them to anyone before it was, you know, super serious."

"Ahhh, right. Good idea."

"Yeah. What's the point in getting their hopes up or anything. I haven't dated much—okay, at all—since they've been born, so I want to keep things, um, safe." I'm floundering here and I know it.

"Well, Alex must really be special to be the first guy you've dated then! He definitely is easy on the eyes, and I am not ashamed to admit that," she laughs.

"Yeah, he looks good in a suit. And not in one," I say, meaning the one and only time I saw him in jeans and a t-shirt. Of course, that's not how it sounds, and Kate giggles.

"Oh, I'm sure he looks very good without a suit, or anything, on."

I dry my hands and we go back to the table. Jerry and Alex are talking about work.

"She's back," Jerry laughs. "Better change the subject." He gives Kate a wink. "And we'll have plenty of time to talk new strategies this week," he says to Alex. "How's your Friday? Mine's wide open."

"That's because we're going to the lake house in Vermont this weekend," Kate reminds him. Then she gasps and gets another big smile on her face. "You guys should come! We have the extra space. It's so relaxing up there. It's right by a vineyard, there's a beach, and there's the cutest little cottage next to the house that never gets used and would be perfect for you two!"

Alex's eyes meet mine, silently pleading for me to say yes. But I can't just go to Vermont. I have my kids, and more importantly, he's not my boyfriend. I don't want to travel anywhere with him.

Only…a vineyard and a beach and cute little cottage sound amazing.

"I've never left my kids," I blurt. "Not even for a night."

"It'd be good for you then," Kate laughs. "It's hard leaving, trust me, I know, but I swear it's strengthened my bond with Heather. Sometimes I just really need that break."

"It does sound like a nice time," Alex coaxes and I flash him a look, daring him to keep pushing it. "And you do deserve a break." He means it and isn't just saying it to try to land a big business deal.

And fuck, I do deserve a break.

"I'll think about it," I tell everyone. "I'd have to make sure my dad could watch the girls."

I'm sure he could. I know he's not working this weekend.

"And I'd have to find a way to get them to and from school on Friday."

I already have a way: Tessa.

Kate smiles. "You'd have fun, trust me. It's so cozy and romantic up there." She wiggles her eyebrows and leans in, lowering her voice. "It will definitely be full of *no suit* time."

If Alex was really my boyfriend—my new boyfriend—the

thought of sneaking off to some picture-perfect lake house for uninterrupted sexy time would excite us both. I force myself to smile back, acting as if I'd love that.

We all walk out together, and Kate gives me a hug goodbye. Alex puts his arm around my shoulder as we walk down the street, pretending to be a happy couple.

"Go to the lake house this weekend," Alex says as soon Kate and Jerry are out of earshot. "I know I'll be able to convince Jerry to come back to our firm over that time."

"Are you serious?"

"Yes," he tells me. "Think of it as a business trip."

"Even if it really was, I don't think I could go. Leaving the girls for a weekend…it's not that easy."

"You'll get a travel bonus."

"A what now?"

"Travel bonus," he repeats. "For your trouble. How does five-thousand sound?"

I come to a dead stop. "Five thousand? Dollars?"

"No, pennies. Yes, dollars," he laughs. "And the company will cover all travel-related expenses."

Five thousand dollars.

Five.

Thousand.

Dollars.

For one weekend at a lake house. Drinking wine while sitting on the beach with a friend.

And living a lie.

But still…that kind of money could do so much for me. I'd have enough to cover rent. Buy groceries. Take the girls shopping for clothes, shoes, new sheets, and even a new toy. It would allow me to breathe.

I can't say no. We need that money. It's one weekend. One. Weekend. I can handle it.

"Fine. Assuming I can get someone to handle school drop-off

and pick-up, and my dad is able to watch them Saturday and Sunday. I'll go."

"Thank you, Harper. I'll get the bonus cash to you when we get back to the office."

Back up. Did he say cash? As in I'm not going to get taxed on this *cash*? That's even better. And definitely not a legitimate bonus, but who cares?

It's five fucking thousand dollars.

~

"AM I CRAZY?" I PACE BACK AND FORTH IN TESSA'S LIVING room. Her dogs are following me, biting at my shoes as I walk.

"You'd be crazy not to take the money," Tessa tells me. "Five grand to go spend a weekend at some fancy-shmancy lake house? Sign me up."

"Yeah, but I'm lying to Kate and you know how much I hate lying."

Tessa nods and lets out a breath. "One lie for five grand, though?"

"That doesn't make it right. And where will it stop? After my fake-wedding?"

"Don't sign a fake prenup and you'll be good."

"Hah, not funny, Tess. I'm internally freaking out here."

"Calm your tits."

I reach up and gently tug on my necklace. "I wish Mom where here. She'd know what to do."

"She'd totally tell you to go for it. Your mom had a sense of adventure."

I smile, eyes getting misty. "She did. And you're right that she would. She'd use that money for something crazy too, like a garden full of giant sunflowers."

"Complete with a giant sundial."

We both laugh and I finally let out a sigh, nodding. "Okay. I'll do it. You're sure it's not an inconvenience to watch the girls?"

"I'd be bringing them back with me anyway Friday after school. Spend the night here Thursday so you can be with them at bedtime. I'll take them to school, bring them back, and your dad said he can pick them up, right?"

"Right. He gets off work around five and then will have them for the weekend."

"He loves having them, you know."

"Yeah, I do. And they love hanging out over there."

"See, it'll all work out, and you'll come back five-grand richer!" I look from Tessa to the girls, who are sitting at the table coloring and eating a snack. It's going to hurt to be away from them, but it's *for them*.

Five grand can really change our lives.

It's just one weekend. How bad could it be?

CHAPTER 19

ALEX

What the hell did I just sign us up for?

A million-dollar deal, that's what. One weekend with Jerry Harold is all I need to convince him I'm the right person for the job. That I'm not some screw-around playboy, even though none of that affects how I do my job, and it's a bullshit reason to not want to work with us. And I'd do just about anything to keep that fucking Reach PR firm from taking another one of our clients.

And a weekend of playing pretend with Harper... It's fucked up how part of that excites me. Putting my arm around her felt so good. So right. I've put my arm around dozens of women and never felt anything close to what it felt like to hold Harper.

And that was all for show.

Just like this weekend. It's all for show. I know she could use the money. I lean back on the couch, stretching my feet out in front of me and resting them on the coffee table. I forward the flight info to Harper, not expecting a reply from her until the morning. There weren't any first-class tickets left on the same flight Jerry is taking, so we had to take an earlier one. We'll land only about an hour before they do, assuming nothing is delayed.

My phone dings with an email alert. It's from Harper, saying thank you, and she has no idea what to bring or what to wear and she's nervous. Seeing how she's up and replying, I exit out of my email and open my texts instead.

Me: The weather is a little cooler up there during the day and temps drop to the high 50s at night.

Harper: That doesn't help with the packing :-

I laugh, imaging her face if she were talking to me.

Me: Bring a variety of clothes? Your friend mentioned a beach, so beachwear, something nice for dinner, and if we are going to a vineyard you can assume we might tour it, so comfortable shoes you can walk through a field in would be helpful.

Personally, I find heels very sexy. I love when the woman I'm fucking wears them and nothing else. But I've gone out too many times where my date has worn inappropriate footwear, and I know how taxing and just plain painful it can be.

Harper: I'm looking up the weather forecast now and I'll bring layers. But I need an itinerary or something so I penis ahead.

Me: Penis ahead??

Harper: P L A N omg I meant plan! Stupid autocorrect

I laugh and reread her text, laughing again.

Me: The real question is, why are you typing "penis" so much your phone autocorrects to that?

Little bubbles show up and disappear three times before she sends a response.

Harper: I don't even know. It corrects duck to fuck now instead of other way around so I guess that says a lot about me. I promise I won't send an accidentally penis to a client.

And I'm laughing out loud again.

Me: That would be awkward.

Harper: Just slightly. I'm headed to bed. Thanks for sending the flight info over. See you at work in the morning.

I look at my phone, rereading our conversation and smiling like a teenage boy who just talked to his crush for the first time. Getting up, I go into the shower and it's no surprise my mind drifts back to Harper.

Something she said earlier has stayed in the front of my mind all day. She said she didn't care what those asshole moms at the school thought of her, but she didn't want them to treat her children any different because of it.

It's the exact opposite of my own mother, and if Nicole and I had grown up with that kind of love and support...fuck...I don't even know what it would be like. I have a fear of ending up exactly like my own father. It's not something I like to admit to myself, and Nicole might be the only one who has an inkling that thought crosses my mind.

But there's another fear paired along with it. What if I did have a kid and I was that shitty father...and the kid had a shitty mother too? I know others have had it a lot worse than I did as a child.

We had money.

A nice house.

Went to the best schools and drove expensive cars.

But I was beaten by my own father. Verbally and emotionally abused by him as well, all while my mother sat back and did nothing. She cared more about herself and what the people in her social circle thought than my own wellbeing.

I've worked hard to repress most of my childhood. There's one moment in particular I like to pretend never really happened. I have the memory of it because I saw it on TV or in a movie... something like that.

Not because it happened to me.

Because it still hurts, mentally as well as physically. I look at my left hand and feel the bones shattering all over again. Dad was drunk, mad a deal fell through at work, and threw a bookend at me. It hit the top of my left hand and broke two bones. I needed

155

surgery to fix it, and Mom told everyone I was "messing around like boys do" and knocked a bookshelf over on myself.

I was eight at the time.

Looking back, I wish I could yell at my younger self to tell someone. The nurse at the hospital. A teacher. Juan, our driver who seemed to suspect something was going on. He'd always ask Nicole and I over and over if we were okay, and his prying got him fired.

But I was scared. Scared I'd get taken away and end up in the foster system—a fear put in my head by my own parents. I didn't want to get separated from Nicole, or worse, have her stay at the house without me to protect her. And I was scared nothing would get done and I'd be left alone with my dad, who'd be even more pissed I ratted him out.

I turn up the temperature of the water and look up, letting it wash over my body. A shrink would have a field day with me, I'm sure of it. I've lived through childhood trauma, hid my desire to settle down and start a family by excessive drinking, meaningless sex, and partying.

Yet I'm successful, and I suppose underneath it all, work is just as much of a mask as the other vices. It's the one thing I have that I'm more or less in control of. It's the one place I know I can get validation. Well, not from my father, but from the others around me. It gives my life meaning, drives me to keep pushing, but in the end, when I retire and step down just like my father is doing…that'll be it.

No one will remember me. Someone else will take over the company, will move it in a new direction and bring it more success.

It used to be enough.

But now…now I want more. Not more money. But *more*. I tell myself I don't know what that is, but really, I do.

I just won't admit it to myself. Not now…probably not ever.

∾

"I CANCELED YOUR FRIDAY LUNCH AND MOVED THE NINE AM VIDEO call to tomorrow at two PM," Harper tells me, looking down at her notebook. It's bright and early the next day and she just set my coffee down and started going over notes.

I pick up the coffee and suck it down. I didn't sleep well last night, tossing and turning and trying to avoid the thought of how unfulfilling my life is despite the millions I have in savings, the name I've built for myself, and how big the company has gotten over the last five years.

Finally, I fell asleep and slept for a whole four hours before my alarm went off. I almost didn't go to the gym in the morning, but pushed through. When I start letting my thoughts interrupt my routine, then I know I have a real problem.

I do have a problem, I know, but it's easier to pretend I don't when I'm still able to function in my everyday life.

"Thank you."

"And Mr. Walter called and said he's stuck in traffic, so expect him to be twenty or thirty minutes late. You had an open hour for lunch penciled in after that meeting, so it won't affect the rest of your day. Just your lunch. I can pick something up for you if you want, though."

"Yeah, that'll work. Order something for yourself too."

"What do you want?"

I shake my head, looking into Harper's pretty eyes. She's wearing another dress today, and it looks amazing on her. This one is blue with red and pink flowers. It's flowy at the bottom and longer in the back than in the front. She's wearing low heels today and her hair is hanging straight down her back. It's long, shiny, and I really fucking want to run my fingers through it.

"You can pick. Order what you'd like and get me the same thing."

"What if I want a fully loaded Chicago-style hotdog and a beer?"

My lips curve into a smile. "Then I'd say that sounds pretty damn good, actually."

"For real?"

"Yeah. I haven't had a good Chicago dog since a Cubs game I went to last year."

"You probably have awesome seats, right?"

"They are pretty damn good. You like baseball?"

She shrugs. "I don't dislike it, but it's not my favorite thing. My mom used to love the Cubs, though, so I turn on the games in the background sometimes."

"Used to? She likes another team now?"

Harper's eyes immediately fill with tears. She brings her hand to her face and I have no idea what's going on. "Sorry," she says, voice tight. I get up and rush around the desk, gently putting my hand on her shoulder.

"Are you okay?"

She nods, lip quivering. "Yeah," she squeaks out and wipes her eyes. "It just hits me sometimes, all of the sudden like this." She sucks in shaky breath and closes her eyes. A single tear rolls down her face. It guts me to see her like this, and I have no idea what is wrong.

I step back and grab a tissue. She takes it and blots at her eyes. "My mom died."

"I'm so sorry."

"Thank you. It's been nearly six years, but sometimes...sometimes it just hits me, ya know?"

I shuffle closer, fighting the urge to pull her into an embrace. To wrap my arms around her and tell her everything is going to be okay.

"Yes," I say honestly. I don't know what the grief is like, but I do know how startling it can be to get hit with emotions or a memory all of a sudden. "It comes out of nowhere."

She blinks back more tears and looks up at me, right into my eyes. I angle my body toward hers, aware of nothing else but her.

The way that little lemon charm rests right above her breasts. The way she smells like floral shampoo and freshly washed clothes. How fast her heart is beating, hammering along with mine.

Another tear rolls down her face and I don't think. I just reach out cup her cheek, brushing the tear away with my thumb. Harper closes her eyes and leans into my touch. Heat sparks through me, and my heart flutters. She brings her hand up, closing her fingers around my wrist.

Then the phone rings, and Harper jerks back, blinking rapidly as she looks around. Did she forget we were standing here in the middle of the office too?

"I...I should get that." She sniffles and hastily walks out of the office. I swallow hard realizing that my heart is in my throat. I shove it back down into the pit of my chest and go back to my desk.

I look out through the open door at Harper. She's writing something down, cradling the phone between her ear and her shoulder. Her eyes are still misty, but she's pulled herself together. I get the feeling she's used to doing that, to putting on a smile and acting like things are okay.

She's just so unlike anyone I've ever met. Maybe this weekend was a terrible idea. Because as much I want to pretend my life is fine and I have everything I need, I know it's a lie.

And for some reason, Harper reminds me of that. Maybe part of me wants what she has: close friends and a good relationship with her family.

Or maybe it's because I want her.

CHAPTER 20

HARPER

"I love you," I whisper, blinking tears out of my eyes. It's super early in the morning on Friday, and I'm up dressed, and ready to go to the airport. The girls are sleeping on an air mattress on Tessa's living room floor, and I spent the entire night cuddling them and looking at their baby pictures on my phone.

It's pathetic, I know. I'm going to Vermont, not Mars, and it's just for a weekend. We'll be back Sunday evening, so really, the only day I won't see the girls is Saturday.

Giving them each an extra kiss, I take one last photo of them snuggled up together and then grab my purse. Alex is sending a car to pick me up, and we're meeting at the airport. It should be here any minute now, and I want to go outside before the dogs start barking and wake the girls up.

If they cry and ask me not to leave, there's a good chance I'll end up caving and staying here. I trust Tessa. She's a kinder-garten teacher, for goodness sake. She's CPR certified and has been helping me with the girls since they were born.

And I trust my father, of course. But still…they're not me. No one knows the girls like I do. I'm their mother…and I'm leaving them.

"No," I whisper to myself. "Stop it right now." I'm going on a business trip, not a girls' night out to Vegas, even though that does sound wonderful. Having a little time apart could be good for us too. Dad will love having them for the weekend, and already has activities planned for both Saturday and Sunday, including taking them to the free zoo downtown.

I lug my heavy suitcase to the door, not wanting to roll it. The sound of the wheels on the tile makes the dogs bark. I unlock the door and then double back, giving the girls one more kiss.

"Love you, Mommy," Violet says, slitting her eyes open for half a second.

"I love you too, baby. So much." I kiss her forehead and then give Penny one more kiss. "And you too, my little love bug."

Finally, I force myself out of the house. Just a minute later, a black Caddy rolls up. The driver gets out and puts my back in the trunk, and then opens the door for me. I'm surprised to see Alex inside.

"Oh, hey." I slide in, slightly cursing myself for thinking I could do my makeup on the ride to the airport. My hair is still in messy French braid pigtails as well. I had this whole plan of do my makeup the way there, pull the braids out as I walked inside the airpot, and shake the waves loose right before seeing Alex.

But it's not like I wanted to look good for him or anything.

"Hey," he replies. Somehow, he looks just as put together at this hour as he does at nine when he steps into the office. Though instead of a suit, he's wearing blue athletic shorts and a black t-shirt. It's a casual look, comfy for wearing on a plane, and yet seeing him out of his regular suit and tie throws me again.

In his suit, there are multiple layers keeping that firm body from me. An undershirt, then the button-up. A tie. The jacket. It would take longer to strip him of his work-clothes than it would to pull that t-shirt right over his head. There's no belt to unbuckle, no button to pop or zipper to pull. I could just stick my hand right inside and feel his—*I need to fucking stop.*

"I didn't realize you'd be in here," I rush out, pulling the seatbelt so hard it gets stuck. I yank it a few more times and then release it completely.

"When I gave the driver the address, he said we'd be driving right by here on the way to the airport from my place."

"Oh, makes sense. Save gas and all, right?"

He nods. "That's your house?"

"No, it's my friend Tessa's house. She'll take the girls to school with her in the morning."

"Tessa the teacher?"

"Yeah. That's, um, how we got into Briar Prep. She had a good connection."

Alex just nods again. He doesn't have children of his own, but seems involved in his nephew's life, which is not attractive at all. Nope. Definitely not. He probably doesn't know the exact monthly tuition that school costs, but he's has to know it ain't cheap. There's no way I could afford one kid, let alone two, on an assistant's salary.

"Kate sent me some pictures of the little cabin we'll be staying in." I get my phone out of my purse and feel a tug on my heart when I see the photo I just took of the girls. They'll be fine, I tell myself again. My throat starts to get tight and it's hard to swallow when I think of all the things that could go horribly wrong.

Bad weather. Violence at school. Choking on toys. Choking on food. Car accidents. Kidnapping. The zombie apocalypse. Stomach flu. Alien invasion. The possibilities are endless.

"It looks really cute." I don't care if Alex wants to see these photos or not. I need the distraction. "And it's a two bedroom, which will be nice so you don't have to sleep on the couch."

"I'd be the one sleeping on the couch?" he asks with a smile.

"Oh totally. As far as I'm concerned, I'm doing you a huge favor."

"You are, but doesn't the bonus I paid help even things out?"

"We'll see." I swipe to another picture. "That view alone almost makes up for it. Isn't it gorgeous?" I show him a photo of the lake the house in this one, complete with a man-made sandy section of beach. "And the vineyard...just wow."

"Have you ever been to one?"

I let out a snort of laughter. "No. But I have been to a tequila farm."

"You mean distillery, right?"

"No, I mean a tequila farm," I laugh. "My uncle in Mexico opened his own distillery, but one night after sampling his own product a little too much, he forgot how to say the words in English and called it a tequila farm. We still make fun of him for it today."

"Do you have a lot of family in Mexico?

"My mom's side is still there. We used to go visit them once a year but I haven't been able to, um, get things together to take the girls."

"I tried taking Spanish in college and really struggled with it," he tells me.

"I would say it's a hard language to learn, but I feel like that's a lie," I laugh. "And it came easily to me. Obviously, my mom spoke fluent Spanish, and my dad was okay with it when they first met. He's pretty fluent now too. It's kind of fun, actually. I'm like super pale and don't have a Spanish-sounding name, so people area always surprised when they find out I can speak it."

"That would be fun. It's always nice to surprise people by being smarter than they assume you are, right?"

"Right," I laugh. My phone screen blacks out and I bring my hands back to my lap. I'm tired, nervous, and still not sure if this is a good idea or not. If Alex had asked me last week, I would have laughed in his face.

But I saw something in him that night in the school and he was so gentle when I started crying in his office. He didn't make a

EMILY GOODWIN

big deal about it, in fact, he didn't even bring it up. He just asked if I was okay the next time I came in to relay a message.

The rest of that day, as well as Thursday, were super busy since all of the Friday appointments and meetings got crammed in to any open time slots. Alex told me to leave an hour early on Thursday so I could spend extra time with my kids.

He's really not as beastly as I thought, and I almost feel bad for assuming there was no other side to him.

Almost.

∼

"Wow," I say when I get out of the car. "It's even prettier than the pictures." I set my carryon bag down and turn around. "Everything is so green."

It's a little past noon and we've finally arrived at the lake house. Tired from being up all night, I fell asleep on the flight and got a solid hour and a half nap in. I'd never flown anything other than economy before, and found the seat to be really comfy.

"I feel like I'm on a movie set." Alex sets my suitcase on the ground and closes the trunk.

"Yes!" My head starts spinning with story ideas. "So Kate said to head to the main house and her cousin Lynn will be there to give us the key to the cottage."

Alex locks the car and starts to lug both suitcases up toward the house.

"I can take mine," I tell him.

"No, I got it. Though I am curious what all you have in there. We're only going to be here for a weekend."

"I had to get creative with my murder weapons so TSA wouldn't catch on."

"You're planning on murdering me now?"

"And then take your identity."

"Well this is awkward." He comes to a dead stop. "I was planning on doing the same to you. I bought a wig and everything."

"Ohhh, awkward is right. Because now we're going to be waiting for one of us to strike the first murder blow. Though maybe this can be a rare instance where we agree to just assume each other's identities without having to kill each other. Disposing a body is much harder than it seems, and there aren't gators or sharks in this lake to eat you."

"Fine, but only if you agree to some Parent Trap style lessons where you teach me how to be you. I really need to sell this or I'll revert back to my original plan full of lots of murder."

I laugh and roll a piece of gravel under my foot before we start walking again. "I'm glad you don't think I'm a total weirdo."

"Oh, I do. But I like that about you."

I remember one of the interns saying a compliment by Alex is as rare as an honest politician. We're not at work...so does the compliments being out of the norm thing not apply?

Technically this is a business trip. Alex is here to try to win over Jerry and needs me to be his cover. But not work related for me. My job is to drink wine, sleep in, and pretend to be madly-in-lust with my new boyfriend.

Which isn't going to be that hard to do. *Dammit.*

"Good. Because I can control it in small doses, like a work day, but a whole weekend...all bets are off."

He laughs again, and seeing his face light up makes me feel a little squishy on the inside.

Leaving the luggage on the cobblestone path leading to the lake house, we go up the steps and knock on the door. Everything is so beautiful here, like something from a postcard. The house is set back a good ways from the road, and tall trees line the driveway. The yard alone is impressive, and the lake behind the house is massive.

Even though I saw a picture of the house, it seems bigger in person. It's crazy to think this is a second house for the Harold family when it's probably bigger than most people's one and only house. The cottage is in the woods to the side of the house, and I think I can make out a roof through the trees.

The sounds of nature surround us, as well as the gentle lapping of the lake. If I lived here, I'd never leave. It's so serene, so peaceful. Plus the maple syrup here is supposed to be to-die-for.

The front door flies open. "Hi! You must be Harper and Alex." A short, peppy blonde woman with a glass of red wine in her hand steps onto the porch. "I'm Lynn. Come on in." She waves and takes a step back, bumping into the door.

"Are you hungry? Thirsty? How was your flight? I've only been to Chicago once and I liked it. I'm from Vermont, born and raised. People who live here don't usually move, so Uncle Jerry is a bit of a black sheep. I'm kidding, of course." She's talking a million miles an hour. Alex gives me a look that I return with a smile that says *yeah, she's freakishly hyper.*

"We got something to eat at the airport," I tell her. "But I could use a drink."

"Couldn't we all?" she laughs. "Water? Wine?"

"Water for now, please."

She takes a drink of her wine and leads us through the impressive foyer. There's a formal dining room to one side, an office to the other, and a curved staircase leading up to a catwalk on the second floor.

Stunned doesn't begin to cover how I feel right now. I thought lake houses were small cottages by the water. Smelling like lake water and sunscreen would be expected as well.

The kitchen is just as impressive, all white and bright and full of expensive appliances. Lynn takes a big drink of her wine and sets the glass down on the counter with a *clink*.

"Sparkling or still?"

Her question throws me and I don't know what the heck she means.

"Still," Alex answers for me. "Harper isn't a fan of sparkling water."

Oh, right. Duh. I feel stupid. Alex looks at me in question, not sure if that's even true. I give him a small nod. I wish I could like sparkling water, but I just can't. It has a funky taste I can't get over.

Lynn gets two water bottles out of the fridge.

"Thank you," I tell her and look around the house. The kitchen opens into a living room. The decor is heavy on the nautical theming, too much for my taste, but still pretty none-theless.

"Oh wow," I say when I look out the large windows in the living room. "That view is amazing."

"Isn't it? It's been a while since I've been up to the lake. I forgot how stunning it is. So good for the soul too, healing really. The full moon over that lake at night…" Her hand flies to her chest. "It's gorgeous. Just gorgeous." She opens a drawer in the kitchen and pulls out a key. It's attacked to a large sailboat keyring. "Here ya go! I'm assuming you want to go freshen up or something." She gives a big wink and leans in. "Kate mentioned you two just starting dating. I remember how that is…and then how quickly it falls apart," she adds under her breath. "Here." She takes two bottles of wine from a little wine fridge in the kitchen and thrusts them at me. "You have got to try these. This one is my favorite."

I grab one bottle and Alex takes the other.

"Thank you," he tells her. "And you're right. We do want some alone time." He gives me a look that's supposed to be playfully sexy, and fuck, that's exactly what it is.

"The door can stick a little," Lynn tells us as we go back to the front of the house. "Don't be afraid to give it a little butt-bump."

"Okay, thanks again, Lynn," I say and wonder if she's going to follow us out to the cottage as well. She stops on the bottom porch step, thankfully. I put the water and the bottles of wine in my carry on, regret it as soon as I hook that sucker over my shoulder, but grin and bear it anyway.

The cottage is a good distance from the house, and is charming as fuck. "It's like something out of a fairytale," I muse, stopping in front of it. A smile pulls up my lips, and my mind goes to flowing dresses, evil curses, and a handsome, brave prince, swooping in to save the day.

But then he's captured, and it's up to the princess to save him. Oh! And she has magical powers. *Let it go, bitch.*

"Should we go in?" Alex asks, shaking me back to reality. "Or do you want to keep staring at it for a while."

"I'm good with staring for another minute or two. Though I actually have to pee. And I want to open that bottle of wine that said it has hints of maple syrup flavors. It's either going to be wonderful or disgusting."

"My money is on disgusting. It looks cheap."

"Hey now," I start and take my heavy bag of my shoulder. "Cheap doesn't always mean bad."

"But it can."

"Oh, of course it can. You get what you pay for with a lot of things, but you can also get ripped off." I stick the key in the lock, turn it, and dry the door knob. It turns, but the door sticks, just like how Lynn said it would.

It's cooler here than in Chicago, but with the lake so close, it's humid. I butt-bump the door and it squeaks open.

"Oh my goodness," I gush. "How freaking charming is this? Seriously. It's like Snow White and Rapunzel put their decorating styles together and built this!"

The cottage is a mixture of whites, grays, and natural wood. It's very simple while having traditional accents, and though it's not big and fancy like the lake house, it's perfect.

The downstairs is mostly open concept, with a living room to one side, and the dining room/kitchen combo to the other. I set my heavy bag on the table and pull out the wine.

There's a bathroom behind the staircase, and a sliding glass door off the living room that leads to a screened-in porch.

"Do you want to pick your room first?" Alex asks me, picking up my heavy suitcase as if it weighs nothing.

"Um, sure." I twist off the cap to one of the bottles of wine and open and close cupboards in the kitchen until I find wine glasses. I pour two generous glasses for both and Alex and myself, and follow him up the stairs.

There are two rooms upstairs, and each has its own bathroom. Perfect. Alex and I can stay separated when the lights are off and no one will be none the wiser.

The rooms are similar, both in size and decor. I go with the room that has the best view of the lake. Alex puts my suitcase inside and takes his to the other room across the hall.

We go back downstairs and take out the wine onto the porch. You can't see the lake from here, but we're completely surrounded by the woods. It makes me feel like we're all alone in the world, and no traces of civilization can be found for miles.

"So Lynn was very...peppy." Alex takes a small sip of the wine. "This is actually pretty good."

"Told you. It's the maple syrup one." I take a drink. "Okay. I love this."

Alex laughs and takes another drink. He sits on the porch swing, going to the side instead of sitting in the middle. It makes the swing unbalanced so sit I next to him.

"I think Lynn is recently divorced and the fall out of her marriage was due to her own insecurities and her desire to have children when her husband didn't want them. She gave him an ultimatum she didn't' think he'd follow through on, and when she said she either wants a family or nothing at all, he left, and is already engaged to a younger woman, because—surprise—she's pregnant."

"That's oddly specific."

"I have this weird thing where I like to make up stories for

169

people. Give them dramatic backstories that explain their behavior."

"Do you have one for me?"

"I do." I raise my eyebrows and take another drink of wine.

"Well, what is it?"

"I'm gonna need another glass or two of wine before I tell you that." Planting my feet on the porch, I get up. "I'm going to take a shower and then lay down until Kate and her husband get here." I suck down the rest of my wine, hoping it'll help me take another micro-nap, and go back up to my room.

I pull out only what I need from my suitcase and go into the bathroom. It's a little dated, with teal tile in the shower, but it's clean. I take my time washing my hair, and make sure I shave off every single last strand of unwanted hair.

I dry myself off and then wrap my hair up in the towel. I'm not girly by any means, but I have a routine I'm used to after a shower. Put my face toner on, lotion on my body, and then moisturizer on my face once the toner has dried.

I left the lotion in my suitcase, and this bathroom is so steamy it's making me start to sweat already. I'm naked, and stepping into the cool air is going to feel so fucking good.

I throw up the bathroom door and am face-to-face with Alex.

CHAPTER 21

ALEX

The bathroom door opens, and I'm hit with a billow of steam and the sweet scent of Harper's shampoo. She hadn't been in the shower that long, and I thought I'd have time to set my suitcase down and leave before she got out.

Turns out, I was wrong, and when I look up, startled, all I see are boobs. Big, round, perfect boobs. They're right at my eye level and I stare at them for three seconds, but it's three seconds too long.

"What the hell?" Harper jumps back, trying to get into the bathroom and close the door. I turn away, and a second later, I hear her slip and fall to the ground.

Holding my hand up to block her from view, I take a step around the bed and stop. Blinking, I get a flash of her naked body once again. Fuck, she's gorgeous.

"Are you okay?"

"Define okay," Harper huffs. The bathroom door clicks shut and I lower my hand. "What the fuck, Alex?"

"I am so sorry." I move to the door. "Kate is here."

"So you came in to tell me? The door was closed. I didn't think I'd have to lock it to. Oh my god. You saw me naked!"

"You look good, if that helps," I say and then wince at my own words. "I'm really sorry, Harper. I thought I'd be able to put my suitcase in here and leave."

"And why the fuck would you do that?"

"Can you open the door?"

"No!"

"Can you hear me?" I ask, lowering my voice.

"What?"

"Can you hear me?"

She shuffles behind the door and then unlocks it. The door opens just half an inch. "What?" she snaps.

"Kate and her husband are here. In the cottage."

Harper shakes her head. "Okay?"

"They're staying in the cottage with us. In the other bedroom. I needed to get my suitcase out of that room before they asked why we were in separate rooms."

Harper, who's wrapped in her towel now, lets the door open another inch or two. "Oh shit. That means we have to be in here together? Share a bathroom and sleep in the same room?"

"I'll take the floor," I tell her, having already thought about that. It's all hardwood throughout the house except for the bathrooms, but there's a very worn-looking rug next to the bed that will provide some cushion, and I'll fold up a blanket to help as well. "And Kate said something about about going out with the girls, so we won't have to see each other the rest of the day."

"Thank God," Harper huffs. "I still can't believe you saw me naked."

"Want to see me naked?" I ask with a smirk. "Level the playing field?"

Harper glares at me. "Maybe later. For now can you just...get out?"

"Yes, of course. And I am sorry again. I didn't mean for that to happen and really thought you'd be in there longer."

"Short showers are habit, I guess. The water doesn't stay

warm long in my apartment, and I'd rather save it for the girls to have a hot bath than for me to take a long shower."

Once again, Harper's love for her children hits me right in the heart. She's selfless, kind, caring...and is still basically naked and just a few inches from me. I've never been so tempted to reach out and kiss her than I am right now.

"You have nothing to be embarrassed about, you know," I tell her as I push off the wall to leave.

"I've had two babies and have a big c-section scar on my belly," she says, but I think it's more to herself than to me.

"I didn't notice," I tell her. Probably because I was too distracted by her glorious, wonderful, large tits. I want to put my face in between them and then kiss my way down her stomach, slowly parting her legs. I'll find her wet already, hot with anticipation for what's to come. "And I have scars too."

"You do?"

"Yeah." I turn and lift up my shirt, showing her a three-inch long scar on my right side of my back. I got it when Dad pushed me and I feel into a glass coffee table. Mom told the ER attendants I was playing ball in the house, after she told me not to, of course, and I tripped and fell.

The nurse actually lectured me about how important it is to listen to my parents.

"It's not as cool as your scar," I go on and drop my shirt back into place. "Nothing living came out of me."

Harper smiles. "Thank you."

"For what?"

"For trying to make me feel better."

"Did it work?" I ask.

Her smiles widens. "Yes. Now get out of here so I can get dressed."

$\approx$

I SIT ON THE PORCH SWING, FEELING THE BREEZE PICK UP AND BLOW in the scent of rain. The sky is patchy above us, barely visible through all the leaves, but I can tell a storm is coming.

Not that I can sense it or anything. No, I'm not that in tune with nature. A weather alert popped up on my phone, letting me know. I don't think Harper is going to get to to down to the beach with Kate, and it doesn't look like taking the boat out and fishing with the guys is happening this afternoon either.

I haven't been fishing very many times, but I actually do enjoy it. There aren't many things I do in my life that involve sitting still. Not doing something, not keeping myself insanely busy…it puts me at risk for thinking.

For *feeling*.

The front door opens with a creak, and Harper steps out onto the porch. She's holding the wine we opened earlier, and two empty glasses. She's done her makeup but her hair is still a little damp, plaited in a lose braid going down her back. She's wearing a short black dress with a gray sweater over it. The little lemon necklace rests right about those big, beautiful tits, and it takes a great amount of willpower not to look at them again.

"I'm pretty sure they're up there having sex," Harper tells me and comes over, stopping just a foot from me. She sets the glasses on the wooden railing and fills them both up. After handing me a glass, she sits on the swing next to me.

"All right. Get up and strip down."

I look at her and laugh. "Right here? Right now?"

"Oh, right. I did forget my phone."

"Ha-ha. Nude photos will cost you."

"Please. I can look at free porn all day, every day."

"True…and also why we had to put blocks on certain websites at the office."

Harper laughs. "People were looking at porn at work?"

I nod. "The most uncomfortable day in my entire career was when I had to fire an intern for jacking off at his desk."

"No way!" Harper brings her wine to her lips and takes a drink. Her eyes sparkle when she's happy and she's just so damn beautiful. "You're making it up."

"I wish I was. Turns out the guy had a form of a sex addiction, but that still doesn't make it okay to jerk it at work. Though it did explain why we kept finding empty boxes of tissues in the break room garbage."

Harper's nose wrinkles. "The break room? Where we eat?"

I nod. "Yep. Everything was sanitized, don't worry."

She shudders. "It grosses me out to think about all the public surfaces you sit on—or eat on—that have...you know...gross fluids on them."

I laugh. "I try not to think about it."

"I'm just glad I don't have to rely on public transportation anymore. Taking two little kids on the subway..." She shudders and takes another drink of wine. I think she's getting a little tipsy, and I don't want to ask personal questions while she's not in her right mind. It's not fair, and I don't want her to answer anything she wouldn't say if she hadn't had a glass of wine.

"So the girls' father..." I ask carefully.

"He's not in the picture at all." Harper takes a big drink of the wine and sets the glass down on the porch. She leans back and pushes the swing back. "We met at a party, hooked, up, and about a month later I realized I was pregnant. I never got his number and I never saw him again after. It was the one and only one-night stand I ever had."

"Oh. Am I supposed to say I'm sorry?"

She shrugs and then laughs. "I don't know. I was in college... never partied...hardly ever drank...I made a few reckless choices that night but it brought me my girls, and I wouldn't have it any other way. And it wasn't a completely terrible experience. We had this magical connection and the sex was good...but it ended that night."

I hate that part of me likes knowing she has no ties to the

girls' father. She's single. Available for me to—nope. I don't date my employees. Hell, I won't even sleep with them.

Though today feels like a good day to break the rules.

"Do you think less of me now?"

"Why would I?"

She lets out a sign and shakes her head. "A lot of people do."

"Lord knows I've made a lot of reckless choices while I was drinking." It's probably a miracle I've never gotten anyone pregnant, really. "I think it's unfair and hypocritical for men to be praised for hooking up but women are chastised for it."

"Yes, that's what I say all the time. Because we do...I do." She bites her lip and look away. "Micheal was his name," she says quietly. "And it wasn't just a random hookup. We spent the whole night talking but didn't exchange numbers. I know...it sounds dumb. But I was young."

"I don't think it sounds dumb. And you don't have to explain yourself, Harper," I say gently. "I'm not one to judge. My moral compass is..." I trail off shaking my head. "I think the needle fell off a long time ago."

"Nah." She playfully elbows me. "You're not that bad." Leaning forward, she picks up her wine. "Want to walk down to the lake with me?"

"Yeah, that'd be nice."

She finishes her wine and I take a big drink of mine and then set the glass on a small glass table on to the side of the front door. Harper jumps down the steps and looks around the house.

"We should take that path." She points to a grassy trail going away from the lake and into the woods.

"I don't think that leads to the lake."

"But it might." Her eyes light up. "Where's your sense of adventure?"

The wind picks up right as we get into the trail, and Harper shivers. She pulls her sweater around herself and looks back at me, smiling.

"It smells good in here."

"Yeah, it does. The air feels clean."

She laughs. "Right? I don't think there are steel mills around here like there are in Chicago. If my girls weren't back there, you might not get me to leave."

"Maybe we'll have to do one of those lame team building meetings up here for work in a few months."

"Do you seriously do those?"

"No fucking way," I laugh, though if it gets me up here alone with Harper again, I would.

We walk silently through the woods for a while, enjoying the sights and sounds of nature. After about a half-mile in, the wind really picks up.

"Maybe we should go back," Harper says, looking up at the trees swaying. "I don't want a tree to fall and kill us."

"Good idea."

Right as we turn to leave, a crack of thunder rings out, and rain starts to patter down.

"We better run," I say and grab her hand. We race through the woods but only a few seconds later, the sprinkle turns into a downpour. Harper lets out a little shriek and then starts laughing. Lightning flashes and more thunder rings out.

"Hurry!" she calls and give my hand a squeeze. The ground squishy beneath our feet and the rain comes down in buckets. Finally, we reach the cottage and dah onto the porch.

Standing in front of the door, Harper stops and turns toward me. "Well, that was an adventure, wasn't it?"

"It was. That storm came on fast."

"Hopefully it'll be over fast too." She looks out at the trees blowing like crazy. Rain mists us, and we step back, closer to the house. Harper is right there next to me, so close I can feel the heat coming off her skin in waves.

If there ever was a perfect time for a first kiss, this is it. I brush wet strands of hair out of Harper's face. She shuffles closer, and I cup her chin. I lean in, lips parting and heart racing.

Another crack of thunder sounds above us and a brilliant flash of lightning illuminates the gray sky. Harper blinks, bringing her long, wet eyelashes together. She rests her hand on my waist, pressing the cold, soaked fabric of my shirt against my skin.

Her eyes meet mine and then fall shut. She wants me to kiss her just as much as I want to kiss her. I close my own eyes and go in for the kiss.

But then I stop.

Harper isn't interested in a hookup. She's not one to have a one-night stand. She wants commitment and I...I don't know if I can give that to her. She deserves the world but there are so many *what ifs* when it comes to a longterm relationship I don't know if I can get over it.

The biggest one isn't what if she doesn't make me happy. It's what if I don't make her happy?

CHAPTER 22

HARPER

*A*lexander Harding is going to kiss me.

The wind and the rain pick up, blowing in on us even though we're standing on the covered front porch. Thunder echoes above us, my clothes are drenched and in that moment, I forget that Alex is my boss.

That he's a cocky asshole.

Right now, he's just Alex, and I'm really starting to like him… and I also really want him to kiss me. My let my eyes fall shut and my lips part. Alex's hand is on my cheek and I can feel the heat of his skin coming off in waves.

If he kisses me, everything will change. One kiss might not be a big deal for him, but it is for me. I meant it when I said I'm not a one-night stand kind of girl. And even though Michael and I never spoke again, we shared a connection that night.

Not just a naked, physical connection, but a real one. We got each other, and if I wasn't so drunk by the night's end, I so would have remembered to get his number or even his last name so I could stalk him on social media like any normal twenty-year old girl would have done.

Alex shuffles closer, brushing his hips against mine. A shiver goes through me and suddenly I feel too young and innocent, too inexperienced and clumsy for someone like him. I've had my fair share of crushes, and a decent amount of boyfriends over the years. But Alex is no innocent crush, and he's certainly far from the boys I dated before.

There's nothing innocent or boyish about him, not at all. He's a *man*. Tall. Muscular. Commanding. My heart jumps into my throat. Even though my eyes are closed, I can sense Alex moving closer. Can smell his cologne. The fresh scent of laundry detergent. *Him.*

But then he hesitates.

I don't want to open my eyes and see the look on his face. Did he suddenly realize what he was about to do and regret it? Or maybe he wasn't going to kiss me at all and now I've made things a million times more awkward than him walking in on me naked.

Then the front door opens and we jump apart, feeling we've been caught in the the the act.

"Oh my goodness!" Kate laughs. "Got caught in the storm?"

I look down at my wet clothes. "Just a little bit."

Alex turns away, looking at the rain coming down through the trees. "It came on fast."

So did you, buddy. And I liked it.

"I just checked the radar," Kate tells us. "It should pass in about an hour. Are you hungry? I'm starving."

"Yeah…I'm, um, hungry." I look at Alex. He's still staring off into the woods. I drop my gaze to his crotch and force myself to look away. "Alex?"

"Yeah?" he turns, brows furrowed, and looks at me as if it's my fault he wanted to kiss me.

"Are you hungry?"

He nods. "I am."

"We should, uh, change then."

He just nods again and I head in, going up to the room as fast as I can to avoid dripping on the hardwood floor. I grab new underwear and a blue dress and go into the bathroom to change. I'm toweling off my hair when I open the door to go back into the room.

And Alex is standing there wearing just his boxers. His back is turned to me, and I get another look at that scar…and his body. My God, what a perfect body. He's fit and muscular, but not obnoxiously so. Men aren't supposed to actually look like that. Besides that time Tessa forced me to go running with her in the morning and we saw the college football team shirtless and jogging around the tract at school, I've only seen men this in shape on TV.

His chest muscles are defined, leading down to well-cut abs and that perfect, lick-able V of muscles that disappears into his boxers.

"Trying to cash in on our deal already?" he asks and steps into dry jeans.

"If I was, I would have stepped out of the bathroom a few seconds ago. Unless you're willing to do a Magic Mike style dance for me."

"You got a bunch of dollar bills?"

"Unfortunately, I left those at home," I laugh and run the towel over my hair once more. "Should I find an ATM?"

"I might be willing to strip for other things?"

"Oh really?" I pick up my brush off the dresser and run it through my hair. "Do I want to ask?"

He chuckles and gives me a wink. "You'll find out later."

Shaking my head, I grab my hair dryer from my bag and go back into the bathroom to dry my hair. Alex is confusing me, and I don't get what's going on.

He's flirting, that's for sure. And I'm flirting right back. I was sure he was going to kiss me and then he stopped, acting like it was the last thing he wanted to do.

Once my hair is mostly dry, I put it up in a French braid, fix my smeared makeup, and go back into the bedroom. The rain has slowed down and Alex opened the windows. He's standing by one, looking out.

"It really is serene here," he says quietly.

"It is. The girls would love exploring the woods."

He flashes a cheeky grin. "As long as it doesn't start raining."

"Oh, they'd love the rain." I feel a tug on my heart thinking about them. Only a few more hours until they're out of school and we can FaceTime. Man, I miss those little kids so much already even though I'd normally be at work. Just the fact that I *can't* see them is what's making me miss them. It's not like I can just leave work whenever I wanted to, but if I really did want to, I could.

I can't drive over and see them now.

"You okay?" Alex asks me. "You seem sad all of the sudden." He takes a step away from the window.

"Yeah, I'm thinking about the girls and missing them. We've never been apart before. It's good for them, I know, to spend time away from me like this."

"Yeah, it's healthy for you both. You're a good mom," he adds, and it's like he know just how much I need to hear that right now because here I am day drinking and hanging out and having fun.

"Thanks. That means a lot." I put on another sweater and Alex closes the window most of the way, leaving it open maybe two inches to let the cool air in.

Kate gives us one large umbrella to share. It wouldn't be a big deal if we were a real couple. I pull my sweater tight around my body when we get onto the porch. Alex opens the umbrella and extends his arm toward me.

He saw me naked.

We almost kissed.

I'm starting to really like him.

And now that he's putting his arm around me, pulling me close to his body so we are both under the shelter of the umbrella...nope. I need to stop. It's such a me thing to do. I get carried away, read too much into things and make up my silly stories with usually impossible happily ever afters.

There is no way Alex would be interested in someone like me.

He's about to inherit the family company and has already been in *Forbes* twice and he's only thirty. I'm a broke single mom who never finished college.

Yeah...me and him...it will never happen.

~

"WE CAN EITHER STAY HERE WITH THE OLD FOLKS," KATE TEASES, loud enough for her parents to hear. "Or we can brave the rain and go into town for something to eat."

"I'm fine with whatever you guys want to do," I tell her. We're sitting in the living room of the lake house, enjoying the warmth from the fire in the big, stone fireplace. It's weird to have a fire going this time of year. It's still hot as hell and humid as fuck back home in the midwest.

Alex is next to me, and put his arm around my shoulders when we sat down. I know it's all for show, but it felt like he did it without thinking, as if he wanted to put his arm around me.

"I vote for braving the rain," Leo, Kate's husband, says.

"I'm fine with that too," Alex says and slowly pulls his arm from around my shoulders, fingers brushing across the nape of my neck. It sends chills down my spine and heat between my legs. I'm a little surprised he'd vote for going out. The whole point of coming here was so he could talk to Jerry and convince him to work with his firm again. "What about you, babe?"

I'm going to implement a new rule once we're alone: no pet names. I'm not really a fan of them to begin with, and it's starting to feel weird because I'm starting to have feelings for him. Playing pretend is confusing me, making it impossible to read the signals.

If there even are any, that is.

But the times when I thought he was feeling something too weren't times when we were around others and needed to put on a show. It was when we were alone, and what others thought didn't matter.

It was just me and just him.

Dammit. This is getting too complicated. No wonder so many actors start dating after playing romantic couples in movies.

"Great. There is the cutest tavern downtown that has surprisingly good food. The whole downtown area is to die for." Kate smiles and gets up. "Lynn, are you coming?"

Lynn, who's been talking nonstop to Kate's mother, waves her hand in the air. "Nah, I'll pass and will let you couples go out and have fun. But thank you."

"You sure?" Kate asks, making my story of Lynn getting over a breakup or divorce more likely.

"Yeah. I'll catch up with you later and the sun is supposed to be out all day tomorrow so we'll have a beach day."

Kate smiles, but her eyes don't convey the same happiness. Is there discord between them as well? Ohhh, this could be interesting. I don't think the divorce would have to do with Kate at all. I mean, she's happily married and lives all the way in Chicago. But maybe—stop.

I'm getting ahead of myself again, and using someone else's drama to distract me from my own.

"Take the Escalade, sweetheart," Kate's mom tells her. "The roads might be slick."

"We'll be fine, Mom," Kate says, going over and giving her mother a kiss goodbye. She gets her southern accent from her mother, and she told me just today that after her parents met at college, her father moved from Vermont to Georgia, where he got started in the "toy business" and started his own company. His success story is an interesting one as well, and just goes to show how big money can land on anyone, really.

A bigger toy company bought them out, and then that

company got into trouble with the IRS and declared bankruptcy. Jerry, who invested all the money he got from selling his company, had enough to buy the company back, get them out from the hole they were in, and turn it around into one of the largest toy manufacturers in the nation. I never would have thought there was so much money in making toys.

I check the time on my phone, doing a mental count down until I can talk to my girls. I hope they're having a good day, and it's starting to hit me that I won't be there to tuck them in bed tonight.

Going out is a good idea. It'll distract me...I hope.

The rain slows down to a drizzle by the time we get into town. There's a big sign outside the little tavern Kate talked about, letting us know Trivia Challenge Hour is starting in just twenty minutes.

"Do you guys want to play?" I ask when we get to our table. "I know a lot of useless information."

Kate laughs. "Sure, it sounds fun. I don't know lots of useless information, but if any of the questions pertain to running nonprofits, I'm your girl."

I look up at Alex and my heart swells in my chest when our eyes meet. I never noticed just how vibrant and complex his eyes are. At first glance, they appear brown, but on closer inspection, I can see flecks of green and yellow in there, making them more of a dark amber than brown.

"Do you want to play?" I ask him, suddenly breathless. Dammit, Alex. Leave it to you to take my breath away without even trying.

"Sure." He leans in, narrowing his eyes and grinning. "I'm rather competitive, just to warn you."

"And I play to win."

"Then we'll make a good team."

We put in our food and drink order just in time for the game to start. Feeling like I already had more than enough to drink this early in the day, I got an iced tea. Kate got wine, and both guys ordered a beer.

All participating teams in the trivia challenge are given white boards, and the simple rules are explained. Write down your answers within thirty seconds and don't cheat.

"Ready?" Alex asks, wiggling his eyebrows as he uncaps the dry-erase marker.

"Oh yeah."

"All right, let's get started!" the host says into the microphone. "What is the only state in the US that only borders one other state?"

"Maine," Alex whispers as he scribbles it down.

"Damn, you really know your geography," I say.

"Not really. That question was asked on a TV show where the characters were playing trivia," he admits with a laugh.

"Hey, as long as we get it right, I don't care how you know it."

The time is called and we hold up out boards. Anyone who got it wrong has to hand over their board, and will continue to do so until only one team remains.

"Next question: how many children are in the Weasley family from the *Harry Potter* series?"

"Seven," Alex and I both whisper to each other at the same time.

"Easy-peasy," I say, though that question causes three teams to surrender their boards.

"What is the only vowel on a keyboard thats not on the top line of letters?" the hosts asks for our third question.

I close my eyes and hold my hands out in front of me, as if I'm typing. I use my computer every day but my mind is blanking. The only vowel? I imagine typing out the alphabet.

"A," I whisper and Alex write it down. We get that right and move onto the next question.

"What is a group of ferrets called."

Alex goes right to the board again and writes down *business*.

"Really?" I ask in a low voice.

He nods. "Don't ask me why I know this, but it's right." And it is. Kate and her husband get eliminated with that question, along with four others. We're down to three other couples along with us, and the stakes are getting higher.

"What is the name of the prince in Disney's 1959 film, *Sleeping Beauty*, that Aurora is promised to marry?"

Alex looks at me and shakes his head. I know the answer to this, but right now I'm getting lost looking into those pretty eyes.

"Do you know this?" he asks when I don't even respond. I shake myself and smile.

"Yeah. Prince Phillip."

Alex quickly writes it down.

"Yes!" he cheers when we're one of the two couples to get it right. He holds up his hand for a high-five.

"Next question," the host says, looking down at his paper. "Which Chicago Bears running back was known as "The Galloping Ghost"?"

"I hope you know this one," I tell Alex.

"Of course. He's a Hall of Famer and we're from Chicago." He writes down *Harold Grange,* and I can honestly say I've never once heard that name despite being from Chicago.

We get it right, as do the other couple we're up against. The next question is laughably easy, for us at least. *What fictional city is Batman from?*

"All right, next question," the host says, reading off his list. "What crime-fighting dog has S.D. written on his collar?"

"S.D.," I repeat, thinking. "A crime-fighting dog?"

"Scooby Doo," Alex excitedly whispers and jots it down.

"Yesss!" I raise my fist in the air when we get it right. I look across the tavern at the other couple. They're not much older than us, and are staring daggers our way.

We're mostly likely beating their record and are—gasp—

tourists and not locals. Four more random questions are asked and we all get them right.

The host rings a bell and says we're going into a speed round of category based questions. He grabs a jar from the bar top and takes it to the closet table, asking someone to pull out a slip of paper.

"Disney," she reads out loud.

"I am not very familiar with the singing and dancing and princesses." Alex picks up his beer and takes a big drink.

"Don't worry, I got this. I really want to take my kids to Disney someday, so we watch a lot of YouTube videos about it in preparation for when we can go…you know…in like twenty years most likely since that place is so damn expensive. And as a mom of twin girls, we're all about the princesses in our house."

Alex laughs, gaze locking with mine. We really do make a good fake couple. No one would have any idea we we're not actually together, and it's almost a shame we're not.

We get along.

He's made me laugh multiple times just today.

I'm on the taller side of average for a woman, and he's tall enough I could still wear heels and not be taller than him.

And he likes Harry Potter. That's a must, by the way.

"I'm going to start this category round with an easier question," the host says. "How many eggs does Gaston eat for breakfast?"

"That's mentioned in the movie?" Alex asks and I giggle.

"In a song. Five dozen."

He writes it down, and no surprise, we get it right. So does our competition.

"This next question is a little tougher," the host goes on. "Who gave the opening speech at the 1971 Disney World grand opening?"

"Walt Disney?" Alex asks and I shake my head.

"He was dead by then. I think. Shoot." I bite my lip. "I want to say it was Roy, but now I'm second guessing myself."

"Don't do that. Go with your gut, and your gut told you this." He writes down *Roy* and I was right. The other couple just barely got their answer on their board in time.

"And now it's time for a hard one," the host says. "What is the name of the little girl referred to as "Boo" in the Disney/Pixar film, *Monsters Inc?*"

"I know this!" I get way too excited and jump out of my seat.

"What is it?" Alex asks, getting just as excited as I do. The other couple seems stumped.

"Mary," I whisper and he writes it down. The other couple is still scrambling and the ten second warning is going off.

"Five…four…three…two…one. Time!" We hold up our board and the other team doesn't. They don't know if, but if I got it wrong, then we're both out.

"And the correct answer is…Mary!"

"Yes!" Alex lowers the board and turns to me, pulling me in for a one-armed hug. It's an innocent gesture, but I'm all hyper-aware of his firm body. My breasts crush against his chest, and his hand slips down my waist a few inches, fingers resting on the curve of my hip.

"How the hell do you know that?" Kate asks.

"Penny wanted to be Boo for Halloween two years ago and insisted she know her real name so I looked it up. It's not mentioned in the movie, but you see it written on a picture that's hanging in her bedroom."

"Damn, you Disney fans are die hard," Kate's husband says.

"I told you I know a bunch of useless information. Most of it is probably dated but now, but it's how I stayed entertained on the long flights or car rides to Mexico as a kid."

"It paid off." Alex is still smiling and his arm is still around me. I don't want him to take it off. I'd like to slip into his lap, hook my arm over his shoulders and take a drink of his beer.

I was in a dark place right after I had the twins. I was grieving the death of my mother, the fact that she'd never meet her grandchildren and how they'd never meet her and know how wonderful a woman she was. How she inspired me everyday to be kinder than I was the day before, to push myself but not exhaust myself. To stand up for myself and not take any shit.

I was on my own, trying to juggle work and being a mom and having to accept the fact that I'd most likely not be able to go back to school.

My friends were graduating, going out and having fun, and didn't give me a second thought. I grieved the loss of my carefree life too, and felt guilty the whole time.

Going out like this, no matter how simple it may be, just didn't happen. It took me a good year and several months on medication to get a handle on my emotions. Now they're older and I'm in a better mental space and want to go out. I just can't afford it.

So this…this is nice. I thought being here with Alex would nullify the whole *spend some relaxing time away from the kids* thing, but right here and right now, I can't imagine being here with anyone else.

CHAPTER 23

ALEX

It's strange, how this doesn't feel like a business trip. I don't know Harper's friend Kate at all, let alone her husband. I should be coming up with ways to stay at the house and talk to Jerry, but here I am, holding Harper's hand as we walk down the main street of this small town.

It's starting to feel weird pretending to be her boyfriend. Lying never really bothered me before it if didn't hurt anyone and got me what I wanted in the end. But something about this is bothering me, and I think it has a bit to do to with me asking Harper to lie to her friend for money...and a lot to do with wishing things could always be like this.

I'd give her the money she needs if I would, but I know she wouldn't accept it. She mentioned wanting to take her kids to Disney but couldn't afford to. I can afford it. I'd put them up in the nicest room in the best hotel and make reservations to have breakfast, lunch, and dinner with the princesses and Mickey Mouse.

But...I can't. Because at the end of the day, she's my assistant. We're out here in this weird little town that makes you feel like the rest of the world doesn't exist anymore and it's messing with my head.

That's all it is.

Not the fact that Harper is so fucking hot.

And funny.

And smart.

And kind and caring and probably the single most genuine person I've ever met in my entire life.

Jerry and his wife are going out to dinner tonight, and I opted to stay with Harper and her friends. It would have seemed weird to say no and go off with Kate's parents, so really, it made the most sense to stay with Harper.

And I want to.

Because I know once this trip is over, I won't get to see her like this anymore and it already makes me upset.

The rain has stopped and the sun is starting to come out again, shining down on us before it sets. It's becoming quiet humid out, and Harper sheds out of her sweater.

She's wearing that blue dress I've seen her in before, and it looks just as good on her now as it did then. The sleeves slide a little off her shoulders, and the hem flows around her ankles as she walks. I'm positive she has no idea how good she looks. Though even if she did, she wouldn't go around flaunting it. That's not Harper and it's yet another thing that I like so much about her.

We go into an antique store—Kate collects some sort of jars made in the 1920s and she wants to look for some—which is something I'd never do. Yet seeing Harper's interest for some odd reason, makes me interested. I've never actually been in a store like this. It smells just as I assumed, like musty forgotten dreams, dust, and old-lady perfume.

Harper looks at the random assortment of junk on the shelves as we follow Kate. Her husband turns around and rolls his eyes. Kate somehow sees and elbows him in the ribs, making Harper laugh.

"I swear that thing is watching us," I whisper to Harper, pointing to a doll sitting on a shelf at the back of the store. She turns and startles.

"Holy shit, that thing is creepy! I think it's supposed to be a prop from that *Annabelle* movie." She takes a few quick paces to the side. "The eyes...watch the eyes. It's totally following me." Narrowing her eyes, she starts to inch forward toward it. I duck behind a shelf and stand perfectly still.

"Did you see that? It's moving, and I'm not joking." She gasps. "It just moved again." She whirls around, looking for me. "Alex?" I dodge behind the shelf with the doll and reach through, pushing the doll at Harper.

She screams, I laugh, and then she jerks back, jumping into another shelf. A glass vase topples over and she twists around just in time to catch it, pushing it back into place.

But when she steps back, her hair catches on the doll's outstretched hand. She turns fast and the doll comes with her. She screams again and the doll crashes to the floor.

"What is going on over here?" Kate asks, hurrying over.

The doll landed face down on the floor, revealing a large crack in the back of the head, mostly covered by the hair. Three fat mice come rushing out of it. One runs onto Harper's shoe and she flicks her foot, sending the mouse flying right at Kate.

Kate screams, jumps back, and bumps into Leo, who knocks over a display of old Pez dispensers.

"Oh my god!" Harper shrieks, madly running her fingers through her hair as if she's afraid the doll still has a hold on her. I'm dying of laughter and Leo is looking around, trying to make sense of what just happened.

The owner of the store comes rushing to the back.

"Is everyone all right?" she asks, eyes going wide when she sees the mess.

"There...there were mice in that doll," Harper stammers. Her eyes go to me, giving me a death stare, and then she starts laughing. "I thought it was alive and trying to kill me."

"I'll pay for that," I say, coming back from around the shelf. "Ring up the damages."

"Meet me up front," the owner says. "Then I think it's best you leave." She lets out a heavy sigh before turning to go. Harper punches me in the bicep.

"Seriously? I have never been kicked out of anywhere before!"

I'm still laughing. "I couldn't resist."

"Jerk," she tries to act mad but is laughing too. "I almost peed my pants!"

I laugh even harder. "I would say I'm sorry but I'm not. It was worth it."

She takes a step closer, eyes glimmering. Her mouth opens to say something else, but then her phone rings. With impressive speed, she pulls it out of her purse.

"It's the girls!"

"Go outside and take it," I tell her. "I'll handle this."

Harper nods and speeds off. I help Leo put the Pez dispensers back on the display and then pick up the doll. If I'm paying for it, I might as well keep it, right? It's been a while since I've played any good pranks.

I find Harper outside, sitting on a bench as she talks to her girls.

"The more you play with it, the softer it becomes," she tells them.

"Not from my experience," I whisper, sitting down next to her.

She laughs and shakes her head. "And a pinch or two of cinnamon to make it smell good." She pauses. "Okay, okay…go play. Call me before bedtime. I love you!"

Her eyes get a little misty after she hangs up.

"Missing your girls?" I ask.

"Is it that obvious?" She sniffles and puts her phone back in her purse.

"It's okay. I got you something to cuddle tonight." I pull the doll out of the bag. "Will you be my Mommy?" I ask in a high-pitched voice, holding the doll up.

"Oh my God, no! Just no!" She jumps up, laughing. "I cannot believe you bought that creepy thing!"

"I need you, Mommy."

"Stop!" She holds out her hands, pushing the doll away. "I am throwing that thing in the lake and then burning it."

"I think you need to do that the other way around."

"Either way, I'm sure I'll wake up to it on my pillow. In Chicago."

I look at the doll. "Throwing it in the lake does sound like a good idea."

She shakes her head. "That's littering though."

I set it up on the bench. "We could leave it here."

"And scare innocent children?" She laughs. "Now I'm imagining it and I wish I could hide somewhere with a camera."

"It would go viral."

Kate and Leo come out of the store, and Kate stops short. "What the fuck?" Her hand flies to her mouth when someone passing by glares at her.

"Harper was missing her girls so I thought I'd get something to tide her over until we get back Sunday."

"That's hilarious." She beams at us. "You two are so good together," she says to Harper, wiggling her eyebrows. "I love the humor in your relationship."

The smile dies on Harper's face, and I wonder if Kate's words hit her the same way they're hitting me.

None of this is real...and being remind of that makes me realize just how much I wish it was.

CHAPTER 24

"I love you, too, my sweet girls," I say for the tenth time. "Sweet dreams." I hang up, and push my feet down on the porch, sending the swing back. They're having fun with Papa and are about to watch a movie and eat popcorn. They still don't miss me and are having fun...and I'm still not sure if I feel jilted or relief.

My eyes flutter shut and I tip my head back, listening to the sounds of the night. It's not even that late but I'm tired. In my defense, it has been a long day and I didn't really sleep at all last night.

It's so relaxing out here. I could fall asleep right—

"Hello, Mommy."

I open my eyes and see that creepy doll staring at me. "Fucking shit, Alex!"

He laughs and my stomach flutters like a million butterflies taking off at once. Why can't he go back to being the cocky boss I didn't like? Things were simpler then. Because I'm starting to have feelings—real feelings—for him. Hating him was easy. But loving him? That would complicate everything.

"Want to go chuck this thing in the lake?" he asks. "Oh, wait, you don't want to litter."

"Bingo. So I'm thinking we set a scene and really do go for that whole hidden camera thing. We need to find a good location to surprise unsuspecting children."

"And you think you're so innocent."

"There's nothing innocent about me."

He sets the doll down on the table by the front door and sits next to me on the swing. My heart speeds up and I can't help but notice how good he looks now that he's changed his clothes. All he's wearing is a black long sleeve shirt and gray sweat pants. I bite my lip and cast my eyes over him once more, *not* noticing that bulge in his pants.

"We never did see the lake."

"No, we didn't." I swallow hard, mouth suddenly dry. *He's your boss. He's your boss. He's your boss.* And not your type. Nope. Not at all. Funny, handsome, fit, rich…those are things you hate.

Dammit.

"Want to walk down to it with me?" Alex asks. "I don't want to look like a creep walking along the shore alone."

"Well, I can't have that. We have a reputation to uphold here."

"Do we now?" He twists to look at me. His gaze is suffocating. Too intense. It's making me feel hot, like I need to suddenly strip out of all my clothes.

"Yeah. We're, um, guests."

Alex pushes the swing back and heat floods my veins. "So help me not be named the neighborhood creep?" he gets up and extends his hand. Swallowing hard to push my heart back into my chest, I take it and let him pull me to my feet.

Is this really happening? Am I really going on a moonlight walk along the lake with Alexander fucking Harding?

Yes, yes it is.

We don't speak as we walk down to the lake. It's chilly out

tonight, and the fact that I took my bra off already is salient in my mind. I zip up my jacket an cross my arms over my chest.

"Cats or dogs?" I ask, looking at the smooth surface of the water. Stars glimmer above us, and if we were in a romantic movie, this would be the part where Alex would lay me down and kiss me.

"What?"

"Don't think, just answer," I say. "Cats or dogs?

"Dogs."

"Do you have any pets?"

He shakes his head. "I don't. Do you?"

"No, but I wish we did. My dad has a cat my kids are border-line obsessed with."

"Why don't you have pets?"

Hello, discomfort, it's been a while. "They're, um, expensive. Or more so, they could be. I know there's no way we could afford an emergency vet bill if one were to come up, and having to put down an animal due to not being able to afford medical bills would just kill me. Why don't you?"

"I'm not home enough, and it doesn't seem fair."

"Two cats would be okay with that."

He just nods and takes my hand, twirling me around. The stars are twinkling above us. If there was a time to fall in love... nope. No. Can't go there.

Something splashing in the lake, startling us both.

"It's the doll," Alex says seriously. "Trying to lure us in so it can drown us and kill us."

"Most likely."

We both stare out at the water. There are several other people out along the shore, and a few bonfires have been lit and smell amazing. There's a gentle breeze and the humidity is almost gone from the air. If I got into a hammock with a blanket, I'd fall asleep in no time.

"You know what?" he says.

"What?"

"I'm glad I told those women I'm your boyfriend."

"You are?" I ask.

"Yeah. This…this is nice." He's looking out at the water, and his shoulders tense. I don't think he shares his feelings very often, and it's strange how I can sense his apprehension, but can tell he wants to open up. I still want to know what happened to him to make him be so closed up. He's not a bad guy like I thought he was, not at all. He's rough around the edges and could tweak his bedside manner at work, but underneath it all…I think he's hurting.

"I mean, as far as business trips go, this has been the most laid back so far," he says.

"It has. And it got me out of Chicago, which hasn't happened in years. So, yeah…I'm glad you told those assholes you're my boyfriend too."

"Asshole is too nice a term for them."

"It is, isn' it," I agree. "Bitches? No, still not harsh enough."

"Butt-crust."

"What?"

"Butt-crust," he repeats with a laugh. "I used to call my sister a butt-crust when we were kids. I have no idea why or how I thought of it, but she hated it so I called her it even more."

"That's sounds like an insult my kids would come up with. I like it…but if you have crust on your butt, you should probably invest in some baby wipes or consider seeing a doctor."

"My ass is fine, trust me."

I hike up her eyebrows. "Is it now? I feel like this is something I should check out."

"How thorough of a check are you doing? Should I casually bend over and pick something up, or is this a squat and cough situation?"

"Definitely squat and cough, but you need to completely

disrobe and put on one of those super flattering yellow, paper gowns. Open in the back of course."

Alex laughs, and puts his arm around my shoulders. "Thank you," I tell him. "For standing up for me. No one ever has before."

He looks right into my eyes. I inhale, feeling every single little thing. The tightness in his hold. The smell of lake water and earth around us.

"They are fools, then," he tells me, and leans in. The gentle sound of the water lapping the shore surrounds us. "You're worth defending, Harper, even if you don't think so."

"Thank you," I say again quietly. "It's hard believing it."

"Why?"

I shake my head. "I don't know."

"You do know. Don't think, just answer," he says, throwing my words back at me.

So I don't. I don't think. I just answer. "I'm a single mom. I'm not in the best shape. I have a c-section scar, stretch marks, I like to eat, and if given the choice of chips and salsa or the gym, I'll choose the chips. I'm broke as fuck financially and even more so emotionally."

"Those are supposed to be reasons why someone shouldn't like you?" he questions.

"Yeah."

"They sound like reasons to like you."

"Then you're obviously crazy," I tell him. "Because I'm so far from having my shit together it's laughable." We come to a stop on the beach. The sand has turned into the natural stone and grass that makes up the shoreline.

"Do you think I have my shit together?" he asks.

"I do. But if you didn't have a PA then I'd say no, you wouldn't."

He laughs. "That's true. And I'm aware how lucky I am to be able to afford a PA. I'm not that organized, you know."

"Oh, I know. I've only been your assistant for a short while now and I know how much you need me."

He puts his arm around me again and turns us around so we're walking back to the cottage.

"I'm tired," I say after we've walked a good few yards in silence. "Is that pathetic?"

"Not at all," he tells me. "It has been a long day. I'm tired too."

"We can go to bed," he suggests. "And I'll, uh...I'll turn on the TV pretend like I accidentally fell asleep on the couch."

"Oh. Right. One bedroom. Want me to take the couch? You're taller than me and it probably won't be comfortable."

"We can switch off tomorrow."

"Deal," I say as a shiver runs through me. It's really cooled down and my light jacket isn't keeping me warm enough. As much as I want to stay out here, I'm cold.

The lights are still on inside the little cottage when we get back, and Kate and Leo are both passed out on the couch with the TV on. So much for Alex crashing on the couch tonight.

"At least we're not the only ones calling it a night at nine-thirty."

"It makes me feel better," I laugh quietly. Alex follows me up the stairs and we both pause when we step into the bedroom. The windows were left cracked open and the room is cold.

"I'm going to get ready for bed," I tell him and go into the bathroom to shower and brush my teeth. I close the door behind me, and am shocked all over again by how cold the room is when I step back out into it. It's good sleeping weather. I love to be all snugged up under a million blankets.

Alex has moved his pillow and one of the quilts from the bed to the floor. It'll be uncomfortable, and he's going to be freezing down there. He goes into the bathroom once I'm out, and I get under the covers.

The comforter is down and is so soft and warm. It's like being tucked under a fluffy cloud. I lay back and close my eyes. My body is tired but my mind is whirling. The smell of campfire comes in through the window. It takes me back to summers spent in Mexico when everyone on the Rodriguez side of the family would come over to my grandparents for a party that went late into the night.

Mom would sometimes let me have a few sips of her margarita, and my uncle let me sample his homemade tequila more than once. I miss everyone down in Mexico. It's been so long since I've seen them all, and going back now as a single mom who's barely making ends meet is, well…I don't want to say embarrassing, because I refuse to be ashamed of my life.

But I also thought I'd be in a better place than I am right now.

Alex comes back out, only wearing the sweatpants, and looks at his pitiful spot on the floor. That man is used to sleeping on Egyptian cotton sheets and a custom-made mattress, I'm sure.

"Come here," I tell him, reaching for on of the decorative pillows I'd moved to the floor. I grab a lumbar pillow and put it in the middle of the bed. "Just stay on your side."

"You sure?"

"Yeah. It's too cold to sleep on the floor and my back hurts just thinking about sleeping on hardwood."

His lips twitch into a smile and I'm pretty sure he's debating whether or not he should make a joke about *hard wood* right now.

"If you get uncomfortable with it, just let me know," he says and turns off the light. The room is almost pitch black, save for some porch light spilling in through the open window. The mattress sinks down as Alex gets into bed, and I'm suddenly wide awake.

I replay everything over and over in my mind, from the day I met Alex in the school parking lot to him telling me I'm worth defending. I've never been more confused in my life, and I wish Mom were here to talk to about this.

Is this some sort of *what happens on a business trip stays on a business trip* kind of deal? I never thought I'd wish we'd go back to cordial conversation over our newfound friendship, but this... this is confusing. Complicated. And probably doomed from the start.

He's my boss and I can't do anything that puts me at risk of losing my job...even if that thing I do is him. Wait—let me rephrase that.

Especially him.

∾

SOMEWHERE BETWEEN ELEVEN AND MIDNIGHT, I FELL ASLEEP. THE bed was so comfy and warm I slept soundly, much more so than I thought I would. I'm a side sleeper, and like to hold onto my pillow when I sleep. Alex sleeps on his stomach, with one hand tucked under his pillow. He kept the sweatpants on and must have gotten hot in the middle of the night and kicked the blankets off. I have most of them wrapped around me, and carefully disentangle myself and toss the fluffy comforter over Alex.

Bright sunlight is streaming through the window, and I take a minute to look at Alex. He's sleeping, completely relaxed, but I'm still able to admire his back and shoulder muscles. He has a tattoo between his shoulder blades, and another over his ribs. I never would have guessed that about him, and I want to reach out and trace the Chinese letters going down his ribcage.

His breathing is slow and rhythmic, and I can't help but imagine what it would be like to wake up next to him every day— after a night of passionate love making, that is. I'm sure he lives somewhere big and fancy, either a penthouse in the downtown area or one of those massive houses on North Orchard Street in Lincoln Park.

My phone rings, and I scramble to answer it before it wakes Alex. It's the girls calling from Dad's phone, wanting to Face-Time. I look at Alex and back at my phone. I'm waisting precious time, and I don't think I can get up and run out of the room before missing their call.

Angling my body away from Alex, I answer and connect to FaceTime.

"Mommy!" they both cheer. Dad is holding the phone up with both girls on his lap.

"Hey, babies," I say quietly. "How was your night?"

"Good," Penny answers. "We're going to the zoo!"

"That'll be fun! What animal do you want to see the most."

"Tigers," they both cry out.

"Have Papa take lots of pictures for me."

"Why are you whispering?" Violet asks. Shoot. I am. I bring the phone closer to my face. It's the most unflattering angle, but the girls are still young enough to think Mom is the prettiest person in the world so they can deal with looking up my nostrils for the time being.

"The other people in the house are still sleeping. It's a small house."

"Did we wake you?" Dad asks. "These two got up early all excited for the zoo."

"You made a rookie mistake there, Papa," I laugh. "I don't tell them before we have someone fun planned."

"Oh, I can't keep anything from these two. I'll let you go. Do you have meetings all day?"

"Umm…" I flick my eyes to Alex. "Something like that."

"We just want to tell you we love you and we miss you," Penny tells me. "And we hope you're having fun, but not too much fun without us."

"I'll have just the right amount of fun." I smile. "I'd have more fun if you were here of course. I love you girls."

"Love you too, Mommy! Bye!"

I end the call and set my phone back on the nightstand before flopping down onto the mattress again. I pull the blankets up and Alex rolls over, kicking the blankets off again. He's on his back now, with one arm out slightly and his fingers brushing against my side. The outline of his cock is visible through his sweatpants, and good Lord, that thing is big. It's not hard, and I'm almost a little disappointed not to see it in all its glory, even though it would do me no good.

I read an online article that said men can get over twenty boners per night. I have no idea if it's true, but now that I'm thinking about it...last night could have been very awkward indeed.

Pulling the blankets back up around me, I close my eyes and listen to Kate moving around the little kitchen. People are out on the lake already, and talking and laughter float on the air and in through the open window.

We're supposed to spend the first part of the day lounging around the beach while the guys go fishing. It seems a bit old fashioned in a sense, to not even ask if any of us want to go out on the fishing boat, but I like the beach too much to get offended. I'm so overdue for a nice summer glow too. I'll make up for lost time today, and being half Mexican, I tan up nice and fast. *Thanks, Mom.*

"Hey," Alex says, voice thick with sleep. He stretches his arms out and slowly sits up. "Did you sleep all right?"

"I did. You?"

"I sat up watching you sleep like a stalker, and perfected my plan on the best way to murder you and dispose of your body."

"What is the best way to murder me?"

"Strategically tripping you so you skin your knee, and then having your cut get infected with that flesh-eating bacteria from the lake I keep hearing about on the news. No one will suspect I was behind it."

"That stuff only lives in brackish water."

"You do know a lot of useless information."

"I was worried about taking the girls in Lake Michigan so I

205

looked it up. You'll get a million other diseases from the lake, but not the fleshing-eating one."

Alex laughs and yawns, turning away and stretching again. "I'm still tired."

"Go back to sleep."

"Nah, I don't sleep in very well."

"How can you not sleep in well?"

He shrugs. "My mind doesn't let me fall back asleep. I start thinking of everything I have to do and get anxious to start the day." I'm seeing a little bit of the real Alex again, the one that's vulnerable and real.

"I get that. Sometimes I'm the opposite. I sleep so I don't have to think about anything."

"I wish I could be like that." His eyes fall shut for another few seconds and then he gets up. "I'm going to jump in the shower."

Nodding, I watch him get up, grab his stuff from his suitcase, and go into the bathroom. Since I showered last night, I just need to get dressed. I wait until the water turns on to get out of bed. I give him a few more seconds, making sure he's actually in the shower, before I strip down out of my PJs and put my bikini on. It's white with little yellow lemons printed all over it. I never thought I'd squeeze myself into a two piece after having children, and when I went bathing suit shopping two years ago, I was feeling so, so low about my physical appearance.

Then I saw this on clearance and felt like Mom was giving me a sign. She was all about body positivity and would sit me down if she were still alive and give me a lecture about how I should be proud of my c-section scar, how I should love the fact that I have a little extra fat on my hips now, and how I should love the stretch marks on my breasts I got from breastfeeding.

I pull on the bottoms and then the top, getting dressed quickly in case Alex comes out of the shower in record time. Once I'm dressed, I look at myself in the mirror. It's so easy to stare at yourself and pick out features you hate.

I want a flatter stomach. A bigger gap between my thighs. No hyper-pigmentation on my face. My ass has gotten bigger just over the last few years, and the muscle definition I had in my thighs back from my cross-country days is long gone.

Mom would tell me that I'd need to validate two things that I do like for every one thing I don't. Taking a breath, I scan my eyes over my body in the mirror and try to find something to compliment myself on.

"You have nice boobs," I whisper. They're not quiet as perky a they were pre-children, but breastfeeding was kind to me and I've even been asked before if these babies are fake.

"And your hair is pretty."

I nod at my reflection and bring my hands down to the bikini bottoms. They're high waisted and cover up both the scar and that little pouch of fat I don't think I'll ever be able to get rid of, even if I started dieting and exercising again.

Going through my suitcase, I find a black sundress with multicolored flowers printed all over it. I pull it over my head and then sit on the foot of the bed to brush my hair.

The bathroom door opens and steam billows out, followed by Alex...who's only wearing a towel. It's wrapped dangerously low around his waist and I've never wished for telekinetic powers more in my life.

There are certain things you want to stare at but shouldn't. The sun, for instance, is one of them. Accidents are another. And your boss, half naked, dripping wet from the shower, is a third. A bead of water rolls down his muscular chest, and my eyes latch to it, following it as it descends past his pecs and down to his abs.

"I forgot my clothes," he says apologetically and I shake myself.

"Yeah...I can see that."

He gives me a cheeky grin, grabs his clothes from his suitcase, and I'm left wondering if he did it on purpose. I brush out the tangles from my thick hair and grab my hair straightener from my bag. Alex is dressed and out of the bathroom by then, and I go in to straighten my hair and put just enough make up on to feel put together.

Alex isn't in the bedroom anymore when I'm done, and I quickly straighten up my stuff, pack up a beach bag, pull the blankets up on the bed, and go downstairs.

"Morning," Kate says, pouring herself a cup of coffee. "Ready for the beach today?"

"I am so ready. I don't remember the last time I just sat on a beach and relaxed. Taking kids to the beach is the opposite of relaxing."

"I know! And you have two. I'm terrified to even take my eyes off of Heather. The undertow in Lake Michigan kills so many people every year."

"I make my girls wear a floaty. They hate it, but it's my rule. If they want to be in the water, they got to put the floaties on."

"That's my rule too. And it's the full DNR approved life vest and everything when we're out on the boat. The water can get choppy."

Kate gets another mug down for me and I fill it up with coffee and creamer.

"Grab your stuff and we'll walk over to the house. Lynn is making breakfast and then we go down to the shore while the guys head out. Leo and Alex already headed over there, but don't worry, you'll still get to kiss your man goodbye."

"What's Lynn's story?" I ask, hoping to deflect the fact that I'm *not* kissing Alex, and hook my beach bag over my shoulder. Kate leads the way outside.

"Her husband cheated on her—with a man—and she walked in on them. She's been really depressed, which is honestly part of the reason why we came up here this weekend. She didn't have the slightest idea he was gay and that is hitting her harder than the fact he cheated."

"That would be hard to accept. I mean, you think you know someone…"

"Right? They were married for eight years."

"Oh, wow. How awful." I can't wait to tell Alex the backstory I came up with for Lynn was more or less right though. I sip my coffee as we walk along the path that leads to the big house.

Leo, Jerry, some guy I don't know, and Alex are all on the front porch. Alex turns, eyes locking with mine, and smiles.

"God, I miss the beginning stages of a relationship," Kate says, slipping her arm through mine. "The way you two look at each other…ugh. Those are some of the best days! You can't keep your hands off each other and you haven't found a million little things that annoy the shit out of you. Right now, you don't care how they eat crackers, but someday, you will."

I laugh, smiling back at Alex. "How does he look at me?" I ask quietly, as we're coming close enough for him to hear me.

"Like you're the only woman in the world that matters."

If this were real, my heart would skip a beat. I'd beam. Probably make that stupid squealing noise and maybe even jump up and down.

But it's not real…and I have to make sure I remember that.

CHAPTER 25

ALEX

I have blood all over my shirt.

It's not mine, and this time, I wasn't responsible for the cause of the bleeding. Keith, Jerry's brother who owns the boat we went out fishing on, caught a fishing hook on his arm and thought yanking it out would be a good idea. It might have been, if it hadn't torn a large chunk of his skin out with it.

Leo can't stand the sight of blood, and Jerry was the only other one who knew how to drive the boat, which left me holding towels around the wound to try and stop the bleeding.

Jerry took his brother to the hospital for stitches, and Leo and I just got back to the cottage to change and shower. The dock is a ways down the lake from the beach were Harper is, and I'm feeling rather anxious to get to her.

I had a chance to talk with Jerry, and he's coming back on full time with us as our client. He's staying in Vermont until Tuesday, but will be in the office Wednesday for a meeting.

Mission accomplished.

Which means now until the end of the trip, I can spend all my time with Harper. *Fuck*, she's so damn amazing.

I pull the bloody shirt over my head, ball it up, and toss it in the trash. I strip out of the rest of my clothes and get in the shower, washing away the smell of lake water and cigars. I don't smoke. Never have, never will, not even when clients like Jerry offer me expensive cigars.

I've invested a lot of time and energy into working out and being healthy. I'm not going to poison my body by smoking. No, I'd rather poison it by drinking and doing the occasional recreational drugs instead.

My mind goes to Harper again, to her big, beautiful tits. Her skin was still red from the hot shower and would have been so warm to the touch. My cock starts to get hard thinking about her.

She was in bed, right fucking next to me last night, and we didn't touch. I wanted so bad to move that pillow and wrap my arms around her. To bring her against my body and kiss her like she's never been kissed before.

My fingers wrap around my shaft, and I start jerking myself off, needing a release. I rest one hand against the shower wall and lean into the water.

I don't believe in love.

Harper is a hopeless romantic.

I think all relationships will eventually fall apart.

Harper wants something that will stand the test of time.

I can't say she's unobtainable, yet there's something about her that makes her forbidden. Our different views on love, perhaps? The way she's a good mom and had a great relationship with her parents?

I move my hand faster, hearing her voice echo in my mind. She's so fucking hot and this whole pretending we're together yet not actually fucking thing is messing with my head. If we slept together tonight, I'd be able to move on by Monday, though I know that's not how Harper operates. She told me more than once she's not a one-night stand kind of woman, which is a shame. We'd have one hell of a good time together, I know it.

I let out a quiet moan as I come. The release isn't as satisfying as I thought it would be. I'm not ready to admit it to myself, but it's there in the back of my mind, telling me I want something more than a one-and-done night with Harper.

But in the end, it doesn't even matter. Even if I was the man Harper wants, I don't think I'm enough to be the one she needs.

∾

"HOW WAS FISHING?" HARPER WALKS INTO THE COTTAGE ABOUT AN hour after Leo and I got back from the botched fishing trip. She didn't put her dress back on over her bikini and her skin is tanned and glistening from oil. I want to run my hands up and down her, part her thighs and step in between. "Did you catch anything?"

My cock starts to harden and I shift my weight on the couch. "Possibly a blood born pathogen."

"What?" Harper sets her beach bag on the ground and steps out of her flip flops.

"Keith cut himself bad enough to have to go to the hospital."

"Oh my god! Is he okay?"

"He will be after he's stitched up. How was the beach?"

"So relaxing." She reaches up and pinches the little yellow lemon charm between her fingers. "I read several chapters of my book and then took a nap. Sounds lame, but I swear I've been perpetually tired since my kids have been born."

"I can only imagine."

"We need to leave in less than an hour," she starts and heads toward the stairs. "I'm going to shower and get ready. I am so excited for wine." She flashes a big smile and goes up the stairs, tits bouncing with each step.

God, she's gorgeous.

"Go on, go shower with her," Leo tells me. We were watching

The Office together while we waited for the girls to come back. "You got that horn-dog look in your eyes."

Fuck. I do. "I'll wait until tonight," I blurt, mind already going to Harper stripping down and getting wet in the shower.

"Ahh, good thinking. Wait until after she's all liquored up. That's the only time Kate gives me blowjobs anymore."

Fuck. Me. The thought of Harper dropping to her knees, looking up at me deviously as she undoes my pants...my cock jumps, hardening fast and pressing against the zipper of my jeans.

A second later, Kate comes in, she's on the phone and sounds annoyed. I grab a pillow and put it over my lap. Clenching my thighs to try and kill the boner, I stare straight ahead at the TV.

"Talk to your father," Kate says into the phone and then thrusts it in Leo's face. He takes it and gets up, apparently talking to their daughter. Kate huffs the whole way up the stairs.

I watch two more episodes before Harper comes back downstairs. This time I can't help but stare with my mouth hanging wide open. Her hair is curled, she has darker eye makeup than usual, and she's wearing an off the shoulder red dress.

"Wow. You look amazing."

"Thanks." She blushes. "I feel fancy."

"You look fancy." I stand from the couch and go around to her. "Are you ready?"

Harper looks into the living room, realizing everyone else is there waiting for her. Kate came down the stairs maybe five minutes ago, so she has nothing to feel bad about.

"I am."

I hold out my hand for her to take, and we all go over to the lake house to ride in the Escalade with Lynn. It's about half an hour drive to the vineyard, and Harper's eyes are wide when we get out.

"It's so pretty here," she says to herself. "Can you imagine this place in the fall? All those trees would look amazing."

"It would." I take her arm again, helping her walk across the gravel driveway. She's wearing heels tonight, but doesn't seem to have an issue walking on the uneven ground in them.

We get seated for our tasting first, and then will move to a different part of the winery for dinner. The tasting is personalized, and we each get to pick out six different types of wine to have brought to us in a flight.

"The closest I've ever come a wine tasting was the night Tessa went a little crazy on the cheap wine from Trader Joe's," Harper whispers to me. "I think she opened like six or seven bottles. I was pregnant at the time, so I just smelled them and watched her drink. And then held her hair back as she puked it up." She looks at the wine menu. "Needless to say, I'm not fancy. I have no idea what to try."

"Do you like sweet or dry wine?"

"Sweet, but not so sweet I feel like I'm drinking sugar water."

"Do you prefer white or red?"

She shakes her head. "I don't even know the difference. Red is dry, right?"

"It can be." I look over my own menu and point out a few to Harper that she might like. I'm no expert, but we represent several wineries and I've made myself familiar with their products. For marketing research, that is.

We write down our selections and only a few minutes later, the wine is brought out. Harper picks up a glass of red wine and brings it to her lips. I'm so wound up that everything she does is extremely sexy, and right now watching her part her lips and take a sip of wine is borderline erotic.

Until she gags, that is.

"Not good." She shudders. "That one is not good." Making a face, she exhales and quickly finishes the little bit left in her glass.

"You know you don't have to finish it if you don't like it, right?"

She chugs her water. "I know, but it seems wasteful. This stuff is like fifty dollars a glass, which I do no understand. I've liked five dollar bottles of pink moscato better than this."

I got the same wine that Harper didn't like, and find it rather enjoyable. It's Merlot, and is dry. We go through the rest of our samples, and Harper's favorite it a red table wine. She orders a glass of it, and we go outside to look at the vineyard while we wait for our table to open up.

"I know I keep saying it," she starts, pace slowing down. "But this place is so pretty!" She holds out her hands and accidentally sloshes some of the wine out of her glass. "Oh shit." She brings her hand to her face and licks the drips of wine from her skin. Tingles rush through me as I watch her tongue make contact with her skin.

Fuck. Me.

"Easy there, drunky," I tease.

"I'm not drunk," she says pointedly and just happens to misstep, sloshing more wine down her hand. She laughs and takes a big drink to keep the glass from spilling again.

"I think you are." I playfully nudge her.

"I'm not. I'm so sober, I could do math right now."

"Math?" I laugh.

"Yeah, math. Drunk people can't do math. I promise."

"Well…if you promise. What's fifty-four plus fifty-four?"

"That's easy." She makes a face and closes her eyes as she thinks. "Just add the fours…and then…" she mumbles to herself. "One-oh-four."

"You're sure about that?"

"Fuck. I mean one-oh-eight. Because two fours is eight." She shakes her head, tossing her hair back behind her shoulders. "Okay. I'm feeling this wine and I don't know why we didn't start the day here because I'm feeling pretty good right now."

"Light weight."

"We had six glasses of wine back there!"

"They were samples," I laugh. "Six glasses of wine would have me on the floor."

"Oh, I'd be passed out for sure. And then waking up in my vomit, most likely. You know I've never drank to the point of throwing up before."

"Really? Not even in college?"

She shakes her head and takes another drink. "I got knocked up before I turned twenty-one and I'm a rule follower."

"I'm not."

"I know." She looks up at me and I can see it in her eyes that she's tipsy. "But it's worked out well for you."

I drop my gaze, admiring her breasts, but also noticing that lemon necklace again.

"I have to ask, what's with the lemon charm?"

She reaches up to touch it. "My mom gave it to me. You know that lemon saying, right?"

"There's a saying about lemons?"

Harper stops walking to look at me incredulously. "You don't know the lemon saying?"

"Sorry?"

She dramatically rolls her eyes. "When life gives you lemons, make lemonade. Or as Mom said, when life gives you lemons, make lemonade. And don't forget the vodka." Harper takes another drink of her wine. "I didn't understand the vodka part until I was older. But sometimes you need a little something extra. Lemons are sour and I'm talking metaphorically but the vodka isn't. It's literal."

I put my arm around her shoulders, not getting what she just said. Maybe she's a little past tipsy and actually drunk. I'll make sure to take care of her if she is. "Sure."

"I've been given lots of lemons over the last few years. I thought you were one."

"You thought I was a lemon?"

She nods. "Yep. A really super sour one."

"Did you turn me into lemonade?" I ask carefully. "Or is this one of those *I don't want to know the answer to it* kind of questions."

"I thought I did, but now I think you did it."

"I'm not following."

"Working for you was a lemon. But the lemonade can be a perspective sometimes too." Her words slur a little. Yep, she's drunk. I protectively pull her a little closer to me. "I'm lucky to have this job. It pays more and has benefits and maybe that lemonade has to…has to…ferment a while, it'll be worth it."

I'm reminded how different our lives are again. How she most likely struggles as a single mom to make ends meet. I've never once felt guilty for what I have, but right now I kind of do. Harper isn't any less of a hard worker than I am.

Harper's phone rings, and she gives me her glass of wine to hold while she gets her phone from her purse.

"It's Kate," she tells me before she answers. "Hey!" she says into the phone. "Somewhere outside. Okay. We'll head in." She ends the call and puts her phone back in her purse. "The table is ready."

"Good. I'm starving."

"Me too." She takes the wine back and hooks her other arm through mine. We walk back in silence, and Harper stops right before we go inside. "Alex?"

"Yeah?"

She angles her body toward mine and it's all I can do not to reach out and kiss her right now.

"Thanks for not judging me. Even before this weekend, I didn't feel like you did."

"You say that like it's a surprise."

She shrugs and some color rushes to her cheeks. "Men like you can be rather judgey…especially toward women in the work place."

"I don't care what's between someone's legs as long as they're doing a good job."

"As long as they're not jerking it in the break room though, right?" She make a face and we both laugh. "But in all seriousness, that's...that's...I want to say admirable, but really, that's just how it should be."

"No one has called me admirable before, so I'm going to go with that one."

She laughs again and takes another sip of wine. "All right. I'll let it slide. Just this time though."

I put my arm around her again, and my hand slides down her back and settles on the curve of her hip. Heat rushes through me, and I feel that tug on my heart again.

All at once, I find myself wanting to do better. *Be* better. I don't want to be anything like my father, and I've let the fear of getting hurt close off my heart. It's easier to live a life like I do now. Alone, but safe. Surviving, but not really living.

Harper has been dished her fair share of what she calls lemons. And yet she's so full of life, so eager to smile and find the good around her. It's inspiring, and no one has made me feel this way before.

I press my fingers into Harper's side heart racing. What the hell are you doing to me, Harper?

CHAPTER 26

HARPER

"I think I'm still drunk." I take Alex's outstretched hand and get out of the SUV. "How much wine did I have? Like seven glasses?"

"You had two," he says with a laugh, guiding me toward the cottage. "And a half if you want to count those samples. You are such a lightweight."

"I don't drink that often," I remind him. "Though you won't think so by how much I've drank this weekend."

"You get a pass. Would you believe me if I said I don't drink that much?"

I raise my eyebrows. "You have a bottle of Scotch in your office. Or I think it's Scotch. That's what rich, white guys drink, right?"

"I'm not that predictable, am I?"

"Is it Scotch?"

"It is," he admits. "But truthfully, I think it tastes like shit. But it was expensive shit, so I kept it."

"Hey, lovebirds," Kate calls. "Can you pull yourselves apart for another hour or so? I want to be basic and put on a flannel shirt, drink pumpkin spice coffee, and have a bonfire."

"It's August," Leo counters, shaking his head. "Is pumpkin spice even available yet?"

"Technically, Disney started their Halloween parties over a week ago, so we can too," I say, giving Kate a nod. "And it feels like fall here. It's hot as balls in Chicago."

"I guess I'll go start a fire then." Leo gives Kate a kiss and walks around the porch to get firewood. Alex goes with him, and Kate and I go inside to change out of our dresses.

"You guys are such couple goals," Kate tells me, and her words are sobering. "Seriously, you're so cute."

"Thanks." I hate lying to her.

"When do you think you're going to introduce him to your kids?"

I lose my balance trying to get my shoes unbuckled and slump to the ground. I'm drunk, but not drunk enough to blurt the truth. "I, um, I don't know. I don't really know how to handle any of it," I admit. "They don't know much about their dad—hell, neither do I—but all I've said to them about him is that he had to go away. I know I'll have to explain it all one day."

"Oh, hun, that's a tough situation. And I don't know what to do either. Maybe just go with your gut?"

I nod, thinking about this whole situation and feeling more and more like I'm going to throw up. I hate lying in general, hate lying to my friend even more, and hate it most when it's confusing the hell out of me.

Alex is my boss.

Not my boyfriend.

We get along. Make each other laugh. I genuinely believe he enjoys my company…but if we weren't pretending, we wouldn't be together at all.

I have kids, and though Alex has a good relationship with his nephew, he doesn't seem like he wants children of his own. Dating is hard enough, dating when you're a single parent is even harder. I need to find someone who likes me, and who I like and who's compatible with the girls.

If I hadn't had that second glass of wine after I finished my salad, I'd probably be having an anxiety flare up right about now. My girls are wonderful, and anyone would be lucky to have them in their lives. Am I going to find someone who thinks so too? Whoever dates me won't only be dating me in a sense, but will have to be dating all of us. Who won't take one look at me, decide I have too much baggage and toss us to the curb?

I finally get both shoes off. I hurry up the stairs, pull my dress off, and put on leggings, tall socks, a long-sleeve shirt, and a sweater. Kate grabs two blankets from the hall closet and we go outside and down to the shore.

Alex and Leo are still trying to light the fire. Kate moves in, rearranges the stack of firewood inside the fire pit, and gets it started in under five minutes.

"Impressive," I tell her, and sit down in the sand. Alex takes a spot next to me. He's not wearing a jacket and is probably cold. I drape the blanket around both our shoulders.

Lynn comes down from the house with stuff to make s'mores. We talk and laugh as we roast our marshmallows. My phone rings, and I walk along the shore looking for the best area with service so I can talk to my girls. They had a fun day at the zoo but are looking forward to me coming home tomorrow.

Me too, kids. Me too.

I go back to the fire and take my spot next to Alex. He wraps the blanket over me and lets his hand linger on my shoulder a moment too long. His touch, gentle yet firm, feels so fucking good. Everyone is still talking, and Alex gets along so well with Kate and Leo it almost feels like we've been friends for much longer than the weekend.

I'm tired, and around midnight, can barely keep my eyes open anymore. My head falls to the side, resting on Alex's shoulder.

"Harper?" he asks quietly. "Are you awake?"

"No," I grumble.

"Let me get you to bed."

"No, I'm fine. I'll stay out with everyone else."

"I'm tired too," Lynn says. "I've been getting up at five to run before work. Eight PM bedtimes are normally my jam. It's after that and I am tired," she laughs.

Alex pulls me onto my feet and wraps the blankets the blanket around my shoulders. "You made it past midnight this time, which basically makes you a party animal."

I laugh. "I used to be able to stay up until two and then get up at seven, even after I had the twins. I feel old."

"Oh shut it," Kate laughs. "You're the youngest one here."

"How old are you?" Leo asks.

"Twenty-five," I tell him.

"If you're old then I'm ancient."

"You said it, not me."

"See." Kate gently smacks her hand against Leo's chest. "We're way too old to have another kid."

I tug the blanket around myself, chilled to be away from Alex. "You want another?"

"He thinks we should have one."

"That doesn't answer the question," Lynn points out. "Do you *want* another?"

"No," Kate says with no hesitation. "It was a chore to get pregnant the first time around. And now she's six and getting independent. The infant stage was hard. The toddler stage was harder. I don't know how you did it on your own, Harper."

"Well, my dad helped a lot, and my best friend was amazing."

"You got help now," Leo says, nodding at Alex. "And maybe you two will have another, huh?"

"Stop it," Kate hushes, smacking Leo for real this time. "They just started dating. They're not thinking about that."

"Well you never know."

Man, I feel uncomfortable. Putting a baby in me is the *last* thing Alex is thinking about, I can guaran-damn-tee that.

"Would you have another?" Kate asks.

I nod. "I think so. I mean, with the right person. The chance of having twins again is slim to none, and then I wouldn't be alone. Baby number three would feel like a breeze. Or so I say now." I turn my head and look at Alex. He's staring at the ground with a weird expression. Is he sad? Mad? A little bit of both?

Tightening the blanket around me, I shake off the feeling like I said something wrong. I didn't, and it's true. I would love to get married and have another baby with my husband. To plan for it, to even feel that disappointment in a negative pregnancy test—only once or twice, that is.

We all go inside to get ready for bed. I change, wash my face, and brush my teeth. Alex goes into the bathroom next, and Kate walks by, peaking into the room. She waves me out into the hall.

"Hey, sorry of Leo made you guys uncomfortable. He can be a real idiot sometimes."

"Nah, it's fine. I just, uh, don't think Alex wants kids."

"But you already have kids."

"We're just not that, um, serious." If I can start to back pedal now, lying about us breaking up later won't come so out of the blue. "I mean, he's a great guy, super hot, but I think his job is his priority and family is mine. There's nothing wrong with that, ya know. But I want to be realistic."

"Wow, you're so mature. You know for being five years younger than me," she adds with a kind smile. "Are you sure you're okay with that though? I bought ten bottles of wine—no joke—from the vineyard. We can crack one open and talk about feelings or some shit. Sorry. I haven't had a close girlfriend in a while."

I want to crash tonight and enjoy my last night with this version of Alex. I have no idea how things will be once we get back to real life, and I kind of don't want this to end. A story of us is unfolding in my mind, even when I know I'm setting myself up for disappointment.

Getting back into bed with him is a bad, idea. A terrible idea. An idea that will most likely feel amazing and have me screaming his name.

But I can't have sex with Alex.

"Yeah, that sounds nice, actually. I'll let Alex know."

"Great! I'll go open the wine."

I go into the bedroom, finding Alex sitting on the edge of the bed. He looks down when I step in. One of the lamps on the nightstand is still on, spilling a golden glow over Alex's handsome face. He's shirtless and wearing those sweatpants again.

Man, I wish this could be real.

"You really think work is my first priority?" he asks, looking hurt.

Oh shit, he heard? Though I didn't say anything I regret. I have to plant the seed that things aren't perfect between us and he knows it. Hell, it was his idea to tell Kate that we broke up so I can stop living this lie.

"I, um, guess so. Sorry if my assumption was wrong. I shouldn't make assumptions at all."

"You are wrong," he snaps and then lets out a sigh, eyes falling shut. "Sorry...I...I don't want it to be my priority. That's all my father cared about and I swore I'd never be like him."

"Then don't. You can always change thing." I offer a small smile, pulling my lips over my teeth. "Kate...she, um...she wants to have some girl talk. Do you mind?"

"Why would I?"

"Oh, right. Okay. I don't think we'll be up late. One more glass of wine and I'll pass out."

"Probably."

I grab my phone from the nightstand and go downstairs. Kate is struggling with the handheld corkscrew, saying she has an electric wine opener at home. I take a crack at it and end up splitting the cork. After searching the internet on how to remedy this, we finally get the bottle open and pour two glasses. We have to pick bits of the cork out, but this wine is good regardless.

"I didn't know you had trouble getting pregnant," I start, sitting on the couch and turning on the TV.

She nods. "It was a nightmare. Six miscarriages, two failed rounds of IVF, and then four months on bedrest."

"Oh wow, that sounds awful."

She shrugs. "But now we have Heather, and our sweet miracle baby is turning into a royal brat."

I laugh. "This is the age where things start to change, isn't it? I'm not ready for that." My eyes get a little misty. "I've worked so much of their childhood away."

"Honey." Kate's hand lands on mine. "They'll thank you for it one day, I'm sure."

"I hope so." I take a big drink of wine. "I might let them play hooky with me one day next week. Since I got a bonus for—" Shit. I almost gave things away. "I got a bonus at work and have a little extra spending money."

"A girls day does sound nice."

"It really does, and there won't be too many beach days left." I take another drink of wine and feel it start to effect me already. We stay up talking for a bit longer, and then are both too tired to stay up any later. I really am a party animal.

Alex is sleeping when I get into the room. I creep in, careful not to wake him, and crawl under the covers. In his sleep, he reaches out, fingers gracing my skin.

I let my eyes fall shut, enjoying the slight touch.

"Thank you," I whisper to him. "For standing up for me and for taking me on this trip. The money will help so much, and... and I had a nice time with you."

He moves again, and for a second I think he's awake. His breathing is slow, letting me know he's still sleeping. He kicks the blankets off the both of us. I quietly laugh and pull them back up, careful not to cover him up or else he'll kick them off again.

Rolling over, he moves closer and snakes his arm around me. My heart flutters and I don't know what to do. Chances are he has no idea what he's doing or is so used to having someone in his bed this is second nature to him.

I should move out of his embrace and put that pillow back between us. But it's been so long since I've had anyone hold me, and dammit...I'm really starting to fall for him.

"MOTHERFUCKER."

I blink my eyes open and roll over. Alex is sitting up, staring down at his phone.

"You okay?" I ask groggily, thinking back to last night and how I fell asleep with his arm around me. Was he still holding me when he woke?

He angrily types something on his phone. "I will be."

"What's going on?"

"A client just posted this." He shows me his phone, showing a screen shot of a fat-shaming Facebook post.

"Ouch."

"Yeah. And you know what his company makes?" he asks and I shake my head. "Women's clothes."

"Double ouch. Is this going to cost them customers?"

"For sure." He rubs his forehead and lets out a sigh. "It's nothing we can't handle though, but someone needs to take this asshole's phone away. He's responding to people calling him out." He scrolls through some of the comments. "Oh for fuck's sake, now he's bringing up politics. I need to make a phone call."

I run my hand through my messy hair and look outside. It has to be early judging by the muted sunlight filtering through the open window.

"Do you ever feel bad representing people like that?"

"Assholes?" He flicks his eyes from his phone to me. "Not really. I'm providing a service, not supporting or spreading his beliefs."

"Good point," I say and wonder what I would do if I were presented that situation. I'd like to believe I couldn't do business with someone who openly bullies anyone, but then again, turning down that type of money would be silly. We could get out of the south side with that kind of cash.

Alex gets up and goes downstairs to make a phone call. I unlock my phone and go online, checking my social media accounts. Alex and I made a point not to take any pictures together, but Kate got a few at the vineyard yesterday. I'd had way too much to drink to think about it, but right now, seeing her tag me on Instagram, I get a little panicky.

There's photo evidence that Alex and I faked a relationship. I don't want to lose the friend I just made, and more importantly, I don't want to hurt her feelings. I lied right to her face multiple times.

This was a mistake and I shouldn't have come here. Nothing good comes from lies, and karma is already delivering.

I've caught feelings.

Though the fake breakup will seem more genuine now.

"Hey," Alex comes back up the stairs. "I'm going to have to take an earlier flight home so I can deal with this mess. Do you want to stick with your original ticket? I'll have someone pick you up from the airport and take you to your house. You're on the same flight as Kate and Leo." He looks down at his phone. "I don't think I can get two tickets for an earlier flight anyway. It looks like there's only one and it's economy."

"Oh, um, sure. I don't mind. Do whatcha gotta do," I say with a cheesy smile and then mentally shake my head at myself. "Can I help? I mean…I am your assistant."

"Yes, once we get to the office."

"Tonight?"

He sees the horror on my face and opens his mouth to say something but hesitates. "No, not tonight. The morning. Monday morning. We'll have to set up a press conference and do as much damage control as we can. Things like this tend to blow over from the public eye, but if vendors stop buying..." He trails off, not needing to explain. If vendors stop buying, the company will be no more and won't pay Alex to handle the PR.

"Right. Well, if I can do anything tonight, just let me know. I can schedule meetings and make phone calls at home."

He nods. "I will."

"There was only one ticket for an earlier flight?" I ask, feeling anxious to just get home and see my girls.

He looks back at his phone. "There's one for a flight that leaves in two hours. Fuck, I don't think I'll make it." He looks at his open suitcase.

"Go," I tell him. "I'll pack up your stuff and will bring it to you in the morning."

"I can't ask you to do that."

"You're not asking. And unless you're afraid I'm going to find your diary or something, packing your stuff will be easy. You're very neat."

"It's a habit." He looks into my eyes and his gaze sears right through me. "Thank you, Harper."

"You're welcome. Now go save the day and stop that fat-shaming, woman-hating butt-crust of a man from spreading hate on the internet."

"I will." His gaze lingers a moment longer before he hurries into the room, getting dressed and taking only what the needs for the plane ride back to Chicago.

I miss him the moment he's gone.

CHAPTER 27

"Mommy, you're squishing me." Penny tries to squirm out of my arms. I have one wrapped around her and another around Violet.

"I just missed you both so much," I say, turning my head to give them both kisses. "I need to hug you again."

"You hugged us so much last night," Violet says dramatically. Her little arms are still wrapped around me though.

"I know, but I'm your mom and I can hug you as much as I want." It felt so good to be reunited, even though I was gone for a short weekend trip. I fell asleep reading to them in their bed, and when I woke up a few hours later, I was so comfy I decided that's where I was sleeping that night.

I showered, brushed my teeth, and put on PJs and then got back into bed with them, holding them both close. It's Monday morning now and we're getting ready to load into the car and drive to school. My heart is hurting again at the thought of not being able to see them until nearly 5:30 tonight.

But I'm also excited to see Alex...and a little nervous if I'm being honest. I don't want things to be awkward, or worse, go back to how they were before where our relationship was strictly business. I'm professional, and know we can't go hiding that creepy doll I brought home in my suitcase around the office. But I hope things are at least friendly.

The sink was still full of dishes from Friday morning when I got home yesterday. I smelled them as soon as we walked in, and my solution was to fill up one side of the sink and let them soak in soapy water. It got rid of the smell and will made them easier to wash, at least.

I was behind on laundry and didn't remember the last time I vacuumed the apartment, let alone dusted. Spending a weekend at such a nice house and then coming back here makes me want out that much more. The girls deserve it.

We don't need anything big or fancy. Just safer, and having carpet that wasn't stained from past occupants would be nice. I cleaned like a mad woman while the girls were taking a shower and the apartment looks pretty damn good if I do say so myself. It'll last a whole day, but hey, we'll enjoy it while we can.

"Oh shit, I mean shoot," I blurt when I look at the time. "We gotta go."

I throw my purse over my shoulder, dig my keys out, and usher the girls into the hall.

"Hey, Harper."

I jump, not seeing Max standing in the hall. "Oh, Max, hi." I lock the apartment door and keep my keys in my hand. That guy gives me the serious creeps. I make the girls go in front of me, putting myself between them and Max.

"Were you gone this weekend? I didn't see you coming or going.

"Um, yeah. I was." Yeah...serious, *serious* creeps.

"Where'd you go?"

"I went and visited my baby daddy in jail. He's getting out tomorrow. We gotta go. The girls have school." I grab Violet's hand. "Hold your sister's hand," I whisper to Penny. "And don't let go."

Max follows us down the stairs, and my heart is back in my throat by the time we get out and into the car. I practically shove the girls inside and then jump into the driver's seat, locking the doors the second I'm inside. I don't want to freak the girls out. They already think Max is a creepy motherfucker. Luckily, they've never said it exactly like that, but they've told me he scares them.

"Is our daddy really in jail?" Penny clicks her seatbelt into place.

Shit, they were paying attention.

"No, Mommy told a lie."

"Lying is bad," Violet says with so much sass I'm not sure if I should scold her or praise her.

"It is, but there are times when it's okay." Like when a stalker follows you and your children around. Was he waiting outside the apartment door? I feel so violated.

"Is Daddy coming back?" Penny asks.

"I, um, don't know," I tell her, looking at her in the rearview mirror.

"If Daddy came back would you marry him?"

"No," I say honestly.

"Why not?" Violet asks.

"Because we don't...we...it's been a while since we've seen each other." I can't tell them I don't actually know their father. We spent one magical night together, but that's it.

"Would he be your boyfriend?"

"Well," I start and watch it all play out in my mind. It would be wonderful to have us all be together like one big happy family. "I'd go on a date with him and see where it goes from there."

"When will Daddy come back?"

Their questions kill me, and I know there's no way to actually convince them that it's not their fault their father isn't in the picture. Telling them he doesn't know about them might be too confusing, or might hurt their feelings even more. I don't know how to go about explaining these things, and everyone on the internet has a different opinion on how to handle a situation like this.

I don't want to emotionally scar the girls, of course, and I don't want to try to explain the truth and have them relay it to others at school, get some details mixed up, and have them treated differently because we're so far from the typical Briar Prep family.

"I really don't know." I turn around and look at them both. "But we don't need him. You got me, and I'm one pretty awesome mom if I do say so myself, right?"

They giggle but agree with me. I back out of my parking spot and catch a glimpse of Max standing in the threshold of the doorway, waving to us as we leave.

I have a bad, bad feeling about this.

∼

"ARE YOU ALL RIGHT?" TIFFANY, ONE OF THE INTERNS ASKS ME when she walks into the break room. "You're all jumpy."

"Yeah. Just a little freaked out," I admit. I thought about Max the way over. He knew we weren't home, which means he looks for me. And the fact that he was outside the door right at the same time we leave for school makes me think he has our schedule down and he was out there waiting.

He might be waiting when we get home too.

"Freaked out?"

"There's this guy who lives in my apartment complex." I shudder. "I think he's stalking me."

"Holy shit, for real stalking you?"

I nod. "He was waiting outside my door this morning and knew I was out of town over the weekend. I didn't tell anyone I was leaving."

"That's serious. Have you reported it to the police?"

"Reported what to the police?" Dan, one of the senior agents, asks as he comes into the room.

"She has a stalker," Tiffany tells him and I give her a look. "I'm not sorry. You need to take this serious. My cousin's friend's sister was stalked in college and guy broke into her house and tried to kidnap her."

"Oh my God. And I have children."

"Then you really need to take this seriously."

"You do," Dan agrees. "Do you feel like you're in danger?"

I get all shaky thinking about it. My heart speeds up and my hands get clammy. I'm on the verge of anxiety taking over and going into a panic. But then Alex walks into the room, and everything quiets around me.

I want to run to him, to feel his arms around me again.

"What's going on?" he asks, seeing me holding his empty mug of coffee. "Are you all right, Harper?" And apparently the fear on my face.

"She has a stalker," Tiffany says. "He was waiting outside her door this morning. I told her she needs to report it."

"Is this true?" Concern takes over Alex's face and he takes a quick step over, extending his hand toward me. He stops himself before his fingers make contact.

"Yeah, kind of. There's this guy who lives on the floor below us was in the hallway right outside the door this morning."

"He lives below you?" Alex asks and I nod. "So he had no reason to be in that hall. It's not like he was on his way down."

"Right."

"You do need to report this."

I nod again and turn away, needing a distraction. Max has always given me a bad feeling, but he hasn't done anything that would prove he's an actual stalker. He could have been visiting a neighbor or just walking around the building. Would the police even be able to do anything?

Alex strides over and takes the coffee from me, laying his fingers over mine. "Do you feel like you're in danger?"

"He's always given me the creeps, but this morning was a whole new level."

Alex's brow furrows and my heart skips a beat. Suddenly, he jerks away. His father comes into the break room along with his assistant. Everyone in the room scatters, and I remember what Tiffany said before about things being tense between Alex and his dad. I look into Alex's eyes for a quick second and then duck out as well.

The controversial Facebook posts from yesterday keep us busy for the rest of the day, and I'm thankful for being on the phone nonstop. It's distracting from both my possible stalker situation, and has kept my mind mostly off the weekend.

Mostly.

Alex has been in back-to-back meetings and then was gone for a few hours handling the press conference. The day goes by fast yet slow at the same time, and I don't get a chance to take an actual lunch break until 3:45 that afternoon. I call Dad as I eat, asking if he wants to come over for dinner and if he can help me put extra locks on the windows and doors. He works until seven-thirty but is coming over after.

Around five, I go to Alex's office and knock on the door.

"Come in," he says, not looking up from what he's working on.

"Do you need me to stay later today?" I ask.

Blinking to refocus his vision, he turns away from his computer and looks at me. "No. I'm going to leave here soon too. I need to get away." He runs his hand through his hair. "Go get your girls. I know you miss them."

"I do," I say with a smile.

"Do you want me to...to walk you into your apartment? In case the stalker is there."

"Um...I...um..." Shit. I don't know what I want. Yeah, it would be nice to have someone walk me and the girls in. "It's not a burden?"

"No." He flashes a cheeky grin. "It would be more of a burden to have to replace my assistant if the current one I had was kidnapped by a stalker."

"Ah, so you want work assurance."

"Yes." His eyes lock with mine and my heart is hammering away in my chest.

"I have to pick up the girls from Tessa's house first."

"Okay. I'll follow you."

"You sure you don't mind?" I ask, needing to hear him say it again.

"No, I don't."

"Thank you. I'll just, um, close up my desk." Close up my desk? What the hell does that even mean? Whatever. My stomach flutters again and Alex stands, coming around the desk.

"Okay. I'll meet you in the lobby."

How am I supposed to believe that this weekend was some sort of alternate reality fluke when he's staring at me like this?

CHAPTER 28

This is where Harper lives?

I wouldn't have guessed it looking at her, which makes me feel all kinds of shitty to make that kind of assumption about people who live in dumps like this.

I don't know what I was expecting. She's a single mom who, until recently, was making barely above minimum wage. I park my Tesla and get out, looking around. Harper parked in a spot several yards away. I briskly walk over, getting to her before she gets out of the car.

The music is up and she and her kids are singing along to the radio. They're smiling and look so damn happy. Is this one of her *lemonade* moments? Harper kills the engine and gets out, opening the door for her kids.

"Girls, this is Alex," she introduces. "Or do you want to be called Mr. Harding?"

"Alex," I say.

"You're Henry's uncle," one of the twins says. I look back and forth between them. Right now, they're wearing matching school uniforms and their hair is done the same way. There's no way I'll be able to tell them apart.

"I am. Good memory."

"That is Penny," Harper tells me. "And this is Violet. Alex is having dinner with us tonight. I'm making enchiladas."

"The ones Papa makes?" Penny asks.

Harper shakes her head. "The one Abuela makes. With the sauce you like."

Both girls get excited. Harper locks the car and puts her keys in her purse. She looks around the apartment before stepping away from the car, taking her kids by the hand.

We go inside and up the stairs without any seeing anyone who I think could be Harper's stalker. Still, she's tense the whole walk in.

"So, this is our home," she tells me, locking the door behind her. "It's not much, but it's home." The twins take off their shoes and dump their backpacks on the ground. "Go wash your hands," she tells them.

The door opens into the small living room, which flows right into a tiny kitchen. My master bedroom is bigger than this whole apartment. Crayon drawings and paintings cover most of the walls, all signed by either Penny or Violet. A framed photo of Harper with the girls hangs on the wall, and toys are piled in the corner behind the couch.

Harper takes off her shoes, and I follow suit. She grabs her phone from her purse and pushes her purse as well as the girls' bsackpacks against the wall and goes into the kitchen to start making dinner.

"Can I help?" I ask, stepping up behind her. The kitchen is tiny, with hardly any counter space.

"You know how to cook?" she asks, grinning.

"Not well, but I can follow instructions."

"That's a start. You can, um, wash the tomatoes and lettuce."

"With soap?"

She gives me a blank stare and I laugh. "I'm joking, Harper. I know how to rinse vegetables."

237

Her smile lights up the whole damn room. "Good."

The girls come out of the bathroom and go into the living room. They squabble over what to watch before settling on *Trolls*. Henry likes that show too, and I've seen a few episodes with him. I'm not ashamed to admit that I find it enjoyable.

Harper turns on music on her phone, lowers the volume, and balances her phone on a can of beans. She dances along to Taylor Swift as she goes about making dinner. I help as much as I can but mostly feel in the way in this small kitchen.

"Did you ever call the cops?" I ask her quietly. "It's good to have something like that on record. It'll help you get a restraining order later if you need one."

"You have experience with them?"

"I do, actually," I tell her. "I've had stalkers before."

"Really?" She puts her hand on her hip, not believing me.

"Yes. Have you seen me?"

"I have. With your shirt off."

"And I've seen you—" I cut off when she flares her nostrils and glares at me. "It was an ex-client. He stalked a few of us from the office."

"Creepy."

"It was, which is why I think you should at the very least have a report filed."

She nods and looks out at her girls before putting dinner in the oven. "You're right. I'll call now." Grabbing her phone, she goes into her bedroom and shuts the door.

Penny,—or maybe Violet?—gets off the couch and pulls an over flowing bin of toys out. She dumps it and sorts out several Barbies and accessories.

"Do you want to play with me?" she asks me.

"Sure." I put my phone down on the table and get up, going over and joining her on the floor. "How do you play Barbies?"

"You make them talk and stuff."

"What do they talk about?"

"Whatever you want. We usually make them have parties. Mommy makes houses out of boxes for us too and we decorate them."

"You've got a good mom, you know that, right?"

"Yeah," Penny or maybe Violet says like it's the most obvious thing in the world. "I wish she had more time to play with me."

"I'm sure she does too."

"She does," the other twin tells me. "I hear her crying sometimes because she's tired and sad."

"Penny," the twin on the floor—who I now know is Violet—scolds. "You're not supposed to tell people that."

Penny just shrugs and looks back at the TV. Violet dumps another bin of toys and I help her find matches to the shoes. She decided we're going to set up a store and have a grand opening.

About ten minutes later, Harper comes out of her room and stops short.

"You got roped into playing Barbies?" she asks with a smile.

"I didn't get roped into anything. This is fun." I put a pair of tiny pink heels next to a pair of neon green boots.

"How'd things go?" I ask.

"Good, I think. They want me to fill out paper work after dinner," she says and sits down next to us. She takes the remote from Penny, who throws a little fit when the TV is shut off. Only a minute or two later, she's down on the floor with us, and we set up one hell of a Barbie shoe store before the timer on the oven goes off.

I stay and play with the girls while Harper dishes up our food, setting four plates on the little kitchen table. They say a simple prayer before eating, and maybe it's the company, but these are the best damn enchiladas I've ever had.

"Want any help cleaning up?" I ask when we're done.

"Nah, it's fine. Thank you though. I'll get it after the girls are in bed. I hope it doesn't take long at the station." She looks at the time. "Maybe we'll wait until Papa gets here," she says to herself. "I'd prefer not to take them."

"I can stay," I offer. "I've invested this much time into that store, I need to follow through."

Harper looks at me, eyes wide and lips slightly parted. God, she's beautiful.

"Really?"

"Yeah. And if they turn *Trolls* back on I'll be fully entertained. I like the troll that farts glitter."

Harper laughs. "You watch *Trolls*?"

"Henry does."

"You've already done enough for me," she says, nervously playing with her hair. "I don't want to put you out."

"You're not, and you did go all the way to Vermont with me this weekend. The least I can do is hang out here while you report your stalker."

"Yeah, you're right." She steps closer and puts her hand on my arm. "Thank you again, Alex." Her head tips up and I'm again fighting the urge to kiss her. "I have no idea how long this will take, but my dad is coming over around seven-thirty. I'll let him know you're here and if some random old guy shows up, make him say the password before you let him in."

"You have a password?"

"No, but I'll make one up. Pineapple juice."

"Okay. I will not let anyone in unless they say *pineapple juice*."

"Good. Verbal passwords are one of the highest forms of security, you know."

"For sure."

Harper gives her girls hugs and kisses and then hurries out the door. I look out the living room window, watching to make sure she got to her car all right—she did.

I go back to the spot on the floor, sitting down next to the Barbie shoe store we're setting up.

"Do you like my mom?" Violet asks, putting another pair of shoes on an overturned tissue box we're using as a display.

"Yeah," I say and feel something loosen in my chest as I speak the words. "I do."

CHAPTER 29

"You should have seen him." I roll over on my bed and rest my phone on my chest. "He was on the floor playing Barbies with the girls."

"Awww, that's so fucking cute," Tessa's voice echoes through the phone. I'm on speaker and she's moving around, unable to sit still and talk. She'd rather text, but this is much too important to tall about via text message right now.

"I know," I groan. "I didn't expect him to get along with the girls like this. They like him and asked if he can come back and play with them another day." I let out a heavy sigh. "I like him, Tess."

"I knew you did."

"I didn't like him before this weekend."

"Bullshit," she says. "I knew you were all hot and bothered by him."

"He did bother me and he is hot, so yeah."

"That doesn't make sense," she laughs. "But whatever, deny how right I am another time. What are you going to do about it?"

"Nothing. He's my boss, and while I'm pretty sure he wants

this—" I motion to my body, forgetting that Tessa can't see me. "I don't know if he wants a serious relationship, which I do."

"Ask. Then you'll now for sure."

"Stop being logical. What if he says no?"

"Then he says no. Maybe he can be your fuck buddy for a while."

Sleeping with Alex will only further my feelings for him. "Ughhh. It was so much easier when I hated the guy."

Tessa laughs. "It doesn't have to be hard, Harp. You like him. Make a move."

"I don't want to lose my job by crossing a line."

"Don't make the move in the office and he can't fire you for asking him out to dinner. And he had you pose as his fake girl-friend so he could make a business deal. You didn't only cross a line, you ran miles past it with that one."

"True. I don't know...I'm just...scared," I finally admit. "I don't want to get hurt, obviously, and I don't want to get the girls' hopes up. They were asking about their dad again." I stick my feet under my covers. "Do you think they're old enough to tell the whole story to?"

"No, not yet. Unless you want to risk getting asked for details on how Daddy put two babies in you again."

"I am not ready for that talk."

"You got a few more years."

"I'm so glad I have girls. I can't imagine being a single mom and and having to talk to my son about not mastrubating into the good towels."

Tessa laughs. "No, you'll just have to deal with synced cycles every month."

"That might be worse."

"It probably is." My phone beeps, and I pull it away from my face hoping to see Alex's number. It's not him but Kate instead. "Kate is calling me. I'll talk to you in the morning."

"Kay. Love you, Harps."

"Love you too." I switch the calls. "Hello?"

"Hey!" Kate says. "How are you doing, hun?"

"Pretty good. I'm in bed already again. I'm so lame."

"I've been in bed. Heather went down early tonight and I got myself some of that sweet red wine and put my ass in bed. I have an early presentation in the morning.

"Oh, exciting! And good luck."

"Thanks, I'm hoping to get at least fifty grand out of these rich old dudes. The money is going to a women's clinic so my chances are slim. Anyway, Heather was going on and on and *on* about having a sleepover over here this weekend."

"A sleepover?" I echo. I know the twins will love it.

"They've never had a friend sleepover before, have they?"

"Is it that obvious?"

She laughs. "Just a little. Is that out of your comfort zone?"

"Kind of, but if they're going to spend the night at a friend's house, I'd feel the most comfortable with it being Heather."

"Aww, thanks babe. Stay for dinner too and you'll feel ever better. Rose and her twins will be there. I don't know if Mason will stay the night but he's coming to play with the girls for a bit anyway."

"They'll have so much fun. Yeah. We'll be there."

I HIT SNOOZE FOR THE THIRD TIME, FINDING IT HARD TO EVEN OPEN my eyes and look at the clock. I have to get up now or we'll be late for school and then work. Running my hands over my face, I sit up only to flop back down.

A text comes through on my phone, perking me up a bit. Who'd be texting me this early? Alex. That's who.

I blink a few times, vision fuzzy, and open the text.

Alex: The McCord case got moved up and I just found out

so I won't be at the office today. Can you cancel/move all my appointments today?

Oh, it's just a work-related text.

Me: Yeah, I can. What do I do without you?

I send the text and then realize how it sounds.

Me: At the office, I mean. Who do I assist?

Alex: Manage the phone and email. Go through my desk and look for incriminating evidence while I'm gone. Hint: there's a secret drawer hidden somewhere.

Now I'm smiling.

Me: What do you think I am, a rookie? I found that hidden drawer and the file full of photos on my first day.

He sends a laughing emoji and I watch as the little bubbles pop up as he types.

Alex: Do you want a bodyguard this morning?

Me: I think we'll be okay. The teenage boys from the floor above are dealing pot in the parking lot. I think they'd come to my aid if I screamed for help.

Alex: Reassuring. Just say the word and I'll come over.

Me: It's like a twenty-five minute drive from the office.

Alex: It'll give me time to listen to a few more chapters of this book.

I can't sop smiling as I get up and deal with two very crabby kids. I get them breakfast, dressed, do their hair, and help them brush their teeth. Then I let them crash on the couch with the TV on while I get myself ready.

We dash out and into the car without running into Max. I take a picture of the three of us in the car, all making silly faces of course, and send it to Alex to let him know I didn't get kidnapped or mugged.

I drop the girls off and then go to work, knowing the day is going to feel weird without Alex. It goes by slowly, and he texts me around three to tell me I can leave early if I have everything handled. I do, and I make it out of there in time to actually pick up the girls in the carline.

It's nice out, so we go to the park, and then I buy the first frivolous purchase using the bonus money. We get ice cream and take it home to eat. Max is outside smoking, and I tell the girls we're going to have a race to see who can get to the doors of the apartment complex first.

We don't stop until we're up on the second floor, and I unlock our door and pretty much shove the girls inside, and close the door.

"Harper, wait!" I hear Max call as the door is swinging shut. I lock it, let out a shaky breath, and debate moving the couch in front of it already. The girls take their ice cream to the table and I wait by the door. I can hear someone walking down the hall. My heart races when they stop by the door, and I'm too scared to move or look out of the peephole.

Then they put their hand on the doorknob, testing to see if it's unlocked. I don't move the couch, but I put a kitchen chair in front of the door and tell the girls it's there to keep our purses and backpacks off the ground.

To distract us all, we watch a movie while we eat the ice cream. Then we have dinner, go over the girls' sight words, and have enough time to play a bit more before bath and bedtime. Alex texts me around nine, saying he'll be in court again tomorrow. I'm not familiar with the McCord case, but I know they're a client and are suing another company for stealing their patent or something like that.

So the next day is filled with rearranging Alex's schedule, answering phones, and filtering through emails. I leave at three-thirty and have another good evening with the girls—sans stalker this time thank goodness.

Alex is back at the office Thursday, but is so busy playing catchup from the two days he missed, I hardly have time to even look at his gorgeous face.

I hope things are better by on Friday, but he's just as busy, and his father has been in and out of his office. I do my best to stay out of their way.

The girls are going straight to the sleepover after school. I packed their bags already and will have them change out of their uniforms when I get to Tessa's house.

Alex is on the phone when the clock strikes five, and I stick my head into the office. His face lights up and he smiles, mouthing *have a good weekend* to me. I give him a little wave, and head out, driving to Tessa's house.

The girls are outside walking the dogs when I get their. The dog start yipping and my girls come running, cheering for Mommy. It's such a good feeling to see them excited to greet me.

"You got a hot date this weekend?" Tessa asks as soon as we all get back inside. She knows I don't. Pulling the girls change of clothes out of my purse, I shake my head.

"It was a really busy week at work. I didn't get a chance to talk to him let alone ask him on a date." I give the girls their clothes and tell them to hurry up.

"Next week then," Tessa says. "At some point next week you're asking him out."

"Fine," I say just to make her stop pestering me. I sit on the couch, extending my hand for the dogs to sniff. They've known me for years yet still bark every single time I step foot into the house. Suddenly, I remember that I left my wallet in the top drawer of my desk. I lockmy wallet and my phone in there when I leave my desk. I was on my phone a lot today, adding things to my calendar, and had it *on* my desk more than *in* my desk.

Oh well. I can swing by on the way back from Kate's and get it. The building is open until eight. I'll have time to run in and grab it.

After hollering at the girls to hurry up, we say goodbye to Tessa and are out the door. I enter Kate's address in the GPS. She lives in Lakeview and her house is gorgeous. Her cook made a delicious dinner, and if I didn't have to go back to the office for my wallet, I'd stay and sit out on the patio with her and Rose and enjoy some of that Vermont wine.

I hug my girls goodbye a hundred times, and then have them pose for a picture. It's their first friend sleepover. It's a big deal.

"If you want to come home, just have Heather's mom call me," I remind them. "And I'll come get you."

"Mom," they both sass at the same time. "Stop, we'll be fine," Penny tells me.

"Can we go play now?" Violet asks.

"Of course. One more hug?"

They smile and throw their arms around me. I kiss their foreheads and then go back out, letting out a heavy sigh when I start back to the office. I've never been here this late and the mostly-empty parking garage is a little creepy. I rush to get into the lobby.

"Hey, Trevor," I say to the security guard in the lobby.

"Back already? What, you couldn't get enough of the place?"

"You know it," I laugh. "I left something upstairs."

"Yeah, your boss."

"Alex is still here?"

"He's usually here late," he tells me.

"I'll make him leave." I get into the elevator and go up to the fourteenth floor. The lights above the secretary's desk have been dimmed, as have the rest of the lights with the exception of Alex's office. I can see him sitting at his desk, hair all messy from him running his fingers through it.

He jerks his head up when he hears the elevator doors. "Harper?"

"Yeah, it's me."

"What are you doing here?" He gets up and walks around his desk as I head back toward him. My heart skips a beat.

"I left my wallet in my desk."

"Oh."

"What are you doing here?"

"Working." He makes a face and lets out a sigh.

"I think you should call it a night."

"I will...soon," he promises. "What is that?" His eyes go to a gift basket on my desk.

"Oh, it's from that whiskey distillery you went to like two weeks ago, I think? You were so busy earlier I didn't want to bother you with it. They sent a bottle of their finest whiskey and then a bottle of Malort. I think it's supposed to be a joke."

Alex smiles. "That is funny. I haven't had that shit since college."

"I've only seen people drink it."

"Oh, you've got to try it."

"No way."

"You can't live in Chicago and have never tired it. Half a shot. Hell, a fourth of a shot."

"Fine, but you're trying it with me."

Nodding, he goes into the break room to get two bottles of water. I take the Malort into his office and twist it open. Alex sets the waters down and picks up two fancy glasses from the bar cart in his office. I pour tiny amounts in each.

"On three," he tells me and picks up his glass. "One. Two. Three."

I toss the liquid in my mouth and gag. "It takes like poison!" I stick out my tongue and gag again.

Alex laughs. "You should see your face!"

"Oh my God." I pick up the water and chug it. "Why does anyone drink that?"

"I think because it's so bad. Though Dan likes it. Says it tastes good." Alex laughs again and picks up his bottle of water and takes a drink. "Want some more?"

"No, thank you," I laugh and perch on the edge of his desk.

"Where are the girls?" he asks.

"They are at their first friend sleepover at Heather's. She's Kate's daughter."

"Fun. How are you holding up though?"

"I'm okay. They were eager or me to leave, which I wasn't expecting. I don't want them to be sad, of course, but it's different. They're growing up so fast."

"You're doing a good job with them. They're good kids."

"Thanks." I reach up and play with the little lemon hanging around my neck. Alex steps over, eyes meeting mine.

"You have a fuzz," he tells me and reaches out, pulling a piece of red fuzz from my hair. "From your dress."

"Oh, right."

He drops the fuzz to the ground and puts his hand back in my hair. My eyes flutter shut and I lean into his touch. He steps in, and his other hand lands on my waist. My breath leaves me and I bring my hands up, resting them both on his muscular chest. He took his suit jacket off and is standing before me in black dress pants and a teal button up, with the sleeves rolled up to his elbows.

He caresses my face and turns my chin up to his. This time there's no doubt about it. There's no hesitation. Alexander Harding is going to kiss me.

And, Lord have mercy, he does.

CHAPTER 30

HARPER

Alex's lip press against mine. Soft. Full. Warm. I stand there stunned for half a second, and then melt against him. I slide my hands up his chest and around his shoulders. He wraps me in his embrace, kissing me harder. This tongue slips past my lips and he dips me back as he kisses me.

Warmth floods through me. It starts in my heart, causing it to skip a beat. Then it explodes, sending tingles of desire to every single nerve in my body. He moves one hand to the back of my head, burying his fingers in my hair.

Then he suddenly breaks away, eyes wide, and looks at me. The same look is reflected in his eyes, the one where he's searching for something he desperately needs, something he's certain he can't find because he doesn't even know what it is he needs.

It's a look I recognize because I've felt it too, except I've known all along what I need: someone.

Someone I want. Need. Love. Someone who makes me laugh. Who reminds me every single day that while I am a flawed human, I am enough.

Could that person be Alex?

"Harper," he breathes. "If you don't want—"

"I do," I pant, and as soon as the words leave my lips, Alex is back against me, cupping my face with his large hands. He kisses me hard and desperate, stepping in close. His hips press against mine, and the of his cock through his pants almost does me in.

My knees weaken and the heat between my legs intensifies. I can't recall a single time in my life where one kiss has gotten me this turned on. Gathering my hair in one hand, Alex moves it over my shoulder and puts his lips on my neck. I moan softly as he kisses my neck, lips traveling down toward my collarbone.

His hands to around my waist, gripping me tight as he sucks at my skin. I hold tightly to him, afraid my knees will give out completely if I let go. Putting his lips to mine again, he slides his hand down my waist and to my thigh, fingers disappearing under the hem of my dress.

I gasp when he sweeps them up my thigh, gently grazing my core. I'm already so hot, already wet for him, and he knows it. Suddenly unable to multitask, I pull my lips off his and suck in air, looking at his chest. There's too much to do and my body is in overdrive, heart racing.

Unbutton his shirt?

Undo his belt?

I'm so wound up I can't pick one. I need him on me, against me. In me. Now.

I reach for his shirt, thinking I should start with the top and work my way down. Alex pushes my hands off his broad shoulders and picks me up. My dress rides up around my waist as I fasten my legs around him. His cock is hardening against me, and holy shit, that thing is big. I already knew it was impressive in size, even flaccid, from when I saw him sleeping in bed next to me.

But now that it's hardening, I'm not entirely sure it's going to fit inside of me. The thought excites me and sends chills through me at the same time. It'll fill every inch, and it'll feel so fucking good.

He steps forward, kissing me as we walk. Desperation burns inside of me, and I know Alex is feeling it to. He sets me down on his desk, reaching behind me to shove papers and folders and even his empty coffee mug to the ground.

Planting both hands on the either side of the desk next to me, Alex gives me one more passionate kiss before dropping to his knees. My breath quickens and my core spasms with anticipation.

Alex parts my legs and takes one in his hands, kissing the inside of my knee. Chills run rampant through my body, causing goosebumps to break out on my skin. He trails kisses up, stopping at the inside of my thigh just inches from my pussy.

I arch my back, lifting my bottom off the desk so he can take off my panties. He slides them down my legs and drops them off the floor next to his desk. My heart is racing, body begging to be touch.

Alex buries his head between my thighs, breath hot against me. My pussy quivers, making me even more desperate form his touch. But instead of lashing his tongue against my clit, he quickly stands, trailing his fingers up my thigh.

He puts his lips to mine as he brings his hand in, right between my legs, and sweeps his fingers over my core. Moaning I wrap one arm around him and toss my head back. Alex move his head down to my breasts as he continues to rub my clit.

I could come already. He slowly circles my entrance and then dips his finger inside, pressing against my inner walls. He adds another finger, and it's a tight fight. Holy fuck, his cock is going to feel so good inside of me. It's been so long since I've been touched, and I've been denying what's right in front of me all week: I've fallen for my boss.

I am in love with Alexander Harding.

Alex takes his hand from between my thigh and I gasp, not

expecting the pleasure to stop already. He unzips my dress and slowly pulls the sleeves down my shoulders. Lips parted and breath coming out in huffs.

"Alex," I groan.

"Yes, Harper?" He lets my dress fall the rest of the way down my arms and then puts both hands on my knees, parting my legs again between stepping in between.

"I need you."

"I know." He slowly slides his hand up my thigh again, teasing me like crazy. His fingers stop not even an inch away. He's so close and it's driving me crazy. I reach down and wrap my fingers around his wrist, moving his hand back against me. I rock my hips, rubbing myself against him.

"Patience," he growls and snatches his hand back. "You can come when I say you can come."

Holy shit. I swallow hard and look at Alex with wide eyes.

"Now stand up and take your dress off."

He takes a step back and looks at me with hunger in his eyes. I've never been with someone so commanding, someone who knows exactly what he wants and isn't afraid to demand it. It's the hottest thing I've ever experienced.

My fingers tremble as I push myself off the desk. The dress falls to my feet as soon as I'm up, leaving me standing before Alex in just a pale pink bra.

"You are so fucking gorgeous," he tells me, voice deep and guttural. His cock is hard, pressing against the tight confines of his pants. I inhale, breasts rising and falling, and part my lips, not sure if I should tell him to take his clothes off now or go back go begging for him to touch me.

Alex takes one more look at me and then comes back to me, hands going to my ass. He squeeze it as he kisses me, then pushes me back onto the desk. This time he doesn't tease me. Doesn't make me wait.

He drops to his knees, parts my legs, and puts his mouth over my pussy. His tongue flicks over my clit, sending a jolt of pure pleasure through me. I'm holding myself up by my elbows, head back and eyes closed. Alex turns his hand, kissing and sucking at the flesh of my inner thigh, and then dives back, circling my entrance with his tongue.

I'm so turned on. So hot. So close to coming against him face. Alex groans as he eats me out, reading my body and knowing I'm about ready to finish. He slides a finger inside of me, pressing against that sweet spot and pushing me over the edge. My mouth falls open as the orgasm rolls through me, hitting me hard and fast. My thigh quiver and my pussy goes crazy with spasms. Alex doesn't stop, and keeps licking, keeps kiss and sucking.

Another wave of pleasure goes through me, and my ears start to ring. My mouth is hanging wide open, but I'm too caught up in pure pleasure to even make a sound. The orgasm makes it way through every part of me, leaving me breathless.

Holy. Fucking. Shit.

Alex stands, wipes his mouth with the back of his hand, and pulls me to him. My eyes are fluttering open and shut and my heart is racing.

"Can you stand?" he asks, lips brushing against my neck as he talks.

"No," I pant. "Not yet." I suck in air and bring a feeble arm up, wrapping it around Alex's shoulders. He kisses me, gently this time, and I taste myself on his lips.

"You are so hot," he groans and presses his hips against me. He's still fully clothed, and we desperately need to change that. I rest my head against him, taking another few seconds to recover from that intense orgasm. Then I push him back just enough so I can get to his belt.

He gets a devilish glint in his eyes as he watches me undo the buckle and pull it through the loops. I let it fall to the ground next to my panties, and bite my lip as I pop the button on his pants. The force of his monster cock makes the zipper go down on its own. Swallowing hard, I lower my eyes, seeing the gleaming tip sticking out over the top of his boxers.

Alex starts to unbutton his shirt, and all I can do is sit there and watch as he slowly strips down, revealing that gorgeous, impossibly fit body to me. I take over when he gets to the last few buttons, needing to get him naked and on top of me.

The shirt falls to the ground, and I grab the hem of his undershirt and yank it over his head. He hooks his fingers inside his pants and pulls them down, and now he's standing before me in only his boxers. Unlike me, though, Alex isn't shy. He looks good and he knows it, and more importantly, he feels it.

In a swift movement, he picks me up and carries me to the couch against the glass wall of his office.We've exposed on both sides, and if anyone in the neighboring buildings were to look in, they'd see us. I should care, but I don't.

Alex lays me down and moves on top. I welcome him between my legs and reach down slipping my fingers inside his boxers. I push them down and he kicks them off and rests one hand on my cheek, staring into my eyes for a second before he kisses me.

I angle my hips up, heart racing. The wet tip of his cock rubs against me. I suck in air and angle my hips up, needing to feel that big cock push inside me.

He kisses me hard, tongue slipping past my lips. Then he move his mouth to my neck and enters me. Oh my God. He fills every single inch of me, and it feel so fucking good. I cry out as he thrusts in deeper, driving that big cock in and out of me.

Hooking one leg around him, I rake my fingers down his back. He speeds up his movements, and I press my fingers into his flesh. I'm getting close to coming again. I wrap my leg tighter around Alex, mouth falling open.

The second orgasm hits me just as hard, and feeling my pussy contract around his cock pushes Alex over the edge. He drives his cock in balls deep, letting out a groan as he comes, filling me even more.

Panting, he rests his forehead against mine.

My ears are ringing. Stars dot my vision and I can hardly catch my breath. Alex kisses me once more and then pulls out, reaching down to grab his boxers off the floor. He gives them to me to use to clean myself up with. Then he pulls me back to him, rearranging how we were laying so he can spoon his body around mine. It's a tight fit on the couch, but feeling his warm, strong body feels so fucking right.

CHAPTER 31

ALEX

"Come home with me," I say, heart in my throat. I don't want this to end. Harper is everything I ever wanted, and suddenly, I'm terrified she's going to sit up, look at me, and walk out.

If I'm the one to leave, if I'm the one to send her on her way, it takes out that risk. The ball will be in my court, so to speak, even though deep down I know that's bullshit.

Harper doesn't hook up. She doesn't do one-night stands. She wants a relationship, and sleeping together had to mean something to her.

I know it did to me.

"I'd like that." She wiggles closer. "Should we get up and get dressed before someone sees us?"

"Probably," I tell her. "I don't even know what time it is, but security does come up and do a sweep through the office."

"Oh. Then we should get up and get dressed," she says but neither of us move. I kiss the nape of her neck.

"Yeah," I agree. "In a minute."

"Mh-hm." Harper rests her hand over mine and takes a deep breath. Then she rolls over and almost falls off the couch. She shivers and I hook my leg over her, trying to keep her warm. Kissing her forehead, I tell myself I'm going to get up. It's getting late and having someone walk in on us would embarrass Harper.

We both sit up and quickly pull our clothes on. Harper grabs the papers I shoved to the ground and puts them back on the desk. I grab her when she stands and pull her to me, kissing her again.

I like kissing her. Love fucking her. And I really care about her. I want her to know that, but I'm not good at this kind of thing.

"Are you hungry?" I ask as we walk out of the office. I lock the door behind me and Harper goes to her desk to get her wallet that she left.

"Kind of. Are you?"

"I am. Want to get those hotdogs and beer now?"

Her full lips pull up into a smile and she nods. I take her hand and walk to the elevator. Her hair is messy from our love making. I can still taste her on my lips, and I want to lay her down and fuck her again as soon as we get to my penthouse.

I'm still holding Harper's hand when we walk out of the office and onto the busy downtown street.

"There's usually a street vender the next block over," Harper tells me. "I don't know if he's still there. It's getting late, but it is Friday and it's so nice out."

"That's on the way to my place too." I give her hand a squeeze before letting go so I can wrap my arm around her shoulder. She rests her head against me, and everything is so fucking perfect.

"He's still there!" she exclaims when we round the corner. We get the hotdogs, but no beer. We eat as we walk, enjoying each other's company. It's nice not having to feel the need to fill every second with pointless conversation. I'm comfortable just to be around her.

I never thought this was possible.

Yet it's happening, and I never want it to end. Harper is doing so much more than filling the void inside of me...she's making me think love isn't bullshit after all.

≈

"Wow," Harper takes off her heels and looks around the penthouse. "This place is gorgeous."

Normally, I'd say thanks and go on to subtly brag about how new or expensive something was in here. It was what I had to do in order to validate myself, to keep myself interesting and desirable to whoever I was with.

But not Harper.

"It's a little over the top, I know."

"Hey, if I could afford a place like this, I'd take it." She spins around as she walks, looking around in awe. This place is impressive, I'll admit. You walk into a two-story foyer with a curved staircase taking you up to the loft that leads to my rooftop patio—complete with a hot tub.

"Where's the bathroom?" Harper asks. "I have to pee."

I show her were it is and then go into the kitchen. I grab two wine glasses and a bottle of the sweetest wine I own. I have the wine poured by the time Harper comes in.

"You are so beautiful," I tell her, feeling my heart do that skip-a-beat thing the moment I lay eyes on her. I pick up a wine glass and hand it to her.

"Do you want to sit on the balcony?" I ask, motioning to the balcony off the kitchen. Harper takes a drink of wine and nods. I grab a blanket off the back of the couch and lead the way. I drape the blanket around Harper's shoulders and lean against the railing, looking at the city below us.

Harper takes another drink of wine and sets her glass on the glass table. She comes over and wraps her arm around my waist. I turn, taking her into my embrace, and kiss her.

Still holding my wine, I break away to set it down on the table next to Harper's. Then we're back to kissing, and the next thing I know, Harper is undoing my pants again.

I am so fucking lucky.

I pick her up and go inside, stumbling our way into my bedroom. Our clothes come off in a mad rush, and Harper pulls me between her legs. I kiss her and line my cock up to her sweet cunt, ready to push inside and fuck her into oblivion again. But then Harper plants her hands on my chest, pushes me away, and shoves me down on the mattress.

I'm already rock hard, cock aching to be inside of me. She climbs on top, fingers wrapping around my cock. She lines my cock up with her pussy, ready to sink down on it. She's looking so fucking hot I'm afraid I'll nut the second I enter her.

She slowly lowers herself down and pitches forward, hands landing on my chest. I buck my hips and reach down, rubbing her clit as she fucks me. We both come hard and fast, and after Harper uses the bathroom, she climbs back into bed with me. Pulling the blankets up around us, I wrap her in my arms and intent to never let go.

"Harper?" I whisper after a few minute have passed. She doesn't answer. I sit up, and see that she's asleep. I kiss her forehead and lay down, falling asleep with a smile on my face.

$\sim$

"ALEX." HARPER'S HAND LANDS ON MY ARM. "ALEX. SOMEONE IS AT your door."

I blink my eyes open, seeing her sitting up and holding the sheets over her breasts. Her hair is a mess and the makeup she fell asleep in is smeared around her eyes. It's hot, knowing the reason she's looking like that right now is because we fell asleep after making love.

"Who the fuck?" I mumble, grabbing my phone. I pull up the security camera. "It's my sister. Don't worry. I'll get rid of her."

EMILY GOODWIN

Yawning, I throw the blankets back, get out of bed, and pull on a pair of sweatpants. Harper gets up and goes into the bathroom while I go deal with my sister.

"Morning!" she says cheerfully when I open the door.

"What the hell, Nicole? It's early."

"It's eight thirty."

"Yeah, early." I step aside and let her in.

"I was supposed to go into surgery but my patient stopped by McDonalds on the way in. This is the second time we've had to rescheduled surgery because he ate a very full meal before going under. I canceled and am about ready to tell him to find a different surgeon."

"So you came here?" I laugh.

"I said I'd take you out to dinner, but since we can't seem to find a time that works, I thought we could go out for breakfast—oh, sorry. I didn't know you had someone over."

I turn, seeing Harper timidly coming over. She's wearing her dress as well as one of my white button up shirts over top. My God, she's gorgeous.

"Sorry," Nicole says again. "I'll leave."

"No, it's fine," Harper tells her. I can't help but go to her and put my arms around her. "I need to go pick up my kids from a sleepover anyway."

"Oh, right." I put my lips to hers, not wanting her to leave. "I'll, uh, see you at work on Monday then."

Harper gives me a look, but kisses me again. She grabs her purse and heads out, giving Nicole a little wave goodbye.

"She looks familiar." Nicole watches Harper walk out of the penthouse. "Oh, she has kids that that go Briar Prep. Twins, right? I've seen her in the drop off line."

"Yeah."

"They why did you tell her you'll see her at work?"

"She's also my assistant."

Nicole's eyes widen. "You're sleeping with your assistant?"

262

I run my hand over the back of my head and get flashes of last night. "Yeah, I am."

"What's with that gooney smile on your face?"

"What gooney—" Oh. I am smiling. "Nothing. I guess I just like this one."

"So you sent her off with *I'll see you at work?* Seriously?"

"What's wrong with that?"

Nicole smacks the back of my head.

"Ow!"

"Good!" she tells me and goes in to smack me again. "Let me get this straight. You like this woman, like actually really care for her?"

"Yes, I do. She's…she's incredible. She smart. Funny. Unbelievably kind and caring."

"And she works for you?"

"Yes. I also paid her five grand to pretend to be my girlfriend last weekend so I could get a client to sign back on with us. It worked."

"You hired her to be your fake girlfriend?"

"In a sense."

"And you like her?" she asks again.

"Yes, I do." It feels good to say it out loud. "I really do."

Nicole looks at me like I'm the biggest idiot in the world. "How can you be so fucking dumb yet be as successful as you are?"

"What?"

Nicole pinches the bridge of her nose. "I'll admit I don't know her and don't know what she's into, but from what I saw, you sent her off with a pat on the butt and an empty promise of *see you at work* which means you don't give a flying fuck about her."

"But I do."

"Again. How are you this dumb?"

Nicole's words start to sink in. Fucking shit, she's right. And Harper doesn't want a one-night stand. She told me several times that's not who she is and it's not what she wants. I don't want her to think that's all she was to me.

"I want you to be happy," Nicole says gently.

"I am happy."

"Are you?" She puts her hand on my forehead. "You're my brother and I love you. You're not dumb, so don't act like it."

"I'm not acting like anything," I protest. "I like Harper. I like sex. So I really like having sex with Harper."

"But don't you want more?"

"There isn't anything more." As soon as I say the words, I know there's no use trying to sell myself the same old lie. The drinking. The partying. Hooking up with different women every night. It was a mask, a way to hide my true self behind the man I thought I had to become in order to find happiness. It was easier to be the fake version of who I thought I was meant to be, than to be myself and be alone. Rejection doesn't hurt when people aren't rejecting the real you.

But to give someone my heart and have it handed back, bloody and bruised...there was no way I could have put it back in my chest. It's different with Harper. I didn't give her my heart. She reached out and took it, and I don't want her to ever let go.

I want more and I want it with Harper. I've fallen in love with Harper Watson...and now I hope it's not too late to tell her that.

"She is more," I say, brows furrowing. "I need to tell her."

"Shower first," Nicole tells me, patting my arm. "You smell like a brothel."

"Oh, right. Okay." And she's not going straight home. She's picking up her kids first and then is going home. I have some time.

"You got this, Al. Put yourself together and then go get your girl." Nicole smiles up at me. "I'll come visit another time."

"Thanks," I tell her.

"Call me later and let me know how things go?" she asks as she heads toward the door.

"Fine. Later. Like much later."

Nicole laughs and leaves. I lock the door and jump in the shower, thinking about what I'm going to say to Harper when I get to her house. You're everything I didn't know I wanted? No. Sounds lame. You complete me? Fuck. Even lamer.

Can't I just kiss her again? Show her what she means to me?

I'll start with that. Just thinking about Harper's lips against mine gets me turned on.

"You'll get some later," I say, looking at my cock, and then I realize what I need to do: I'm going to ask her to be my girl-friend. She wants a serious relationship, and that's a damn good place to start. I'll take her and the girls out for breakfast, and then maybe we can all spend the day together.

I dry off, get dressed, and practice another lame speech before scrapping the idea of preparing anything completely. Finally, I'm ready to go and maker Harper mine.

Except, I get stuck in fucking traffic on the way out of the downtown area, and the drive to Harper's takes twice as long. The company Lexus is in the parking lot, which means Harper is home. I park my BMW and get out, running to the apartment. I fly up the stairs, taking them two at a time and pound on Harper's door.

It takes a few seconds, but she opens it.

"Alex…what are you doing here?"

"I came to see you. I have to tell you something, Harper."

"Can it, um, wait?" She brings her hand to her forehead and closes her eyes. The skin around her eyes is red, as if she's been crying. I'm suddenly on the defense, ready to fuck shit up if someone hurt her. Is that stalker back? Did he scare her?

The floor creaks behind her and I look inside the tiny apartment. A man is standing in front of the couch, holding a pink sheet of paper in his hands.

"Is this a bad time?" he asks, eyes flitting from me to Harper. "Should I come back?"

"No," Harper says and when she opens her eyes, I can see tears welling in them. Who the fuck is this guy and what the hell is he — "Alex," Harper starts and hearing her say my name soothes my soul. I want to scoop her up, crush those perfect tits against my chest and put my lips to hers, kissing her like she's never been kissed before.

"What's wrong, Harper? Are you okay?" I step closer.

"I'm...I'm...I'll be fine," she says. She turns and sweeps her hand out at the man in her living room. "This...this is Micheal." She inhales and lets out a shaky breath. "He's the girls' father."

∾

Alex and Harper's story continues in HARD TRUTH, book two in the Hard to Love series, coming October 3rd. Check out Emily's reader group and/or Instagram for updates, teasers, and chances to win an early copy!

THANK YOU

Thank you so much for taking time out of your busy life to read Hard Place! This is my first new romance series of 2019, and to say I was nervous was an understatement. But Harper's voice rang so loudly in my head I just had to write her story down. I LOVE this story and these characters. It's funny, actually, that I set out to have this be a light-hearted rom-com and my beta readers say this is one of my more angsty stories! I loved watched the story unfold (in my head, that is) and I hope you fall hard for Harper and Alex too!

I appreciate so much the time you took to read this book and and would love if you would consider leaving a review. I LOVE connecting with readers and the best place to do so is my fan page. I'd love to have you!

www.facebook.com/groups/emilygoodwinbooks

ABOUT THE AUTHOR

Emily Goodwin is the New York Times and USA Today Best-selling author of over a dozen of romantic titles. Emily writes the kind of books she likes to read, and is a sucker for a swoon-worthy bad boy and happily ever afters.

She lives in the midwest with her husband and two daughters. When she's not writing, you can find her riding her horses, hiking, reading, or drinking wine with friends.

Emily is represented by Julie Gwinn of the Seymour Agency.

Stalk me:
www.emilygoodwinbooks.com
emily@emilygoodwinbooks.com

ALSO BY EMILY GOODWIN

Contemporary romance:

Stay

All I Need

Never Say Never

Outside the Lines

First Comes Love

Then Come Marriage

One Call Away

Free Fall

Hot Mess (Love is Messy Book 1)

Twice Burned (Love is Messy Book 2)

Bad Things (Love is Messy Book 3)

Battle Scars (Love is Messy Book 4)

Cheat Codes (The Dawson Family Series Book 1)

End Game (The Dawson Family Series Book 2)

Side Hustle (The Dawson Family Series Book 3)

Cheap Trick (The Dawson Family Series Book 4)

Fight Dirty (The Dawson Family Series Book 5)

Paranormal romance:

Dead of Night (Thorne Hill Series Book 1)

Dark of Night (Thorne Hill Series Book 2)

Call of Night (Thorne Hill Series Book 3)

Still of Night (Throne Hill Series Book 4)

Immortal Night (Thorne Hill Companion Novella)

Dystopian Romance:

Contagious (The Contagium Series Book 1)

Deathly Contagious (The Contagium Series Book 2)

Contagious Chaos (The Contagium Series Book 3)

The Truth is Contagious (The Contagium Series Book 4)

Made in the USA
Columbia, SC
27 August 2020

17961683R00152